I0575388

SAVE THE GIRL

SAVE THE HUMANS | BOOK 2

AVERY BLAKE

JOHNNY B. TRUANT

STERLING & STONE

Copyright © 2019 by Sterling & Stone

All rights reserved.

No part of this book may be reproduced in any form or by any electronic or mechanical means, including information storage and retrieval systems, without written permission from the author, except for the use of brief quotations in a book review.

The authors greatly appreciate you taking the time to read our work. Please consider leaving a review wherever you bought the book, or telling your friends about it, to help us spread the word.

Thank you for supporting our work.

SAVE THE GIRL

1

HOLLIS PARKER — 36 years of age, Caucasian, raised Baptist but current devotee of the Church of I Don't Give a Fuck, six days' worth of beard growth on his face because *man* if it hadn't been hard to keep a shaving routine lately, what with all the aliens invading and cities going to war and the closest people he had to friends (which were none too close) trying to kill him — stood atop an overlook ridge off the side of route 360, also clumsily named Capital of Texas Highway, while flesh-eating vandals ran right up his ass, ruining his day. And to think: It wasn't even noon yet.

Hollis considered the jump, considered how dead it would probably make him, and turned back to the dirt path. That's when the vandals showed up right where they'd been all along, hauling ass behind him. And the path, unfortunately, was the only way down.

"Hey, look," Hollis told the gang, raising his hands. "I didn't realize that path went up. I figured I at least had a shot to make it to the water so I could swim to that golf course over yonder. How about a do-over?"

The leader — a kid who Hollis was already thinking of

as "Fishbone" due to the large whatever-it-was piercing his septum to create an ivory mustache, and who'd probably displayed his pierced awesomeness as a Starbucks barista before the ships had arrived and he'd decided to become an outlaw king — showed his teeth. They were very white, perfectly aligned. Back when Fishbone had been in middle school, Mrs. Bone had definitely laid out for the best orthodonture. In Hollis's opinion, it'd be a lot easier to take him seriously if he filed them down to points. Or if he at least pissed off a drunk soccer hooligan, so he could take a few de-aligning punches to the mouth for improved cred.

Fishbone didn't respond. The leaders, in situations like this, never talked unless they had Australian (or at least British) accents. Instead, a very broad twenty-something who in a hilarious world would be named "Moose" spoke for him.

"You owe us a toll," he said.

"Come on," Hollis said, still with his hands up, still smiling. "It's ... what ... Day 12? I'm pretty sure the Macy's at the mall is still selling Dockers. *Half off.* Don't you think it's a bit early to go all Road Warrior?"

Moose slipped a knife from his waistband. A really big one. Because, see, you don't go right to guns if you want to be a post-apocalyptic gang. Soon they'd be manufacturing steampunk weaponry, but not until all the gas went bad and the man with diesel became king.

"Is this where I say, 'That's not a knife. *That's* a knife!'?"

Moose advanced. "I'm gonna cut your balls off," he said, "and wear them as earrings."

Beside him, Fishbone flicked his tongue like a serpent. It was, of course, bifurcated. With silver studs through both of the points. When he went down on a girl, it must be like stonewashing jeans, except the jeans were a vagina.

Hollis shuffled back. Tiny rocks and dirt spilled over the ridge behind him, crying all the way down to the surface of the river.

"Look," Hollis said. "I don't have any money."

It wasn't exactly true. This morning, he'd helped stop two warring factions from going to battle downtown, and thereby kept an alien bomb from destroying the city. After the air had been let out of that particular balloon, what might have been a huge battle had devolved into petty bitching. They were using their words, just like their kindergarten teachers taught them. Hollis, feeling he'd done well, had robbed an armored car in celebration. It'd just been lying there, by the side of the road, on his way from HQ at the Spider House Ballroom to Brendan Banks's Compound of Misplaced Manliness. The way Hollis figured it, money was useless now that aliens were occupying the planet. That's why he took it, why these assholes wanted it, and why he still didn't really want to give it all up even though he was literally inches from dying. When you were holding actual sacks of cash, Hollis supposed old habits died hard.

And besides, there had to be another way. The money might open doors — and right now, Hollis needed some serious doors opened. Brendan had stolen two ladies that Hollis had gotten rather used to, and what Brendan wanted as ransom had already been destroyed — not that Brendan knew that yet, of course.

On the cell phone in his pocket, a text message from Sonny Malone: YOUR FUCKING DEAD. Complete with incorrect grammar.

And on the note Brendan had left at the Spider House, after tracking and then snatching Carol and Mia: BRING ME THE CASE OR THEY DIE.

Everyone with the all-caps around him lately. All caps,

but no exclamation points. In Hollis's mind, that particular construction was like a raised voice without any teeth. It was talking loud in a nightclub so as to be heard.

I REALLY LIKE THIS SONG. LET'S DANCE OR MAYBE JUST HAVE SEX IN THE BATHROOM.

Or:

SO YOU DO ORTHODONTURE ON BARISTAS WHO FANCY THEMSELVES WARLORDS? THAT MUST BE INTERESTING.

Not that Hollis even *had* the case anymore. Sonny Malone, by proxy, had destroyed everything inside the attache Hollis had stolen from Thomas Davies what felt like six thousand years ago. Sonny'd thought he was using the real combination instead of the self-destruct combo Hollis had given him before running off in Sonny's little restored Chevelle with emergency lights duct-taped to the grill. He'd gotten his nasty surprise some hours later.

So: *cash.* Cash might still be king, right? And now these douchebags wanted to take all that Hollis had. If Hollis went to the trunk and pulled out a few hundred bucks for their bullshit "toll," he didn't think they'd let him keep the rest — money he might be able to use to buy Mia and Carol's freedom. No, they'd probably want to take it all, once they saw he had it. They weren't like that polite mugger Hollis had once encountered in New Orleans. But that was another story.

"If you don't have money," Fishbone said, "we'll take the toll out of your skin."

Except that he didn't say "skin."

Thanks to all the crap in his tongue, he said, "thkin."

Hollis forced himself not to comment. He backed up another step. More rocks and dirt suicided off the cliff to their death.

"Tell you what," he said. "I know the guy who controls all of North Austin. He—"

"*We* control North Austin," said Fishbone, making a dramatic and sweeping wave with his left arm, indicating all of the North Austin kingdom around them.

They were in West Austin.

"Uh ... okay. Well, then, he's up the road a piece. You might know him. Brendan Banks?"

A chuckle went through the group. They were keeping inside jokes and not letting Hollis in on it. What a bunch of assholes.

"We know Banks." *Bankth.*

"Then you know he's Governor Garrett's right hand man."

"He *was* Garrett's right-hand man, until Garrett went soft."

"So *Garrett's* the problem," Hollis said, trying to get inside their opinions and become them, like a chameleon. "Banks is the guy who had the right idea all along?"

"Banks is a piece of shit."

"Ah. So nobody wins."

"I think," Moose said, still with his tired knife, "we should just kill him and be done with it."

"Why, though?" Hollis asked. "Again: *Day 12.* You guys aren't seriously eating flesh already, are you? Tell me that's just the name of your gang: 'The Flesh-Eaters.' You know. Like 'Kiwanis' or 'Bodacious Grannies.'"

"Smart ass," Moose said, stepping forward again — this time to close the deal.

Hollis, acting shocked and elated, jabbed a finger behind the gang, just to the left.

"Look! Defenseless babies!"

They all looked, because that's what you do when

someone says something with conviction that makes no sense. And when they did, Hollis was ready. He'd already subtly shifted his weight forward, so all he had to do was to rush forward and throw his shoulder hard into Moose's arm. The man was huge; Hollis knew he couldn't actually dislodge him. But at an oblique angle, caught off guard, he thought he could get *past* him. And he did, sort of, and also sort of got by the two punk rockers behind him. The three further down the path, though, hadn't even really made the clearing (that's what you got when you were just a nut-licker in a gang, Hollis thought — you didn't even get to hear the leader speechifying) and, in the narrow space, were all hands. They had Hollis around the neck and one arm, sloppy in their tackles.

Hollis had sort of been planning for them, too, and sort of had a response ready. He hit one in the gut, then tried to elbow the other in the face. This did not go well, and a second later Hollis was eating dirt with the others turning to pile up behind him. Only Moose was saving him. The man's bulk, still not recovered, was blocking the way.

He kicked, thrashed, found some daylight.

Then he was barreling down the path, dodging rocks and branches like a man on an obstacle course, with the closest pursuer just two seconds behind him.

2

THE WAY this inverted sock of an exit worked, the gang's senior members were now at the back of the line, while the young panty-sniffers were closest to Hollis's heels. He was now thinking of those juniors — owing to their faces and attire — as Mad Max and Booger. You know — from *Revenge of the Nerds*?

Not that Hollis's cleverness and knowledge of classic cinema was going to get him very far today. The city had just had a very bad morning, and the real sticky part was that it was actually the best morning it could have had. Hollis kept wanting to tell the ruffians he met that he was the reason Austin hadn't been reduced to ash by the mothership and the bomb-thing it'd dropped. Or maybe there was a shirt he could wear that said the same. Perhaps even a tacky blazer, like golf tournament champions were allowed to wear, so that all who saw him would recognize him as the savior he'd been.

Maybe it wouldn't matter. The gang — the Flesh Eaters — didn't really seem to care. Nor did they seem self-confident enough to just let him go and figure they could find someone else to torture. He'd seen their bikes around town and thought, from the start, that here was a post-apocalyptic gang just waiting for an apocalypse to make things official. The speed with which they'd logo'd up motorcycles and found jackets that more or less matched to complete the look felt (to Hollis, anyway) as downright opportunistic, perhaps even desperate. Sort of like when someone drops a could-have-been-awesome one-liner in conversation, except that everyone knows he's been saving that line all night — grooming it, perfecting it, nudging the conversation so an opportunity would arise to use it.

That's what the Flesh Eaters were to Hollis. They were the ultimate sad Your Mother joke.

But that didn't stop the gang — Mad Max and Booger first, then the entire band behind them — from being a very serious problem in the moment. Hollis's bobbing and weaving had given him daylight, but not more than a few feet of it. The path was still thick with brush, still bumpy underfoot. Which was a real pain in the ass, when he thought about it. For years, he'd driven this stretch of highly trafficked expressway and wondered at the constant flow of people interested enough to pull off to the side and take the path he was now re-approaching the mouth of. It *had* to be a miles-long path that explored the whole shoreline, right? It *had* to lead to the river. Because if it was nothing more than a short climb to a scenic overlook, people would stop going there. And if that's what it was, the path should be wide and clear by now, just from force of numbers tromping through it.

He hit the gravel that served as an ad-hoc parking lot, nearly slipped, and managed to regain his footing in a series of moves that must have looked dancelike. The danciness of his maneuvers slowed his forward roll enough that Booger was able to close the gap and almost grabbed him, but a swanlike kick (lucky, but also beautiful) took the man in the teeth. Mad Max seized the opportunity and turned on his afterburners, got Hollis by the shirt, then came up short when Hollis planted his feet and let the kid run into his back. He'd had awesome plans to duck low and use his chaser's momentum to vault him over his back, but all that happened was a dick-to-butt bump that set Mad Max on his rear and left Hollis with a painful coccyx.

With his shirt again free, Hollis ran again.

The wrong way, he realized fast.

He'd run toward the bridge, which was way too high to jump from safely. But at this point it was too late to try and buttonhook back up the slope, toward the housing community — the kind of place that looked like it might have a golf course. Or, for that matter, across 360. There was another path into the trees over there, although maybe it was also a dead end.

So he doubled down. Pumped his legs fast, immediately feeling the accumulated (and, thus far, ignored) beatings of the past days — or, really, the past two weeks. Two weeks ago, life had been simple. There'd been no aliens, no gangs quite this organized or fashionably coordinated, and a whole lot less soft tissue trauma on Mr. Hollis Palmer. He'd been kicked, punched, threatened repeatedly with firearms (often point-blank, their muzzles against his excellent hair), sleep-deprived, psychologically tortured, and generally beaten-the-shit-out-of, as the kids said these days. And only some of those beatings had come from Mia.

Mia.

Hollis wondered, as he sprinted down the concrete with his reserves draining fast, what was happening with Mia and Carol right now. Not much, probably — Brendan had only just snatched them, and with all the war mongering on Brendan's schedule, he probably hadn't had much time for abuse. But that could easily change if Hollis took his time, and it would almost *certainly* change if Hollis showed up empty-handed. That right there was the sticking point. He'd gotten quite a bit of loot from the abandoned armored truck, but as it turned out, cash was both bulky and heavy. He'd filled his trunk and as much of the cab as he could still cover with a blanket so as not to be obvious, and it still couldn't be anywhere near what the original attache case had been worth. Maybe there'd been hundred-dollar bills in that truck once, but by the time Hollis found it — perhaps after other bandits had robbed it and discovered, as he had, that cash wasn't very portable — there'd only been twenties. If he was lucky, his entire stash might be worth $2 million. *Might.*

Hey, Brendan — I know you said you wanted that $60M attache case we had last time we visited ... but how about two instead?

Not to mention that cash was going to mean less and less if this little "alien invasion" trend continued for much longer. Not to mention that (based on what Carol and Sonny Malone's computer guy Theo had discovered), the contents of the case were likely to have *more and more* value if it really was information the aliens themselves kept accessing.

Tell you what, Brendan. You give me the women, and I'll give you this worthless pile of shit.

Yeah, that wasn't going to go over well. And it's not like he could appeal to Brendan's sense of civic responsibility. Maybe what Hollis knew about the database could be used to stymie the aliens' plans or at least get one up on them, but it's not like Brendan would give him Carol to help figure it out "just because." Brendan wanted the database's side uses. Information, in the coming economy, would be the real power.

Face it. You're fucked. In like ten different ways.

This, Hollis told himself as his muscles' glycogen stores ran dry and lactic acid filled his thighs, making them burn. The gang behind him — in addition to likely having slept last night, unlike Hollis — was full of young men. Hollis wasn't used to feeling old, but he felt it now as a hand began to find purchase on his bouncing shoulder.

Still, he wasn't done yet.

He stooped, slid left without slowing, and avoided the tag. Booger's, as it turned out. Then the hand was back, and again Hollis dodged. The third time, huffing and puffing now, he waited until the hand almost had him. He reached back with his own opposite hand, got it by the wrist, and threw his weight hard. Booger spun out, did a wild little dance of his own while trying to regain balance, then lost the battle to momentum. From what Hollis could see, he broke the fall enough to not plant his face, but the sound when the rest of him hit the deck still made Hollis's stomach roll. It was like sandpaper on a rough-hewn board. Booger would be needing Bactine in the morning.

His victory was short-lived. He somehow managed the end of the bridge (Booger's toppling helped; it gave the others something to tangle their feet in), but did so light-headed, moving more on habit than anything resembling real power. His vision was going black, fatigue finally catching him, spots rising before his eyes.

He did manage to make a right turn onto the grass, aiming for the river shore beyond. But that's when the first of the gang tackled him, making him taste turf. Another followed, then another.

He was roughly turned over, breathing so hard his lungs

hurt, vision swimmy, barely able to remember his name or why anyone with any name would have run instead of just giving up his car full of cash. That was what stupid people did, and here he was: irretrievably moronic.

"Hey, I—" was all Hollis managed to say.

Moose was above him, sitting on his chest.

"Wiseass," he said, barely panting despite his bulk.

Then a punch, like a truck colliding with a bridge stanchion.

For a while after that, Hollis saw nothing at all. Until—

3

—PUNCHED AWAKE, like the little slaps you give someone who's fainted to bring them around, only a whole lot harder.

The pain was immediate and intense. Whatever had hit him — and this, Hollis couldn't see as he lay on his back on what felt like a dirt floor — was like a battering ram. He could only see bars above and clouded sun beyond, as if he was in a jail cell that had been tipped onto its back. His head hurt. Things were happening too fast to be sure, but he suspected he'd just taken a 1-2 that'd blended into one unpleasant awakening without order: something striking Hollis; the back of Hollis's skull striking the floor.

His overhead view of the bars and sun was eclipsed by the world's ugliest moon. It had a boxer's broken nose, a shaven head, and two big hoop earrings made of gold. It had a neck like a broad triangle that began just under its chin, muscular like an action figure that some kid has covered in lump after lump of Play-Doh.

"Giddup," the monster above him said.

"Fuck you, Mr. Clean!"

The big man slammed his open hand into Hollis's

crotch, thumb on top and four fingers beneath. He took a grip, then, and hauled Hollis across whatever-this-was by his nuts. The pain was excruciating. For a moment it seemed he might be trying to bring Hollis upright that way but was confused by the fact that balls had ended up on top instead of the head.

Hollis, somehow aware enough to summon a few of his scattered wits, took advantage. He couldn't manage an eye for an eye from this position, but he was perfectly lined up to take a sack for a sack.

He threw a fist, hard, into the big man's crotch. He yelled out and dropped Hollis, who folded the wrong way. This asshole couldn't do anything right.

Somewhere in here, Hollis became aware that someone was cheering. He was still fighting off the last threads of rudely-woken unconsciousness and now throbbing pain of face and groin, but his brain was — in emergency mode, surely — taking the lay of the land. The cheering was from above. There was little down here. No light from anywhere other than the sun, featureless walls that weren't that far away, bars in two different places around the space's walls.

What the hell was this? How'd he gotten here?

Oh, right. The gang. The Flesh Eaters who, true to noncommittal form, hadn't even eaten his flesh. He remembered the tackle, Moose's punch, and then not much else. He'd been in the open then. Wherever he was now, they must have carried him.

Now the behemoth was putting up his dukes like a comic-book pugilist. He was shirtless, revealing that kind of big-fat that's not lean and shiny, but can still crush a Buick into a wad like spent tinfoil.

"C'mon. Fight like a man!" he bellowed.

"I've never understood that," Hollis said, finding himself

to be conversational despite the situation. "How do women fight?"

"With their pussies!"

"Now that ..." Hollis abandoned the sentence and decided he was confused enough to start again. "I don't even know where to begin."

"Hit me!"

"Don't we need a safeword?"

Cheering and jeering from above. Hollis chanced a look up and saw some of the Flesh-Eaters (eating fruit, ironically) standing on what must be solid land above, looking down into whatever pit they'd made in the ground. A storm drain, maybe, with bars welded in place to make a cell? It sure smelled like a sewer. Or maybe it was just this asshole in with him.

Hollis crouched. "Fine. As soon as I find my contacts."

The big man made a sound of confusion. Hollis grabbed a handful of whatever crap had lined the floor — sand, silt, maybe decomposed shit — and threw it at the mammoth's face. It might as well have been butterflies. Without pausing, the man crossed to Hollis, grabbed him around the neck with one meaty bicep, and hit him on the top of the head like trying to pound a stake into the ground. Hollis swayed, then slumped like boneless meat.

More jeers. Now the sportsfans above were throwing the fruit they'd been eating. Apples, oranges, even grapes. Who throws grapes? It was insulting.

"I'm gonna break you in half," the big man said.

Hollis's head was spinning. He had too much orange pulp in his eye. He couldn't even think of a witty response.

The man picked him up and threw him. It didn't even seem difficult.

Hollis crashed to rest against one of the sections that'd

been barred-off. He did so untidily, face against the metal, and saw that yes, those welds were new. Enterprising little bastards, the Flesh Eaters. They'd made a man-fighting hole. How delightfully end-of-the-world of them.

Hollis saw: One of the welds, at the top, had come loose. All he'd have to do would be to goad his opponent into charging him, then bend the bar down on the weakened lower weld and dodge at the last minute so the guy would impale himself on it. It'd worked in so many movies, it had to be the solution.

"Your mother ..." Hollis said.

But when he turned he saw that the guy was already running, chest lowered for attack. Perfect. Hollis could get him through the heart if he moved fast.

He grabbed the bar and pulled. It didn't move even a fractional millimeter. He wasn't able to dodge fast enough, either, and a quarter-second later the man's sweaty chest hit him, arms wrapped around, turning Hollis into the pastrami in the middle of a man-and-bars sandwich.

A literal rotten tomato hit Hollis in the face as the man pulled back. At least their food attack was improving.

The behemoth paused, looking not at Hollis's pancaked form but beyond it. Then he grabbed Hollis's shoulder and pulled him forward, away from the grate. He moved past, and Hollis rolled to see that he, too, had noticed the loose bar. As he reached for it, Hollis thought, *Joke's on you, asshole.*

But of course the big man bent it easily. The lower weld snapped and a second later he was holding a sawed-off pipe that'd been flattened on one end to better conform to the surface it'd been welded to — something that in technical terms is called a disemboweler.

A roar went up from above. More food was thrown. This

time, it included lettuce. There must be a farmer's market up there. God knew, Austin had enough of them.

"Kill him!" someone shouted.

"Fuck him up, Bruce!"

Watching the big man think and slowly respond, all Hollis could think was, *Of course his name is Bruce.*

Bruce raised the pipe like a sword meant for stabbing. The end, where he'd snapped off the lower weld, looked very rusty and sharp. As stupid as this guy seemed, he probably couldn't hit Hollis's heart in one strike. That meant things were about to become very unpleasant.

"Do it!"

"Don't do it, Bruce," Hollis said, trying to squirm backward as he lay chest-up on the culvert's filthy floor. "Think of the Boy Wonder."

He raised the pipe, arching his back for dramatic effect, and began to make a guttural roar. It wasn't authentically an animal roar, but clearly he meant it to be one. Hollis, for his part, was in no position to criticize. He was scared enough to piss blood. Internally injured enough, too.

That's about when Hollis heard a loud report and watched his vision go blind.

At first, he thought he'd been shot. Only seconds later did he realize that he'd actually just been sprayed with goo. *Lots* of goo — like a whole case of rotten farm-market produce's worth of goo.

And, when Hollis wiped the goo away, he saw that Bruce was still more or less on his feet, swaying. Most of his face was gone, though, owing to the bullet exit wound where his nose had been. Some brainstem part of him was still fighting, like chickens and cockroaches must fight when they lost their heads. By force of instinct, he refused to fall.

Then he tipped. Hollis saw it coming, unable to move in time.

Three hundred pounds of shit-sack hit him all at once, flattening his lungs.

A face appeared above. Unlike all the others he'd seen from this side of town so far, this one looked almost normal. He could go into an office and work, if it the dress code was business casual.

A woman. Probably in her 40s, stern-faced, dark-skinned, black hair. A middle manager that everyone at work knew not to fuck with.

She was tucking a pistol back into a holster at her side, the chuckleheads from the Flesh Eaters giving her a respectful berth. When the pistol was stowed, she reached into her pocket for a phone, tapped a few buttons, and tossed it to Hollis. Hollis couldn't catch it, of course; he'd been tenderized and was still trapped beneath a corpse with the world's worst B.O. But it landed nearby, undamaged and face up. He could see that it wasn't actually a phone. It was a walkie talkie.

"Give him whatever time the call takes," the woman told the others, "then clean him up and get him out of there."

4

WITH EFFORT — especially given how beaten-up he was — Hollis managed to extricate himself from the dead man far enough to reach the walkie. It was a partial thing. His lower half was still under the body, but getting free of it could be a project for later.

Hollis held the walkie. But he didn't speak into it right away. All at once the adrenaline of the past few minutes — or the past half hour, if he counted his chase by Fishbone's crew as part of the same continuous experience — left him. What remained of his strength and confidence went with it, as did the analgesic effect on his body. He was suddenly aware just how much everything hurt, how exhausted he was (mentally *and* physically), and how, sarcasm aside, he was actually really freaked out. The fear was surprisingly raw. Hollis seldom looked so directly at his fear, preferring to mask it with a devil-may-care attitude. He didn't like what it showed him. With fatigue heavy and defenses battered, it threatened from the corner of his mind, imbuing that simple walkie-talkie with sinister connotations he'd rather not speak into it while feeling.

But he did anyway, walling off the fear as best he could.

"This is Hollis."

"Hollis," said a voice he recognized immediately. "Keep your fucking mouth shut for once in your life, and listen."

"Listen, Brendan. I got your note. I'm just—"

"Maybe you didn't hear me. I said, 'Keep your mouth shut and listen.'"

Hollis bit back the impulse to respond — even just "Okay." Something had changed in Brendan's voice. He'd always struck Hollis as equal parts insane and friendly, but that's not how he sounded now. When Hollis and Mia had shown up at Brendan's compound last week, the greeting they'd gotten had been perfectly in line with what anyone who knew the man would expect: a gun to the head, then lodging and a hot breakfast. Brendan was a high-operating criminal who took care of his mama, a cold-blooded son of a bitch who, when it all came right down to it, cared more about honor and fairness than getting what he wanted — even if he wanted something very badly.

But that's not what Hollis was hearing in Brendan's voice now, and it wasn't what Hollis had seen in Brendan since he'd hit the man with Thomas Davies's attache case and jumped the fence. The man who'd stood beside Governor Franklin Garrett had looked like a worse version of the man Hollis knew — and that first version had been plenty nasty. This Brendan had been activated by the arrival of the war he'd spent his adult life preparing for, soured by the almost-battle with Forest McCafferty's left-leaning Austinites, spurned by the way Garrett had turned on him, and infuriated by the way his and Garrett's army had stopped being *his* and somehow become *Garrett's* ... and the way that army, in the end, had turned away from conflict rather than toward it. It didn't matter that if they'd fought, the alien bomb would have blown and they'd all be cinders now. Blame for all that'd gone wrong had to lay somewhere, and if Hollis had to guess, Brendan planned to lay it on him.

"I have your women," he said.

"They're not 'my women.'"

Brendan took a meaningful pause.

"I have your women," he repeated. "I told you that if you didn't bring me the case, they'd die. I'm torn. I don't have the case, Hollis. So by the rules of the game, they should die."

"You have to give me time. I—"

"I can't track you like I tracked her," Brendan went on. "I just assumed you'd be smart enough to come. Or rather, I assumed you'd be smart enough to at least *decide* whether to come or not. I thought, 'I'll give him a day.' You know where I live. I haven't moved. Unlike a lot of the chicken shits in this city, I ain't goin' anywhere. Within a day, I figured you'd get past whatever bullshit excuses you were about to give me while you tried to work things out, seeing if there was a way you could have your cake and eat it, too. But of course, you can't have both. Twenty-four hours, I thought I'd at least know: either Hollis is gonna make the trade, or he's gonna let them die."

"I want to make the trade. I just—"

Brendan cut him off again. His words were hard, far less southern-slow than they used to be.

"Either way was okay with me," he went on. "I listened in on the conversations y'all had about the information inside that case. I know what someone in-the-know can predict with the data it accesses, and I know that for some reason, the aliens seem to be pumping from the same pool. Building something with it, maybe. Or *training* something. Don't know and don't care. Because most importantly, I know you're way too dumb, Hollis, to make sense of all that shit on your own. You need the lady I got. Not your girl-friend. The other."

Hollis resisted the urge to protest Mia as his girlfriend, but Brandon was right about the other thing. Yes, he very much needed Carol. He'd considered the issue a hundred different ways, trying to see how the pieces fit, and Carol turned out to be essential every time. Based on what Theo and Carol had both said when they'd looked at the data, the alien fingers probing it were neither innocent nor casual. They were *doing something* with that database, and whatever it was couldn't be good. Theo had said they were building a brain. They were trying to understand humans — and their weaknesses — in ways they otherwise couldn't. Who knew what that incursion might mean, if nobody stopped it? Right now, Hollis was the only free person in the world who knew anywhere near the full extent of what the case promised. But in order to do anything about it, he needed Carol's help.

As happened every time Hollis mulled the issue, the voice of his instinctual, lone-wolf mind asked an obvious question: *What the hell do you care about fighting the aliens? We should run, hide out, and position ourselves to get the best scraps whenever it all goes down.*

It wasn't a flattering comparison, but Hollis knew he was the smartest rat. He could live off of anything, talk his way out of or into whatever he needed. He was excellent at laying low, living off of others, and making his way alone. Having Mia along had slowed him down. Without baggage — and without some stupid, non-Hollis crusade — he'd be just fine. *Better*, perhaps, than he'd been before the invasion.

Why did you try to do what Brendan asked? Why are you still trying? You don't even have the case to trade. It's gone. Turned to acid and pulp.

Well. He did have *something* to trade ... if he didn't care about personal gain. But he'd be even stupider to try and cash in on that, for a thousand reasons.

"Are you still there, Hollis? Or did their man Bruce kill you after all?"

"Are these your people, Brendan?"

Brendan laughed. "They're barely people. They tried to offer me protection. I showed them that they were the ones in need of protection."

"But you know them."

"Does it matter? You got yourself caught. It's worse than running away. If you ran, at least I'd know you couldn't do anything with what you should have given to me. At least I'd be confident in who I already knew you were. Running, at least, would be predictable. I'd be able to move on. And, hey. It's not like I wouldn't have gained some spoils."

Brendan laughed a little. The "spoils" were clearly Carol and Mia.

"Don't hurt them."

"Why? You can't have it both ways, Hollis. You give me the case and I'll give you the women. Once you have the person who can help you access the database, you won't be able to use it anymore. I've got some tech wizards with me, you know. We'd change the passwords. Lock you out. That's why I say I'm happy either way. You either keep the information but have nobody to help you read it, or you get the help but lose the information you needed help with. Either way, you lose."

"Sounds like you're talking yourself out of a trade, Brendan," Hollis said.

"Maybe, maybe not. I already talked to Vika. She said they were going to make sport of you, then kill you. Like they did with Bruce."

Hollis looked down at Bruce. He'd bled Hollis's jeans crimson.

"I hear you pissed them off. Made fun of them. Not a good idea, Hollis. See, I can take it. I know how you are, and I know that compared to me, you're just a pretender. You've got nothing. So if you act like a smartass, I'm mature enough to laugh it off. Not those freaks. All they have is their pride, for what it's worth. You should see the hoops they're jumping through to be respected. If you've heard of the Exchange, that's all them."

"The '*Exchange*'?"

"Hmm. Guess you really *don't* know anything. Now I understand why you were stupid enough to get caught. Stupid enough not to just pay their stupid toll. And above all else, stupid enough to run your mouth. So yeah. You lost your chance for a neutral move. Now it's: deal with me, or die."

"If I deal with you, maybe I die anyway."

"If you don't, you die for sure. But that's not the reason you're going to do this, is it? Because you *are* going to do it, Hollis. You're going to make the trade I proposed: the briefcase for the women. Even if it leaves you just as broke as you already are, now with two more mouths to feed."

The joke was on Brendan. He wasn't broke; he'd found an armored truck. Although still, he wasn't sure money would mean much for long. He'd already heard rumors of an underground economy taking shape, already laced with the paranoia of what might soon come. What had value today were weapons, food, clean water, information, and manpower. And strange creature comforts, he supposed. With the internet now mostly gone and production on most things stopped, filled-up Jukes that weren't zapped by the

EMP would probably become gold just for something to watch. Ditto worthless shit, like Pop Tarts.

"Do you know *why* you're going to make this trade, Hollis? Do you know why, when we're done talking, you're going to let them lead you to Vika's room, where she'll huff and puff before I threaten to blow their house in? Right now, you've got one of the most valuable objects in town, if you could just understand what it contained. But do you know *why* you're about to give it up to little old me?"

Excellent question, said the voice inside Hollis's head.

"Because if you don't," Brendan said, "I'm going to kill them both, as I promised. But not right away. The first thing I'll do, actually, is hand them around. You saw how big the barracks are on my land, right? How many men there are? Or actually, I'm sorry. Doesn't mean to just be men. Some of the women would like to meet your girls, too. How much rape," Brendan asked, "do you think someone can take before their mind breaks?"

Hollis gripped the walkie. He could feel its knurls biting into his flesh.

"I don't care," he said. Because *of course* he didn't care. Brendan was right; this was a lose-lose proposition for Hollis. But he was wily; he could pretend to go along with the plan, get to the office of whoever Vika was, then talk or fight his way out. The last thing he'd do, at that point, would be to head back into danger. Oh, no. He was *done* with danger. If he was careful, once he got free, he could lay low. He could avoid being spotted, this time. He could leave town, seeing as everyone knew him here, and hide in the sticks. With time, he might try another city — maybe a big one like Dallas, or something smaller like Waco or Abilene. Or he could leave the state; breaking the border had proven easily enough last time. Not Louisiana. Oklahoma this time. The Sooner state.

But even that was academic. The main reason he wouldn't take Brendan's deal — the main reason he didn't care what happened to Brendan's hostages — was the simple fact that Brendan was so sure Hollis *did* care and *would* take the deal. Nobody told Hollis Palmer what to do, or how to think.

Yet even as he said those three words — *I don't care* — Hollis found his gut tying in a knot. Maybe he wasn't a total selfish son of a bitch after all.

Or, the voice inside him said, *you're just smarter than Brendan thinks. Don't do your double-cross at Vika's level. Do it at* Brendan's *level instead. Tell him you'll take the deal. What's to lose? Play him like he's trying to play you. Even without the case, there's still a way — so long as you get Carol — to do what needs to be done.*

Yes. The case was gone, but Hollis wasn't ready to give up on it just yet.

"Some of the guys here," Brendan went on, "they like pain. Not receiving it, but causing it. It turns them on. It gets them hard, when someone is suffering. I'm not like that, but some of these guys ... they are. I'm a balanced soul, Hollis. You know I am."

"You're a sick fuck."

"Not compared to some of my end-of-the-world gang," Brendan said, unoffended. "A lot of these people, they were here well before there was any news of aliens on the way. Do you know what kind of person it takes to just give up everything and move into barracks, preparing for a war that might never come? They're like cultists. They're not exactly stable. Every kid who's ever tortured a living thing just to watch it squirm, they're living on my back forty. So after the ladies make the rounds with the picky men, I'll let the freaks have them. I'll have a stern talk with them first, Hollis. I'll tell them that at first, they can only hit. Then they can cut, but only a little — superficial cuts only. There's one guy here, used to be a surgeon. Do you know what a surgeon can do, if he's careful? He won't have anesthesia, of course, but on the up-side I happen to know he's got a few vials of epinephrine. Give them that, and they won't be able to pass out from the pain."

"Stop," Hollis said. But of course Brendan went on.

"Oh, come on. You don't care about any of this, Hollis. Don't let it bug you. After all, based on what you're telling me you plan to do, you'll be long dead. The Flesh Eaters are hardly advanced. Hardly elegant. When they get tired of playing with you and sending big guys in to beat on you, they'll just shoot you. You'll be long dead before I tell my psychos it's okay to start cutting off digits. Some of those fucks, they get so worked up over all that blood. Ever seen a guy jerk off using blood as lube?"

"Stop," Hollis said, this time more forcefully.

There was a pause on the walkie. Then Brendan said, "So we understand each other."

"Yes."

"You'll make the trade. You'll bring me the case, so that — on my honor — I can deliver these two back to you safely."

Teeth gritted, eyes closed, Hollis said, "Yes."

The walkie cut off, the display blinked as the frequency was, he supposed, erased from the device's memory.

Then there was nothing until Hollis began shouting, and the handlers came.

5

CAROL WAS LOOKING between the bars, out the window. And again, like a mantra, she said, "Hollis will come."

Mia glanced over at her, but looked away before the other woman could see her lips curve upward — not into a smile of joy, but one of patronizing. It was so cute, what Carol believed. Like a kid trusting in Santa Claus.

"He'll come," Carol repeated when Mia didn't respond. "Won't he?"

"I don't know."

"But you believe."

"He took the attache case. He knows the combination. He knows what's inside and how to use it and what it's worth. Last we saw him, he was right here in town, and he knows where Brendan lives. Assuming Brendan left the note he said he did and that Hollis found it — which he surely would — then there's absolutely nothing stopping Hollis from coming here to make the trade: the case for us."

"You didn't answer the question," Carol said.

Mia considered backpedaling. Then she decided that

Carol wasn't a kid and that Hollis wasn't Jolly Old St. Nick. Or any kind of saint, for that matter.

"The answer is that I don't know," Mia repeated. "Like I said."

Carol didn't insult Mia or make the moment awkward by fishing any further for assurance. She was, by vocation and temperament, far more practical than Mia. She didn't have Mia's way of picking situations like complicated locks, nor twisting people around her finger — but she was practical plenty. Best she understand where Mia stood, where Hollis may or may not stand, and what chances they had. So far, Brendan had been an active gentleman. It was eerie. But she sensed a new edge to the man just the same, as if his friendly veneer was hiding terrible new depths. The schism with the Governor had broken something in him, and the fact that he wasn't showing it was — to Mia, anyway — more troubling than if he spent his days ranting.

"It wouldn't serve him to hurt us," Carol said.

True. But logic wasn't necessarily in charge here. Sensibilities aside, they were still locked in and there were still bars on the windows. It was the same room she'd shared with Hollis when they'd been here before, with the windows reinforced and minus the tigers. The zoo smell remained. She'd tried digging through the drywall already, figuring she could punch a hole in the exterior siding and make a run for it once she got past the insulation, hoping to subvert cameras and drones and acres of barbed wire — a real frying-pan-to-fire situation, but better than waiting around for the fall of a sword. Sure, Hollis might come. But she was damned if she was going to bet her life on it.

But the house turned out to be more secure than she'd thought. The entire thing was made of concrete blocks, both internal and external walls. Who did that? It was the way you built a prison.

"Do you ... feel anything?" Carol asked when, again, Mia didn't reply.

"I feel plenty. 'Scared shitless' at the top of the list."

"No — I mean from Hollis."

That made Mia's eyebrows bunch. "What?"

"When you told me the aliens would destroy Austin because the human factions kept fighting, I asked you how you knew. You said it felt like Hollis had whispered it in your ear."

Carol paused, waiting.

Then she added, "... from Louisiana, as it turned out."

Mia remembered. It was like a confession made while drunk.

She waved it away. "Right. He was in Louisiana. I was just high or something."

"Those big rocks the aliens are dropping everywhere," Carol said. "I've heard so many people say that when they get close to a line of them, it's like a psychic connection opens to—"

Mia ceased her effort to wave the issue away, upgrading her gesture to a warning hand. "I didn't say that."

"No, but—"

"'No' is right," she said. "Hollis and I aren't in psychic communication. It was just an old-fashioned hunch." The whole question was gross. The people who reported random psychic episodes around the rock lines, it turned out, weren't reporting anything random at all. They connected to sons, daughters, mothers, grandfathers, best childhood friends. And, most of all, lovers. Which, again, was disgusting. She and Hollis had grudge-fucked exactly once in Thomas's bed, and even that had been a manipulation tactic on Mia's part. If the invasion hadn't cut her plans short, that single act of strategic coitus would have been one more link in the chain that framed Hollis for the theft she'd been planning to commit. The idea of letting some dumb stones lump that in with "lovers" was absurd. She remembered the act: every which way, utilizing the dresser and the walls. They'd left a dent in the plaster that Mia had blamed on a renovation crew. There'd been no love to it. Not even close.

Carol seemed about to ask further — probably because the idea of Mia "hearing" Hollis's thoughts would mean a lifeline at best or a source of intel at worst — but wisely decided not to prod. Mia liked Carol plenty and would do everything she could to save them both, but right now her nerves were thin. She had a whole lot less faith in Hollis than Carol did because she knew him better. She'd be damned if she planned to be the damsel to his hero.

Carol sat on the bed. She did so heavily, as if her whole body was giving up. That successfully softened Mia where her questions had failed.

"Hey," Mia said. "It's going to be okay. Whether he comes or not."

"How do you figure?"

Mia shrugged. Aside from her master plot to rob and leave her husband, she'd never been much of a planner. It'd frustrated Thomas to no end, but Mia found that waiting for heat-of-the-moment tended to motivate her and open her eyes. She saw options in those moments that weren't visible from a distance. Because when was an animal most dangerous? When you backed it into a corner.

"I'm choosing to have faith."

"You're kidding."

"We're locked in, Carol. We can't get out. We can freak out about that, or we can do our best to be prepared for when we *can* get out."

"And when, exactly, is that going to happen?" Her eyes went to the doorway, which seemed to be an exit but was actually just egress to a bathroom Brendan had courteously walled them in with. He'd fed them well — lavishly, almost — but had done so through a barred slot built into the bottom of the outermost door. Brendan, at least, had been planning. Whether he'd always planned to capture them specifically still wasn't clear, but he'd revamped this part of the house to hold *someone*.

"Maybe at the next Exchange."

"Why would he let us out for the Exchange?"

Mia shrugged, but she'd already had several ideas that she didn't really want to run by Carol until the time came. Most involved feminine wiles, the request for a form-fitting dress, and a pitch to be arm candy. It was shallow and predictable, but she'd yet to find a straight man who was immune. Brendan clearly liked status; that's why he'd taken the Exchange idea — which she'd heard through the door had been birthed elsewhere — and demanded it be moved to his compound. It had nothing to do with safety or efficiency, which were the excuses he'd given. It had everything to do with being seen as kingpin — especially now that he'd lost official endorsement and his army was on its own. And what said "kingpin" more than a beautiful woman by your side that all the other criminals wanted to fuck? It was ridiculous, but it was also how dudes thought. She'd only really begun understanding that until she'd lowered her standards for rational thought. After that, manipulating

Thomas into things he'd thought were his idea had become so easy, she'd almost been embarrassed.

"I just want to be ready," she said.

Carol inhaled, then let it out in one big puff that deflated her like a balloon. The issue was dead, as it had been for hours. Besides, they both seemed to understand, it was finally approaching evening. It was better to be inside, when darkness came, than out.

Carol was about to lay back when something caught her eye. She moved back to the window, this time shimmying down the length of the bed instead of standing. Mia watched her peek out, making an effort to stay low and unseen. The light in their room/cell was on and the light outside was waning, meaning she'd be obvious in the window to anyone outside — and whatever she was watching, she didn't want to be spotted.

There was a small crashing sound from outside, as of something being knocked over. Carol flinched. Mia moved over to see.

It was Brendan. Out in the dooryard, kicking over a row of tacky, white trash lawn ornaments that, Mia had always assumed, his mother had stuck there. First he felled a goose, then a trio of gnomes done in thin painted aluminum, then finally a wooden thing by the landscaping's edge, made to look like the bent-over ass of someone weeding, complete with painted-on underwear and partial buttcrack.

When Brendan was done with his tantrum, he stalked off into the woods, toward his bunkers full of madmen.

He'd had a walkie talkie in his hand. Whatever had happened in his most recent connection, Mia had to assume, had been infuriating. Or at least been with someone who, just by existing, could piss a person off.

"Good for us," Carol asked, watching the now-empty dooryard and its fallen soldiers, "or bad for us?"

But of course she knew the answer, just like they knew who Brendan must have been speaking to.

Mia, because thinking on it made fear rise in her heart, did not respond.

6

HOLLIS, out of the hole in which he'd so painfully woken and now handcuffed a pipe in the utility room of what (no shit) appeared to be a repurposed Denny's not twenty feet away across a parking lot, was talking to himself. Having a bit of the ol' internal debate, as it were. As usual, the process was depressing. He'd heard, from the self improvement crowd, that sometimes mental voices spoke of encouraging things to buoy the spirit. It'd never been that way with Hollis. His voice, when it spoke, had always been an intolerable asshole.

You told him you'll make the trade. But you can't *make the trade.*

I'll think of something.

He wants the case.

I know.

You don't have *the case.*

I know.

The case, in any helpful form, doesn't even exist anymore. You can't even go out and get it back.

I know.

And if you give him the other thing, it'll only—

I fucking know, okay?

And really, what are you going to tell this lady? That you're going to pull a case out of your ass to make a trade with Brendan that you can't make, and she could help you out by giving you some privacy and some toilet paper, for the shitting I mean, or maybe stand by to hold your butt cheeks apart? You think she hears that a lot? Maybe you can shit out something for her to make it all worth her while, while you're at it. Maybe a nice emerald brooch. You know — nothing with corners.

Hollis frowned, hating himself.

And the voice said, as its final word on the matter, *Fuck your mom, Hollis.*

The utility door opened. Two assbags entered. Hollis knew they were assbags because, like all members of the inaccurately-named Flesh Eaters, these two were wearing cliches, right down to the leather and eyeliner and hair crap that gave them untrendy fauxhawks.

"Sale at Hot Topic?" Hollis asked.

The bigger of the two eyed him, but ever since he'd been pulled from the reinforced storm drain out behind the Denny's, nobody'd laid an aggressive hand on him. Brendan might not like these people and they might not like him, but a deal seemed to be in the making. The woman he'd been waiting to see had shot the man who'd been about to impale him, and Hollis doubted she'd done it without a reason. Tweedle-Dum and Tweedle-Dee, being low-ranking assbags, surely didn't have the clout to do anything beyond what they were told.

"You're pretty funny for a guy who looks like you do," said the smaller one, unlocking the cuff binding him to the pipe.

"You too," Hollis said. "Were you born like that, or did your granny just beat you?"

Instead of answering, Assbag #2 put his thumb in a deep gash in Hollis's side. For the time it remained there, he thought he'd pass out. He'd considered himself lucky that he hadn't already. But then again, who was he kidding? There were no clocks, and he'd felt near death for some time. He might have passed out for hours. Time passed slowly at the home of the Grand Slam.

"Still feeling hilarious?" he asked.

"I don't know. Show me your summer wardrobe."

This time, Assbag #1 punched him in the face. It was the opposite of clever, speckling the concrete wall with fresh blood. In this pair, it was clear to Hollis who was the Lennie and who was the George.

They dragged him out of the utility room and into an office. On the way, they passed a storage area filled with bulk hash browns that had been pulled from the freezer and were slowly going bad. Hollis yelled for someone to make him a skillet, but his prayers went unheard. This shitty restaurant.

Inside the office was the woman he'd last seen shooting bald guys and tossing walkie-talkies bearing bad news. It was also filled with calendars (five or six, because the office's prior occupant had liked to be sure) from Denny's corporate and Denny's suppliers. All of the calendars had May photos featuring staffs so diverse as to be annoying.

"I'm Vika James," the woman said after Hollis was shoved into a seat opposite the desk. She didn't extend a hand. "I run this place."

Hollis said, "Good for you. Bad modern cuisine, though."

"And you're Hollis Parker."

Hollis's attention was elsewhere. She hadn't bothered to redecorate. The nameplate on the desk said, *MR. PLUMMER.*

"You know me?" he finally said.

"In that Brendan Banks wants you very badly."

"Yeah? How badly?"

"He offered to trade six AR-15s and a bag of Beaver Nuggets for you."

"Really. Six." Hollis tried to whistle, but his mouth wouldn't make the shape without bleeding. He was lucky he could still make witty remarks.

"Plus a bag of Beaver Nuggets."

"What the hell are Beaver Nuggets?"

"Like Corn Pops, only shittier."

"Shittier, really?"

"Shittier meaning better," she said. "I'm told you're from Texas. Have you seriously never been to Buc-ee's?"

"Not sure. What's their mascot look like?"

"A beaver. Like this." Then she made a face that was, simply put, horrifying.

Hollis sat back. "I know what Beaver Nuggets are. I just wanted to see how much I could get you to embarrass yourself. Offer me some?"

She laughed. "Like I can afford Beaver Nuggets."

"They're like six bucks."

"Not since the raids, they aren't. Now they're worth at least one-seventh of your worthless life — and that's assuming the guns are worth as much as the Nuggets ... which, considering our new 'cigarettes in prison' economy, they just *aren't* these days. Frankly, I think he's overpaying."

"Someone raided Buc-ee's gas stations? For what, immaculate restrooms?"

"Let's talk about you," the woman said.

"I ain't done talkin' about Beaver Nuggets." Then he cleared his throat and, having gauged the situation and the near-certainty that Lady Warlord's deal meant he'd survive another few hours at least — more than could be said about most people who went into a Denny's — spat blood all over the desk blotter.

The woman considered the blood, decided not to be bothered, and sat forward.

"Tell you a secret, Mr. Palmer."

"What?"

"I've got a bunch of walkies. I listened in on your little chat."

"Ah. And I suppose now you think you know everything?"

"I know that you're not always as cool, calm, and collected as you're preparing to be right now. I know there are things that scare you — things you actually care about. I know that Brendan didn't have much time pushing your buttons, once he had leverage."

"Well, that ain't your issue, now, is it?"

"Actually," she said, "it is. It's *very much* my issue. The world has changed a lot already, Mr. Palmer, and it'll change more and more — and faster — as time passes, especially if the aliens do more of what they did in Moscow and *almost* did in Austin. With the internet mostly gone and no over-air TV still delivering news, we're already falling into a citywide playing of that old game, Telephone, where information gets distorted as it's passed from person to person. I've heard some crazy stuff. A lot of people, right here in town, don't even know there have been abductions. Half don't know there are aliens on the ground here, both the bug- and big-white-types. On top of that, there are tons of rumors that aren't actually true, so far as I know. Like ... that the bugs have established of a compound up north. Have you heard that one?" She didn't wait for Hollis to respond. "The legend is, the aliens have taken over a whole suburb to conduct experiments on the people who live there. I won't even tell you the stories people have invented about New Mexico." She laughed. "It hasn't even been two weeks since we knew they were coming, and already people are falling to shit. So don't tell me that any species of 'knowing' isn't my issue. Anyone with half a brain understands that today, there's one and only one thing that's more valuable than anything else."

"Beaver Nuggets."

"Information." She put her feet on the desk. "Like the fact that Hollis Palmer is, indeed, in possession of the Thomas Davies's attache case."

"Whoopty doo," Hollis said. "So you can listen in to a conversation. Don't mean nothin' to you."

"*And,*" she went on, "that it's the *same* case that Davies was in negotiations to sell to Mobi before everything went bad."

Despite his best intentions, that surprised him. Mobi, so far as Hollis knew, was just an online store — an Amazon rival who everyone agreed was just embarrassing itself. Nobody could compete with Amazon ... unless, Hollis supposed, they had superior knowledge of the customers and a back-door way to reach them. But that wasn't even the interesting part. From what Hollis remembered, there were two newsworthy things about Mobi's founder, Lenna DeLacroix. The first was that in a world where Elon Musk and Richard Branson had set the standard for abstract entrepreneurship as a white boys' club, DeLacroix was aggressively driven to make her mark. The second was that in addition to founding Mobi, she'd founded Blink — an AI firm whose breakthroughs so far threatened to outthink even Google.

Sixty million for the case he'd so recently had, to that particular buyer, suddenly seemed cheap.

"How'd you know that?" Hollis asked.

"Like I said: Information is the most valuable thing in the world right now. So I could listen to Banks, go find the man he's looking for, and shrug as I hand that man over for chump change. Or I could accept that Banks wants you a whole lot more than he'd want some random thief, and that he's got two very good reasons for doing so. That gives me leverage. Do you see?"

"I'm not seeing what any of this's got to do with me. I mean, Banks wants me, but he can join the club. I got fellas all over the place who want me for something or other."

"Exactly. I'm trying to decide if I want to sell you now, or see what price I can get for you at auction."

Hollis chuckled, but she wasn't joking.

"Laugh now," she said. "But I'm the one who started the Exchange. I did it for exactly this reason. Would I be stupid to make a deal without seeing what price you'd fetch?"

Hollis had no idea what she meant by "Exchange," but the important parts of the idea were clear from context. He'd heard rumblings of an underground marketplace for months now — an in-person bazaar sort of like a real-world version of the dark web. The baddest folks met at an undisclosed location and swapped what they had: drugs, guns, trafficked humans, secrets of all kinds. Hollis had never been big-time enough for an invite (not that he'd have wanted to go; it, like the dark web, seriously skeeved him out), but he'd heard it existed — started, apparently, by the woman in front of him before she'd founded the Flesh Eaters. Since the arrival, it appeared to have ramped up. As the old economy began to fail, the Exchange might now be the only real game in town.

And the idea of being auctioned off, finally, knocked the sarcasm right out of Hollis's head.

"Now, hang on a second ..." he said.

Vika looked at the bloody phlegm on her appropriated desk, probably to remind Hollis that the tables had flipped, and that it was his turn to try and win favor.

"I could give you away for a few guns and spun sugar," Vika said, "or I could take a chance at losing a sure thing and see what you're *really* worth." She paused just long enough to let Hollis pre-guess her next move, then beat him to it. "I hear Thomas Davies may be bidding at the next Exchange."

"Wait," Hollis said. "Maybe you and I can make a deal."

"Maybe." Then: "Where's this case he wants so badly?"

"Never mind the case."

"What are you worth without it?"

Hollis thought fast. Then he said, "You don't like Brendan, right? Well, I have pictures of his entire operation. I can show you exactly what equipment he's got, how many recruits he has to run it, what he's got for security ..."

"Schematics of his wiring? Specifically, his security system?"

"You bet."

"Most of it's wireless," Vika said.

"No problem. I spent *days* at his house. He thought we were making a deal for the case. I spent it gathering insurance. I know where all his routers are. All his wireless hubs."

"Show me."

"Nuh-uh. You gotta let me go first."

"Give me a sample. Show me *one* of these photos."

"They were on my old phone. I ain't got it no more. But they uploaded to the cloud, and I *know* someone as smart as you seem has a guy who can get at one of the servers." Now Hollis was talking out of his ass. *Completely* out of his ass, like his ass needed its own microphone. Of course he had no such photos and he had no idea if accessible backups were a thing. But Vika was rubbing her chin. She knew Hollis was a con, but this seemed to be a lie worth considering.

She stood. Then she motioned behind Hollis, to someone he hadn't realized was there. He turned to see Assbags #1 and 2 standing there, possibly behind him the entire time.

"Give him a collar," she said.

The men grabbed him. Then the bigger one produced something narrow, black, and mechanical. It looked like an opened circle, with an hinge in the middle.

One held him down. The other put the thing on his neck, then secured it in the back. Hollis fought, but he had no strength left. After the night and day he'd had, he was lucky to be standing. Seconds later, the henchmen retreated and Hollis was left to stare at Vika with the clunky thing now on him.

"What the hell, lady?"

"You've been to Olive Garden?" she asked.

"*What?*"

"Sometimes you have to wait. So they give you a little thing that buzzes when your table is ready. It's got a limited range, and if you go outside that range, the buzzer will play annoying music until you come back." She pointed to the collar. "This is like that. Except instead of telling you when your table is ready, it lets me track you even without GPS, because it's plain old radio. Not as accurate, but accurate enough. And instead of playing annoying music if you go too far away ..."

"It gives me a hug?" Hollis said.

"... explosives on opposite sides blow your head off your neck," Vika finished.

She nodded to the assbags. One opened the rear door, standing beside it.

"You're free to go," Vika said. "But I'll be watching."

7

GO TOO FAR AWAY, *and it blows.*

Do something that makes me push the manual trigger, and it blows.

Try to remove it, and it blows.

Hollis, because he was Hollis, wished she'd given him a hooker about which she'd said the same things. But no, he was stuck with this stupid collar around his neck, free but not free at all. Vika, before he'd left the property, had laid out the situation for him, just to be clear. If she'd honored her deal with Brendan, she'd have had to let him go; he'd officially no longer be her problem and Brendan, if anyone, would have to wonder whether Hollis would hold up his end or fly the coop. That shouldn't matter; Brendan (and, let's admit it, *Hollis*) knew he'd do what he could or die trying, just because of how deep Brendan had twisted the knife during their conversation. If he wanted to make a deal with Vika, however, things got more complicated. She was delaying payment for Hollis on the hopes of a greater payment later, and for that she couldn't just trust him to do what he said. He'd spun some ludicrous bullshit about insider info on her rival Brandon, and the collar was Vika's way of seeing whether he could deliver. If he couldn't, no big deal. She'd just have her goons track him down, drag him back, and make the Brendan deal anyway.

If you're lying to me, it blows, she'd told him.

But then you can't get your AR-15s and Beaver Nuggets, Hollis replied.

If you're lying to me, she'd responded, *seeing you dead matters more.*

Hollis set out with a problem and no solution, wondering who was the better foe. Brendan would skin him if he didn't deliver. Vika would blow his head off if he didn't deliver. There was, as far as he could figure, a way to play them against each other that would extricate him from the middle — which was what he'd hoped when he'd begun spinning crap for Vika's ears back in the office. Instead, he'd simply doubled the dangers around him. Instead of having one nonexistent asset to deliver, he now had two.

Good going, dickhead, said the annoying voice inside his head. *You found the one way that will get you murdered even if you succeed.*

Now he had to retrieve Carol and Mia without the case Brendan wanted in trade.

And he had to get Vika incriminating photos of Brendan's security setup.

If he somehow got Mia and Carol and ran, Vika would blow his head off.

But if he somehow got into Brendan's business enough to take photos for Vika, he'd be going in without what Brendan wanted ... and at this point, that'd cause Brendan to blow his head off first.

And, of course, he wasn't supposed to go to Brendan's at all. His deal with Vika had him going after photos that already existed. If he went to Brendan's wearing a collar, the jig would be up. Then they'd both kill him, probably at once.

But Brendan couldn't think about that right now. *Wouldn't* think about that right now. Most of his life had been handled like walking through fog (take one step, and only then maybe see far enough to take the next one), so there was no point in trying to plan. He couldn't do what Mia had done — laying a long con on Thomas, complete with skip-town hotel reservations, an escape vehicle purchased with a hidden bank account, and a packed Go bag. For Hollis, he'd always lit the fuse first, and only then thought about what to do with the dynamite in his hand.

It'd gotten him this far. So why worry now?

The fact is, I got shit around my neck, Hollis told himself. *Ain't no changing that. I can't get it off unless I go back to Vika, so first order is to find a way to get back to Vika with what I promised.*

Which was laughable.

Okay, then, he thought, *I'll go to Brendan's. Make the trade, and at least free Mia and Carol. Well, Carol. And Mia can come along for the ride, maybe. But if I got Carol, then maybe we can stop this thing the aliens are up to.*

Which, if possible, was even *more* laughable. Not only did he not have anything to trade; he was also hanging the future on altruism. Did he really want to stop the alien thing, even if he could? That didn't sound like Hollis Palmer, so far as Hollis Palmer knew.

Well then, smartass, he thought, agitated now. *What* can *I do?*

I can walk in that direction.

Toward the road.

So he walked in that direction.

Once at the road, he decided that the next thing he could to was to walk along it. So he did.

The Flesh Eater's headquarters, being in a Denny's, was in a semi-commercial part of town. It didn't take long before Providence showed him a Wal-Mart. It was the first time that anyone, ever, at any point in history, has seen a Wal-Mart as a gift from God. Hollis entered through the broken front window and picked out a loose-fitting turtleneck that was the opposite of flattering. He looked in a mirror and wanted to attack and rob himself. The fact that he was bloody, black-eyed, and barely handsome at all anymore did little to stop the impulse. You see someone in a Wal-Mart turtleneck, you beat their ass. Those are the rules.

But it did the job. It concealed Vika's collar. He looked like he had some serious glandular problems and terrible fashion sense, but at least he wouldn't strike anyone as an obvious mole unless he was searched, which Hollis had no plans to let anyone do. A plan, so far as Hollis made plans, was beginning to take shape.

Step One? Fake it 'til you make it.

When he left the Wal-Mart, he did so with a strut. It was hard, looking like he did and dressed as he was, but Hollis knew that convincing others of what you wanted them to believe was ninety percent attitude. He needed to practice. There was a leather goods store not far up that, owing to the warm weather, hadn't even been broken into. Hollis popped its cherry, then emerged with a leather coat to offset the horribleness of his turtleneck. The ensemble, together, almost worked. He'd gotten a black turtleneck and the jacket was brown, and despite the abuse to his face, Hollis's hair still looked pretty spectacular. He grabbed a pair of Ray Bans from a display conveniently up front at the leather store (if you came in to look cool, then dammit, you were going to *look cool* when you left), and found a pair to complete the ensemble. Wayfarers, it turned out. Of course. Same kind as Tom Cruise wore in *Risky Business*, because no business was riskier than that which Hollis had gotten his stupid ass into.

After that, strutting was a little bit easier.

He was beginning to see the path before him. That was the thing about Hollis's way: Despite looking foolish from the outside, it'd always worked in the past. He'd gotten himself into a multitude of dicey situations, then sleazed his way right on out. Even just in Austin, he'd wronged half of the criminal underground in one way or another, yet he was still alive and cracking wise. That said something.

Now, despite the pain of walking and honestly just existing, Hollis was strutting tall. Strutting for *real, bitches*.

If he understood Vika's collar correctly, it was low-tech enough to still work even without internet, and that meant it didn't *track* so much as *kept track of*. It was a leash that would keep Hollis within perhaps a 20-mile range of its base unit, but it's not like Vika would be able to watch his movements on a map. That meant he'd be free to move so long as he wasn't caught anywhere he shouldn't be.

What's more, he understood his deals with both Brendan and Vika to have some give to them in terms of time. He'd bullshitted Vika about the errand maybe requiring a few days (and what did she care, so long as he had his leash?), and so to buy time for her deal with Hollis to work before she had to act on Brendan's, he knew Vika would tell Brendan that she needed a few days before she let him go off in search of the case Brendan wanted. Why didn't matter; she'd make something up. Hollis, for his part, didn't care. He knew what he needed to know — the fences within which he could attempt his deception.

He could go wherever he wanted, as long as he didn't exceed the collar's range.

And he had 48, maybe 72 hours to work with relative impunity.

Hollis's hatchling plan called for some intel, so he went in search of a place to get it. Finding clusters of criminals wasn't hard; despite the aliens, they were still under bridges dealing drugs, still in run-down hotels dealing whores. For the most part, he could just follow the gunshots. The armies downtown had shifted outward — not disbanding, but no longer at each other's throats — following the city's near destruction, and their separation made them quiet. Ironically, it wasn't the armies firing the shots. It was the underground. Either they didn't know that human-on-human violence triggered the aliens to attack or didn't care, but the result was the same. There seemed to be a threshold. Big, many-person fights attracted alien ships and alien soldiers to break them up with extreme prejudice, but skirmishes flew below the radar unless they happened in front of a bunch of the bug-things. That, Hollis hadn't seen since near-annihilation day. Which, by the time he thought of it, had only been yesterday morning. It was the longest week ever.

But on the first full day away from the Flesh Eaters, Hollis found what he was looking for: a nest of lowlives just sophisticated enough to see his jacket-and-shades-and-beat-up-face ensemble as cool instead of pretentious. Hollis tried to buy some heroin using cash he'd pocketed from the armored car score but was laughed away. He tried again using food to barter. That time, he got what he wanted. Then he threw it discreetly away, because it wasn't what he wanted at all.

He hung around all day, pretending to be high. By the

time he was pretending to come down, he'd made friends. They all had ridiculous nicknames. One was Lefty; one was No Balls; one was Hard-On. There was one woman, but ironically, it was Hard-On. No Balls was a dude.

They talked. Hollis spun a heroic yarn to explain his condition, involving a rival gang and several pipes used as bludgeons. He'd taught them, though. He'd run off with their best motorcycle — something he'd actually done with the Flesh Eaters to rile them up, so elaborating was easy.

And he learned about the Exchange, which everyone in the underbelly seemed to know.

As Banks had told him, the Exchange had moved from wherever Vika had set it up pre-aliens to his own compound, ostensibly because it was a large space, privately controlled, with security up the ass to make sure everything stayed on the level and nobody tried to cheat. That part worked with Hollis's plan just fine. What he needed to know, however, were specifics: Who came to trade? *What* did they trade? Was cash used, or was it all barter? Was there an official barker of sorts, or was the floor open for anyone to swap with anyone? And most importantly, when did it happen and how did you get in?

The heroin dealers, being low-level, knew few of the answers. But they knew enough to give Hollis a start, and by evening he was talking to their bosses, already boasting about a trade he wanted to make — a trade the likes of which the Exchange had never seen. Through artful conversation and careful misdirection, he managed to gain credibility without giving up the contents of his big trade, which of course he didn't actually have. From this group he learned what he needed: Where to go, when, and how to get inside. He still wasn't sure about the trading mechanics or what others brought, and hence what he might pretend to have to buy his way inside.

He learned that the Exchange opened every three days at noon. And that tomorrow was the third day, and all he needed to do was to show up.

He slept in a burnt-out clothing store that smelled like hair, hoping the 36 hours he was spending between his debut at the Exchange and Vika (or, more specifically, Bruce the Behemoth) wasn't healing him too well.

That night, a gang of 16-year-olds who'd apparently laid claim to the clothing store found Hollis inside and beat him until their fists went numb. That alleviated Hollis's concerns about healing, though it required a trip to a similarly burnt-out Rite-Aid, at which he managed to find Neosporin ointment for his many cuts.

The next morning, Hollis dusted himself off, realized he'd traded the last of the food Vika had given him for heroin he didn't want, and ended up finding a hipster scooter with keys in it while wandering around town to distract himself from hunger. The scooter was embarrassing — and didn't at all go with his cool, fucked-up-guy image at all — but it got him up to Brendan's neighborhood with a minimum of sweat.

From there, Hollis milled about to kill the time, then circled the very large block to find a line beginning to form outside of Brendan's gate. Before finding his place, Hollis detoured to the ditch he and Mia had taken cover in after jumping Brendan's fence, before Ricky and Ember had rolled up in their van to offer a ride. The blood stain, where Hollis had collapsed in the street before Mia dragged him to the ditch, was still there. And he thought, *Ah, memories.*

Hollis, still with a working, wind-up watch despite all he'd been through, kept checking the time. It was 11, then

11:30, then 11:45. Time dragged, and Hollis couldn't stop fidgeting with the collar of his turtleneck, suddenly convinced that even its blousy black fabric wasn't sufficiently concealing Vika's device. He searched for a reflective surface to check — a car's side mirror, even a discarded hubcap — but found nothing. So by the time noon came and a captain-of-the-guard type that Hollis had seen when he'd been here before opened the gates with a loud bark to line up, Hollis found himself uncharacteristically nervous.

This is stupid, he thought as he turned toward the line.

Yes, but since when was that new for Hollis Palmer?

8

ON THE DAY of the Exchange, Mia and Carol were given permission for a change of venue. The Exchange itself was in a massive converted barn — almost an arena, sufficient for two large horse shows at once — located on Brendan's property such that it, the house, and the paranoia baracks formed an equilateral triangle. Mia knew this because yesterday, when she'd convinced Brendan to let her gather eggs from the chickens "just to get some fresh air, please" under heavy guard, they'd paused in the barn's old tack room for egg-gathering baskets and on the wall she'd seen an aerial photo of the land. It must have been an old picture, because while it showed the house and the pre-renovation barn, the baracks were absent. She recognized the land enough to know where they'd been built, but back then they'd been a dream in the future.

The barn had been tall and large, but when Brendan had it remade he'd used the old barn as a corner, reusing only two walls and expanding in both of the other directions. Because the end structure was large, he'd kept the roof lower than that of the old barn. He'd still left the original building at full height, however, resulting in a curious-looking structure that seemed to be bulging on one end. Yawning above the large arena roof, in the corner, was the peaked top of a triple-tall barn. He'd turned the crow's nest, above the hay loft, into an office. The loft, which was half above the new roof and half below, looked out across the floor below (if you crouched) or looked across the aluminum roof panels (if you stood up tall and looked out the window).

It was into this loft, locked in a walled-off partition surrounded by windows, that Carol and Mia were moved.

"I can't watch you every second back at the house," Brendan explained.

He was short with them these days, but still hadn't touched them. Something had happened two nights ago that Mia, listening carefully, had partially overheard. She hadn't caught it all — just that Hollis would need more time. It hadn't been Hollis he'd been speaking to. Carol had taken this as a good sign; if Hollis needed more time, that at least meant he was coming. But now more than ever, Mia smelled a rat. Her father had been the procrastinate-until-it's-irrelevant sort, once requesting "just a bit longer, until some money comes in" and delaying Christmas until February. At that point, everyone gave up expecting it to happen, just as Dear Old Dad had hoped all along.

Hollis wasn't late.

Hollis didn't need more time.

Hollis, Mia felt sure, was currently hauling ass from wherever he'd been, through state lines, and back into the good old US of A. If the person on the other end of the phone and Brendan had both believed otherwise — if they'd taken Hollis's "just a bit longer, I promise" as an honest delay instead of a spineless denial — then shame on them. Brendan, at least, had known Hollis long enough to know better.

"Maybe he'll come today," Carol said.

Mia had to stop listening. She respected Carol, and was getting tired of Carol's oft-spoken, Hollis-related hopes ruining that respect. She knew Carol was brilliant and didn't want to hear her being stupid and naive. She supposed Carol, if confronted, would say "hopeful" instead of "naive," but Mia knew the truth when she saw it, and had a hard time believing that such a smart woman couldn't.

They paced the loft, which seemed to be a guest suite of some sort, Mia seriously considering breaking a window and leaping to try and escape. The windows didn't open — probably for security, since no guest in their right mind would care to climb onto the roof or leap toward broken shins from them. She'd have to throw a chair to get through, but she'd been considering it for over an hour now, as crowds began to gather for what Brendan said promised to be a record-capacity Exchange, and thought it might be do-able. It was noisy out there, echoey like a convention center. They kept moving equipment below — shifting equipment to accomodate the larger-than-expected crowd of traders — and that movement, which often required forklifts and trac-tors, was also loud. It was possible nobody would even notice glass breaking, if she timed it so that nobody was below to catch the shards. And if the guard outside rushed in? Well, he had testicles to kick, didn't he?

But ultimately she decided against a daring escape, seeing as it was far more likely to become a daring capture than a true escape. Even if they got down safely, they'd stick out like thumbs. Neither was dressed for the outdoors, like the others, and Carol was terrible at blending in. She was an introvert, used to schematics, code, and computer screens.

She couldn't be subtle in a crowd to save her life — which, Mia reflected, was exactly what was on the line for both of them.

No. Best to keep biding her time, keep mulling her hard-forming plan, keep looking for a way out. They didn't have forever; at some point Brendan would need to face the fact that Hollis had screwed him yet again — and when that happened, who knew how their situation might change for the worse?

"What do they trade, do you think?" Carol asked, looking out.

Mia joined her. It looked like the floor of a less-crowded stock exchange, complete with round-table checkpoints throughout, the way stock floors were pocked islands full of monitors.

"Well, that," Mia said, pointing at a man pulling a child's wagon full of bottled water. "And those, obviously." Pointing at a repurposed department store clothing rack, now lined with rows of automatic weapons. And although Mia didn't want to say it aloud, they could both see the people milling with women on what could only be described as leashes, looking drugged. It was something Mia had considered for her own reasons, and right now she had to imagine Carol was imagining the same.

Carol wouldn't say it aloud, either.

She cupped her hands to the glass and peered out instead. "So many of them don't seem to have anything," she said. "I heard a lot of what the barter with is information."

"How would that even work?" Mia wondered.

"Probably like a blind drop. What they know is written-down inside an envelope, and during the bidding, they'd just give teasers. Whoever wins gets the envelope."

"What if what's in the envelope turns out to suck, like it's something everyone knows? Or if it's lies?"

They both watched the people milling on the floor. At least half had pistols on them, either in holsters or tucked into waistbands. And, Mia remembered from the day of the first Exchange, they'd heard pops like gunshots all the way back at the house.

"I guess the market is self-correcting," Carol said, meaning murder.

Mia turned and sat on the floor with her back against the window. The change of venue, which at first had seemed promising for novelty alone, was only depressing her. Instead of seeing possibilities for a way out, she was only seeing evidence of how bad things had already become. Truth was, this kind of trading had probably been going on forever ... but all it'd taken was a week of occupation to bring it right out in the open, like an institution to be proud of.

She watched them all. What humanity had already become.

And again turned, facing Carol and trying to ignore the chatter beyond.

"If Hollis does come," Mia said, trying to keep hard emphasis off of *does*, for Carol's mindset's sake, "do you think Brendan will trade the case at an Exchange, or use it himself?"

"I've been thinking about that, actually," Carol said. "Remember how I said that that information, in the wrong hands, would be very bad for society and the economy?"

Mia nodded.

"Well, the economy is already not so much a thing anymore. *This*—" Pointing out the floor below. "—is the new economy. Guns and white slavery and ..." She squinted. Mia turned, and saw that Carol was trying to riddle out the presence of one man in particular, crossing the open area pulling a red Radio Flyer wagon filled with what looked like oversized, neon-yellow popcorn in clear bags. "What the hell does *that* guy have?"

Mia looked, but it didn't make more than the vaguest hint of sense to her, either. Something about the bags was familiar, but from where, she had no idea.

She shrugged. "Some sort of snack food."

And Carol, as if granting Mia a point, gestured toward her with one extended finger. "That. Exactly." She pointed below. "They're down there trading *snack foods*. What's that about?"

"Stuff that's had to get suddenly has value, I guess," Mia said.

"Right. *Stuff*. Not money. And not even *smart* stuff! I heard him talking about how this works. They have main-stage auctions throughout the day for big stuff, but a dozen little side hustles all day in between. The right person could trade and trade and trade, working small gains from nothing. There's no sensible governance. The window for arbitrage is huge."

"I don't get you," Mia said.

"It's an inefficient system. The smarter traders are going to win because they'll exploit those inefficiencies. So, you asked about the case? I honestly don't know anymore. First of all, there's no way it'll damage *this*. Second, this Exchange is highly regional. I can see people traveling from other parts of Texas if word gets around, but it won't work for the US proper, nor even well for all of Texas. I still think it's dangerous, but not for the same reasons. It depends what's done with the information. Hollis didn't say much about the case when he got back — I guess he's still hiding it — but he did say the guy he took it to said something about the aliens trying to understand us through it, as if *that* were somehow our collective brain. Or, God help us, what if the aliens get a taste of what's in there and want more, and go to the wider internet? They'll think we process our lives through the filter of spam and porn."

Mia wasn't sure that was entirely inaccurate, but took the point.

"Point is, if someone tries to use what's in there for their own means, the aliens are going to see it unless the owner finds a way to lock them out, which — and this is just a guess, so call me crazy if you want — I don't really think they'll be able to do. What will *that* say to the aliens? And might their opinion on the matter turn out to be just as dangerous as any economic collapse?" She sighed and shook her head. "All of that is on top of whatever the aliens might be doing as they access the data on their own. And I'll bet you anything that even with the internet out, they're still able to get their fingers in there somehow."

Mia sat with that, not feeling better.

"So you don't have a guess whether he'd trade it or not," Mia said. It wasn't a serious question anymore. Now, it was just a joke. Because what did it matter? They were all just as fucked.

Carol, seeing the way she'd put it, laughed. "I don't," she said.

They sat for a moment. Mia's mind was still on their way out, whatever it might be.

In the stillness, Carol, looking beyond Mia and to the floor, said, "It's fascinating, really. I've never seen a clearer demonstration of a universal truth."

Mia turned, looked, and saw nothing different.

"What truth?" she asked.

"That everyone wants something," Carol said, "and is willing to give up something else to get it."

Mia, feeling something, blinked.

"What?" Carol asked her.

But Mia's mind was turning.

Everyone wants something.

She turned and considered the traders, from those with guns to those with nothing but information.

And is willing to give up something else to get it.

"Mia?" Carol asked.

Mia held up a finger, waiting for something to fall into place.

"Hang on," she said. "I think I've got an idea."

9

THE MAN at the front of the line wasn't checking passes, or invites, or otherwise scouring the comers for information that Hollis, watching, obviously wouldn't have. Instead, he seemed merely to be surveying them — asking what they had to trade and, if they knew, what they were hoping to get. All personal weapons had to be checked, and all weapons brought to trade had to have their magazines pulled, chambers and cylinders opened to show that there wasn't still a bullet inside.

Hollis, suddenly realizing something incredibly obvious that had eluded him before, discreetly stepped backward in line. He stepped on a few sets of toes, raising grumbles.

He had nothing to trade.

And, hoping to attend a trader's exchange, that might be a problem.

They were along the berm of the rural road outside Brendan's house, feet in the dirt, lined up before the compound gate. The land was, other than inside Brendan's, wide open. Hollis swiveled his head, looking for somewhere to hide and think. But there was nowhere. If he walked off, it'd be obvious. It'd draw attention. And right now — right here, especially — Hollis very much didn't want an excess of attention.

So he did the best he could. He went to the back of the line, telling himself to think fast.

His backpack contained nothing of value to anyone else. His original bag, containing his gun and phone, had been in his pre-Flesh-Eaters car, possibly still hidden but likely stolen. He'd kept the new bag light on purpose, taking only a few bottles of water and snacks from what remained of the Wal-Mart food section. But he hadn't anticipated finding something to trade, and right now that looked to be a problem.

From the back of the line, he could see but not hear the activity at the front. Everyone, it seemed, had something to trade. Offering apparently wan't optional. You couldn't — at least as far as Hollis could tell — come just to shop. Or to sniff around for prisoners that the Exchange's host might be holding.

Some offered supplies.

Some offered weapons, of all types.

But as he came closer, he could hear what the man at the front was saying to the applicants instead of just seeing. And learned that plenty who he'd noticed didn't have obvious visible goods, came offering information.

Information.

Hollis could do that. Frankly, he had information falling out of his ass. He had *so* much information falling out of his ass, in fact, that he needed a diaper to catch it all.

Cockiness didn't return to Hollis, but it crept a step closer.

When he reached the general-type, the man barely looked up.

"Name," he said.

"Ken Adams."

"Anyone in particular you're here to see?"

"Is Regina Phalange here today?"

"Who?"

"Never mind."

The man scribbled on his clipboard. Seeing it, Hollis had two sequential thoughts. The first was that an operation this big should really be computerized. What kind of half-assed operation was Brendan running? But then he remembered the electromagnetic pulse the mothership had sent out — the one that had flash-fried even Sonny Malone's electronics all the way in Louisiana — and wondered instead if any of the digital-looking things he'd seen the people in front of him holding were, in fact, digital things. If so, how far must they have been shipped from? Or, perhaps more accurately, how many dedicated preppers had built Faraday cages of their own to protect their gadgets?

Although really, what would be the point? The cell network still came and went (he'd had service long enough to get that lovely set of texts from Sonny), but the internet was a lot closer to down for the count. Even if the guy had a working tablet, it'd have to work solo. A good thing in any event, for a guy like Hollis.

"And what do you have to trade?"

Hollis had been listening, searching for the most attractive language to use. "I know the location of three alien ground nests, plus access to a digital cache being used by them for coordination purposes."

It meant nothing. None of those in front of him had been asked to prove their sources (that'd reveal too much prior to the trade, he supposed), so Hollis had just thrown together a bunch of buzzwords. Unless the guy set him up with a trade show table from which he'd need to entertain passers-by, he'd never have to repeat it.

When he was finished writing Hollis's ("Ken's") information on his list, the guard looked up. Once, then twice. Then for ten seconds, like a study.

"What's your name again?"

Asking instead of looking at what he'd already written. Not a good sign. But it was too late to change course now.

"Ken Adams," Hollis said.

"Do I know you from somewhere?"

Hollis thought fast. The cliche was true; the best defense was usually a good offense.

"I do a lot of jai-lai. And I do mean a *lot* of jai-lai." Now Hollis squinted, pretending to think. "I know you from the jai-lai club. You're Chuck, right?"

The man squinted for another few seconds, taking in Hollis's destroyed face. He did still look like Hollis Palmer, but Hollis Palmer having an extreme allergic reaction.

"Never mind," he said.

But Hollis had always believed that any job worth doing was worth doing well. Don't go half-assed like Brendan with his clipboard holders, basically.

"Wait!" Hollis said. "Not Chuck. I mean, that's your name, but we don't call you Chuck." He chuckled companionably, almost secretively. Then, glancing back as if to make sure they weren't being overheard, Hollis stepped toward the general and wrapped his arm around his shoulder. The other was too shocked to respond.

"'*Anus*,' right?" Another laugh. "I'm *so* glad to see you, Anus! How'd you end up here?"

The man pushed Hollis away. "You've got me confused with someone else."

Hollis chucked him on the meaty part of his shoulder,

then again got too close. "Same old Anus. Remember the time we saw how many marbles we could all get up your—?"

The general, homophobia finally kicking in, shoved harder. Enough of a sudden gap opened between him and Hollis that the few people who'd gotten in line behind him started to stare.

"Oh, I see," Hollis said. "So our group's time in Cabo meant nothing to you."

"Go in," the man said, shuffling to straighten his tousled uniform.

As Hollis passed through the gate, he turned and snapped, "You let me know if you ever come around, Chuck."

He walked the intake road, looking for a chance to slip away. There was none. The man at the gate had been just for starters. They'd turned the road into a soldier-lined gauntlet, specifically to prevent straying.

A few minutes later, following the crowd, Hollis arrived at a massive hybrid building that struck him as a barn with glandular problems. From the front it was a semi-modern structure, double-tall but still just one floor. At the rear, he could see the remains of what appeared to be an old multistory barn tied into the rest. He hadn't seen it when they'd been on the property before. This, he'd have remembered.

The large sliding doors, mounted on overhead tracks, were wide open. Beyond, Hollis could see people. A lot of people.

Enough to lose himself in, maybe.

And, as he entered the fray, he thought that if he was very lucky and solved some still-unsolved problems along the way, there might just be a way out of this.

First step: slip the ridiculous number of guards and get away.

After that, all he had to do was to find Carol and Mia, break them out of wherever they were being held in one of the many buildings on this massive campus without being noticed, then get away unseen. Oh, and then he had to go back to Vika, deliver photographic evidence that didn't exist of security loopholes he didn't think existed, and convince her to undo his death collar without taking a pound of flesh.

Impossible, Hollis thought.

Good thing he was awesome.

Or so he felt, anyway, until he solved the problem of how to find Mia and Carol.

He saw them now, front and center, inside a cage on a plinth in the exact middle of the floor. Everyone was looking up at the two women — especially the younger, lither one who'd been poured into a long blue dress, hair done, lips painted fire engine red. Brendan hadn't beaten them, at least; that much was plain just by looking. But that had probably been strategic, because damaged goods wouldn't fetch top dollar.

They were a featured trade, ready for auction to the highest bidder.

It seemed that Brendan had, Vika's pleas for time aside, decided that Hollis wasn't coming, and decided to move forward with plan B.

10

HOLLIS CIRCULATED. Once on the trading floor, there seemed to be no rules. He understood, from overheard chatter, that there were big auctions that would happen from a main stage throughout the day, but otherwise it was an open marketplace. It was also incredibly inefficient, with no common currency established — not even the good old dollar. All trades other than the big auction were one-to-one — a stupid way to do things, Hollis thought, because anyone seeking a thing but lacking something the one who had it wanted would find themselves out of luck. The alternative was to pursue a series of trades, working backward from *have* to *need*. Hadn't these people learned anything from the madcap adventures of many television episodes?

But, problems aside, the marketplace was also pure capitalism in action — a place where Hollis felt intensely at home.

He forced himself to look away from the women and breathe deeply, finding his center.

On one hand, things were very bad. He had plenty of

valuable information, but none he could share — not if he wanted to save it to dangle for Brendan later. That left him with nothing to trade, and that was Problem #1. He was also a wanted and somewhat known man in this crowd (he'd already spotted several people he'd rather avoid, lest a beating ensue), and that was Problem #2. Although he wouldn't need to work to find Mia and Carol (Asset #1), them being in the dead center of a crowd who wanted to buy them actually made them far *less* accessible, far *harder* to run off with (Problem #3). Lastly, he'd have to act now or never. Once the women were traded from Brendan to someone with a thing Brendan wanted more and hence would make him more dangerous (Problem #4), he'd have no way to find them at all (Problem #5) unless he somehow followed them, which of course there'd be no way to do (Problem #6).

So basically, a total and complete clusterfuck.

But on the other hand, Hollis was a wily bastard (Asset #2) with a history of vastly underestimating the obvious problems right in front of his face (Assets #3-10). So it all worked out.

He kept his gaze averted. Tried to go blank. Tried to over-inflate his ego and abilities.

Who'd landed a job with the biggest boss in town even after ripping him off and blaming it on a gardener, then gotten away with fucking his wife before stealing his biggest asset? Hollis had. *And who'd taken a very large lump of money from a small domestic terrorist organization, given them an impressive-looking but ultimately useless box instead of the bomb they'd wanted, then somehow not only got them to forgive him ... but later went into business with the same organization again, only to empty their bank accounts?*

Goddamn right: *Hollis had.*

In the middle of the surging crowd, he closed his eyes. Tried to think.

He couldn't smash and grab. There were too many hands, too many guns. He couldn't find Brendan and try to pry up that corner; Brendan wanted him dead, and he hadn't brought what he'd agreed to trade. Mia would be useless as a co-conspirator. Even if she wasn't locked up, he couldn't get close enough to whisper, nor whisper loud enough that she'd be able to hear it in the crowd without being overheard by others. She probably wouldn't recognize him all busted up, and that meant he couldn't even catch her eye without work.

Then he thought, *Trade for her.*

Calm came. It was right. He had absolutely nothing beyond a shitty protein bar he was willing to part with, but he could do this.

Unearned confidence, filling his senses.

"One red paperclip," he mumbled to himself.

And so it began.

In a trade economy, nothing has a definite value. If, in this kind of economy, you can maximize the value of what you have and minimize the value of what you need, you can parlay very little to a lot if you trade enough times. Such was the basis of the One Red Paperclip principle, and what Hollis — a salesman if ever there was one — began doing now.

He showed his protein bar to the first man who'd listen, extolling its awesomeness. The man had a cube of graham crackers — 1/3 of a box, still wrapped tight. Hollis tested the graham crackers, decreed them to be stale, and "reluctantly" made the trade. He traded the graham crackers for a Boy Scout compass, then traded the compass for a cheap Casio wristwatch. He made what looked like a lateral trade after that: the Casio for a similar watch, but in silver instead of gold. To the woman he'd traded with, this was a great deal: gold is better than silver. But the gold wasn't real, and the watch took a battery. The silver watch Hollis got instead had an eco drive that never needed batteries or winding. A step up, working the system.

As he worked the crowd, he began to notice that the network was not unlimited. He couldn't keep going back to the same people for later trades on better goods, so he needed to circulate. Circulating showed him parties who he'd need to avoid, which made it all harder. Thomas Davies was one: Mia's husband, already stopping wordlessly by the cage containing Mia and Carol to gawk, then to contemplate their value for reasons of revenge. He saw several members of the Flesh Eaters — and while Vika hadn't forbidden him from doing anything, his showing up at the Exchange would look suspicious, if he was supposed to be out finding a phone containing incriminating photos of Brendan's organization. So he dodged Thomas and dodged the Flesh Eaters and practically leaped into hiding when he spotted Theo, visiting not just from another state, but from a whole other country these days as well. Apparently the Texas border was still porous, and it'd let his most recent enemy through.

He was intrigued to see Theo, though — even more so once he saw that Sonny didn't appear to have come with. It reminded him of the data in the case, and sent that same chill down his back. He'd been keeping his eyes on the prize, trying first to escape head-detonation and second to free the women. But now that third priority was back inside his head, troubling because there was no solution: What would happen, with the brain the aliens were building using their continued access to the most intimate and most illegally collected personal databank in the world?

He watched Theo come and go at a distance, measuring his movements, trying to guess his mood and allegiance. It was Theo who'd made the connection between alien attacks and large acts of human-on-human violence, and the reason Hollis had returned in time to help save the city in the first place.

His eyes kept going from Theo to Carol, in the cage. Each had understood Thomas's databank; each had given insights the other hadn't realized from totally different perspectives. If he still had the case, he wished he could get them together.

Forget about that for now, Hollis's mind told him. *One thing at a time.*

Yes. Focus on the trades. Try to read the mood of the audience. Trading was stressful, full of emotional gambits. Few people were truly good at it because most wore their desires on their sleeve. The trick was to not give a shit, yet with aliens threatening the planet and government degrading, it was hard not to be agitated even before beginning to barter.

Hollis found their weaknesses and insecurities, and traded again and again.

He traded the watch for an extra magazine, fully loaded, for a 9mm pistol. Traded the magazine for a bag of those absurd yellow Beaver Nugget things, then for some sort of fully automatic rifle that Hollis found impressive but couldn't identify, then for a cache of insulin, then for an entire palate of canned dog foot. After the dog food, he made huge leaps. He'd heard in the crowd that Brendan's survivalist compound had a few Faraday cages stuffed with electronics that, because they'd been protected, still worked even after the alien EMP. Some gadgets were hotter than others, so Hollis focused on the less glamorous items with lower perceived value, then parlayed up after a long lunch break, after the Exchange was more than half over and the unsatisfied traders started to get nervous they'd come home with nothing. In that frenzy, Hollis's 5-year-old handheld video game system suddenly had value and he was able to trade it ranch-style for an entire cow. The cow — apparently alive and tied up outside — was represented by a slip of paper. Hollis traded the thing away without seeing the actual animal, netting himself a moped. He traded the moped for fifty gallons of increasingly rare gasoline, then split the ten 5-gallon cans into 10 lots and traded them away individually, leveraging the arbitrage on each. That netted him ten assets which he consolidated, after a few more trades, into a late-model Mercedes.

"Man, I really wanted that," said an envious voice beside him.

Hollis looked over, then quickly away. It was Thomas Davies.

11

THOMAS MUST HAVE REGISTERED something askew, because he double-taked at Hollis while Hollis, staying very still in the way you're supposed to outwit hornets, prayed his injuries made him unrecognizable.

"The Mercedes," Thomas said, mistaking Hollis's nerves for confusion.

"Oh. Yeah." *Damn my sexy southern voice.* He played it down, trying to sound nasal like a midwesterner.

When Thomas didn't stop inspecting him, Hollis managed to say, "Do you want to trade for it?" Affecting the voice of a bored clerk at an Office Depot in Ohio.

"I wish," Thomas said. "But I'm thinking I'd better save my stuff for Lot One."

Hollis looked. None of the big-ticket items were labeled Lot Anything, but it was clear what Thomas was referring to: Mia, of course — with Carol tossed in as a bonus.

"Oh. Sure."

"But I don't like my chances. Do you know Beef?"

Hollis wondered if this was a dietary question. Then he saw where Thomas was gesturing and realized that "Beef" apparently referred to a very large black man waddling through the aisles with a ten-man entourage surrounding him. The entourage were dressed in black, all wearing sunglasses. Beef himself was a prince of pimps in their center, wearing enough gold to sink a ship. A gaudy piece of bling spelled his name in diamonds on his chest: BEEF. He hadn't traded for that piece of custom shittery, meaning he'd been balling since before the invasion.

Hollis shook his head, trying only to give Thomas his profile. But this was the thing about Thomas. He was always talking someone's ear off if he wasn't threatening them, and until Hollis found an exit, he'd just have to try and freeze him out.

"He's got all the Nuggets, man."

"Nuggets?"

"Beaver Nuggets. He intercepted a shipment. Has a whole semi-truck full of them." He indicated the trailing member of Beef's entourage, pulling a Radio Flyer full of yellow-filled bags.

"So what?" Hollis couldn't help saying.

It was a bad idea. This made Thomas turn toward Hollis, shocked.

"*So what?* Is this your first Exchange?"

"Yeah ..."

"Man, *every marketplace* this week has been all about the Nuggets. You get a hold of Beaver Nuggets, it's like somehow getting hold of Boardwalk when you already have Park Place. Get some Nuggets and you can buy anything you want."

Hollis was thinking of the bag he'd had half a day ago. The guy he'd traded his ammo magazine to for it was a desperate-looking kid who kept asking Hollis, rhetorically, how he was supposed to defend his family if nobody was selling ammunition for his specific gun. Hollis had had the ammo, but didn't realize how much the kid had apparently overpaid. No wonder the guy he'd traded the Nuggets to for that machine gun has seemed so happy, like he was getting away with something.

"Shit," Hollis said. "I traded mine for some kind of automatic rifle."

Thomas was aghast. "You traded a bag of Beaver Nuggets *for a gun?*"

"It was a good gun."

Thomas just laughed at Hollis's stupidity. "Wow. You get Beaver Nuggets, you're supposed to stop. You either bank that shit for later, or you buy up to the best thing here. Well, the best thing Beef doesn't want, anyway, since he'd outbid you with two bags." He laughed again.

"They don't even taste that good," Hollis said.

"Doesn't matter. They got hot, and now they're hot. You don't get them to eat them; you get them because it's like finding a million-dollar bill. Because of how much buying power they have, while the craze lasts.

"If I had Beaver Nuggets," Hollis said, "Do you think I could get those two slaves?"

Slaves. Yes. Don't call them people; it might make Thomas curious why anyone but him would want them.

Thomas looked at the cage containing his wife. "Probably. But don't think you're going to beat me without one. Certainly not with that Mercedes. I've got a tanker truck full of diesel."

"You're bidding on those women?"

Thomas nodded slowly, staring at Mia, who'd seen him ... and didn't look pleased.

"Maybe go for something easier," Thomas said, his

manner growing dismissive as he bored of Hollis and his bidding competition. "Like the creature."

"What cr—?" Hollis asked. But Thomas had already moved away.

Creature?

Hollis, up-traded to about as best he could do with time to kill, began to pace to clear his mind. People in the crowd stared, noting his broken face and the blood evident even on his black turtleneck. Again he saw Theo; again he saw Flesh Eaters. He skirted both. Thomas hadn't recognized him, but he'd given Hollis long, thinking looks when they'd first started talking and as he was walking away. And that made Hollis wonder: *Did he leave because he was tired of chatting? Or did he leave because he finally placed me and my voice, and went to tell someone with live ammo where to find me?*

No time to think about that. He concentrated on the crowd, and tuned into the chatter snippets of the rumor mill.

"I heard that they're sending a second mothership to Austin," someone said.

"Did you hear? Paulie's cousin Jason? One of those little ships hovered right over the guest house and ..."

"... Nashville? I mean, I've heard about those big muscular ones, but this was ..."

"... Nutri Grain bars, of all things, and then she started ..."

"... named Benjamin Bannister, I think? Anyway, it's not so funny in Moab anymore, especially if ..."

"... right in the face. Look, I don't usually like to kill old people but ..."

"... fifty or sixty, and that's not even including the black ones — the ones that look like big praying mantises? Is that how you say more than one mantis? 'Mantises'? Or is it ..."

"... a whole *group* of them at once! I guess you can shoot them, but every time someone does, they just send more and more ships after you and it's not like you can hide, but the way I see it, I'd rather be shot by a laser beam any day instead of ..."

"... a helmet on it, but I still think it's absolutely insane to bring it in here. I think that if this 'creature' thing is actually happening, it'll—"

Hollis cut this last one off with a hand on the shoulder. The speaker was a kid of maybe 17, and he jumped when he turned to see Hollis's split lips and black eyes.

"What's this 'creature'? Hollis asked.

The kid blinked. Then: "One of them."

"What do you mean, 'one of them'?"

"One of the bug-type aliens. They caught one. You didn't hear?"

Hollis leaned back, finding he wanted the support of the railing behind him.

"How the hell'd they catch one?" he asked.

There was a young woman with the young man, and she was the one to answer. The boy was looking annoyed at Hollis's continued presence, and Hollis realized he'd probably broken up some weird post-invasion pickup scene, with the kid trying to earn his way into the girl's pants by flaunting information and implied status. *Good luck, kid,* Hollis thought. *Your face is like a pizza, and the world ain't been dead long enough for her to fuck you yet.*

"Supposedly a bunch of guys with guns cornered it, backed it into the rear of a truck in a loading bay, and shut the door. Usually they've got friends, but this one was alone. I heard they hunt as if any one of them can see for all of them, like they're psychic with each other. For some reason, this one didn't have that. Like it'd been cut off. I guess they do that — I heard they did, anyway. Usually they work like a hive, but sometimes you'll see one working on its own. They captured it specifically to trade."

That sounded both impossible and like a horrible idea.

"Why would anyone want to trade for an alien?" Hollis asked.

"Dunno," the girl said while the boy still stared daggers at Hollis. Hollis, even tenderized like meat, was more attractive than pepperoni-face. "Like a collection? Or maybe just to fuck with it, because they keep fucking with us. I wouldn't want it. I guess they lost seven people just trying to catch it. And another two trying to put a helmet on it, even through the cage the shoved it into, off the truck."

"They put a helmet on it?" Hollis asked.

"I haven't seen it," she said. "But apparently, yeah."

"Wait ... it's *here* already?"

Now it was the girl's turn to look at Hollis like the most naive person on the planet.

"Yeah, of course. You didn't look through the featured exhibits?"

"No."

"They're back there. You're supposed to look before they go up for auction."

Hollis looked, but saw nothing where the girl was pointing.

"Past those girls in the cage," she explained.

"They're a featured exhibit, too?"

Now the boy talked. Furrowing his brow, he said, "I don't know about them. The tag says they're on offer from Mr. Banks, but the tag is handwritten."

"That's unusual?"

Another of those *well-duh* looks.

"They must be a late addition. Not sure who they are, or if they're anyone."

Hollis, looking, spied Thomas again inspecting Mia. Planning a trade, planning murder.

"Why would that hap—?"

But the boy had pulled the girl away. Nobody wanted to let him finish sentences today.

So Hollis kept his question to himself. If Mia and Carol were last-minute additions, that meant Brendan meant to keep them, and only recently decided to trade them away. And *that*, in all likelihood, was bad news for Hollis. It meant Vika and Brendan had spoken, and after that conversation Brendan had seen right through Hollis's usual crap and decided he wasn't coming. And that made his situation decidedly worse. When he'd gotten here, he'd known he didn't have what he needed for the private, one-on-one trade they'd negotiated over the walkie-talkie. Now, he'd have to outbid everyone in the place. He'd already known that; so far he'd parlayed up to a full-on Mercedes starting with a protein bar. Not a bad day's work — but, by the look of things, still not enough.

He doesn't think you're coming. There's no reason to be here.

Except that he still needed to get Mia and Carol, whether Brendan was a threat to them anymore or not.

You don't need to save them. They got themselves into this.

Except they hadn't. Hollis had broken off from them; Hollis had sent them to the Spider House as HQ. Hollis had failed to realize that the tracker keeping Brendan on their tails wasn't planted on Hollis or in the case, or simply the result of superior surveillance. It was Hollis who hadn't even thought Brendan might be tracking and listening in on Mia, all through that little spy device he'd slipped into her locket.

It doesn't matter. Right now, you can walk out of here. But if you make waves, who knows what'll happen?

He had to try.

But do you?

Yes, because Carol was the only one who could help figure out the database — and, therefore, what sinister shit the aliens might be up to.

Which is irrelevant, because the attache case was destroyed.

Except that Hollis, of course, had painstakingly taken photographs of everything in it before giving it to Sonny. Those photos, unlike the photos he'd told Vika he had of Brendan's security weaknesses, actually existed.

On a phone you no longer have.

He'd left it in the car before the Flesh Eaters had chased him up onto that ridge. The Flesh Eaters had, almost for-sure, retraced Hollis's steps after capturing him and found the car. It was stuffed with all that armored car cash, his pistol, and of course Ricky's stolen cell phone. They'd surely found the car right where he'd parked it, low on gas and needing a refill, before stealing one of the Flesh Eaters' motorcycles from outside a bar and begun that chase.

Unless, of course, the car was still there. Unless, of course, the cell phone containing records of everything that'd been in the case was still in it, whole and untouched.

It's not.

But what if it was?

What are you going to do, hero? Is that really why you're here? To free Carol, so she and the photos you'll never find can save the world?

Well, no. Of course that wasn't the only reason. He was in a very complicated situation, in need of many solutions.

Someone passed by him too close in the crowd. Hollis had been carrying a stack of papers he'd collected like leaflets on a trade show floor. Mostly the papers didn't matter, but the deed to his new Mercedes was among them.

He stooped. The man who'd knocked them out of his hands stooped to help, too.

A thin black man, wearing dark-rimmed glasses.

Theo.

"Oh, man. I am so sorry."

"Ain't nothin'" Hollis said. "I just ..."

The other man had stopped moving.

Probably, Hollis realized, because he'd been caught off-guard, hadn't altered his voice, and had just said a signature Hollisism in standard Hollis dialect.

They were both holding the Mercedes title, still low to the floor. Theo was staring at him, squinting to see through his bruises.

"Hollis?" he said.

12

"Hollis, is that you?"

Hollis tried to backpedal, looking away. "No. You got me confused with someone else."

He stared to move, because the best choice for such situations tended to involve evasion and apathy.

He had no idea what Theo might do. There were no loaded weapons allowed on the floor, and violation of that rule (so said the notices tacked all over) was cause for expulsion from all future Exchanges. So Theo wouldn't be packing and wasn't physical enough to fight him, leaving only the question of whether he'd resort to tattling and screaming. Which came next hardly mattered. Hollis needed to find shelter, to start pretending this didn't happen.

Either way, Hollis wasn't interested in finding out. He moved faster.

"Hollis!"

It was too loud. Heads were turning.

"Hollis, wait up!"

Hollis turned. Then he rushed back to Theo, eyes darting, and took him by the wrist. He pulled him away from the floor's center.

"Goddammit, you tryin' to get me busted?"

"How did you get here?"

"I drove. How the fuck'd *you* get here?"

He didn't actually want to know. He just wanted Theo to stop saying his name loud enough for everyone to hear — including Thomas Davies, who wasn't twenty feet distant.

"Sonny sent me."

"Good for Sonny. He here?"

"No, he's back in Lafayette. Look. I'm glad I ran into you."

Hollis was still looking around, sure he'd been spotted. "That so?" he said.

"Yeah. I'm guessing what happened when Sonny tried to open the case wasn't an accident?"

"You tell him you saw me here," Hollis said, "and I'll pull your balls off one by—"

Theo, so completely undaunted by the threat that it seemed he hadn't heard it, pushed on.

"I need to know what else you know about what was inside," Theo said. "Anything at all."

"Why the fuck should I tell you? Way I understand it, stuff like I know will get you food, weed, a goat ... anything I want. You got a goat to trade me, Skippy?"

Theo shook free of Hollis's grip, but ran nowhere, to tell no one.

"Sonny wants what was in the case," Theo said, "but just because he wants to exploit it. He's fixated on what we said, about the predictions it can make. Before the thing self-destructed, I was trying to figure out how to handle it. He'd have had me start working right away on how to use it to his advantage. You solved that problem for me."

They'd moved into a small alcove. Less seen now. Hollis wasn't positive that he could rough Theo up without getting caught, but the floor was loud and nobody was paying attention. Maybe.

"Why don't you tell me why you're here?" Hollis said.

"I told you why I'm here."

"But the case is gone."

"Yes, but there's a lot of chatter and rumor about that case already. Obviously Davies knows about it, but a lot of other groups, too. This is where it's from. I'm supposed to find out if anyone, anywhere, knows what might have been inside. I have the IP of that shell site in my history, but we didn't write down the password. I remember a lot of what was there, but not enough. But ... now you're here."

"You still seem happy about that."

Theo shrugged. "I am. This makes things so much easier."

"How?"

"I don't want Sonny to use what's inside the case. *You* didn't want Sonny to use what was inside the case. You know more of what was inside and how it fits together. And—"

Hollis pointed at Carol. "Not me. Her. That one right there? She'd the one that knows the most."

"She the one that built the shell?"

"If that's what it's called, yeah."

"Well," Theo said after a few seconds considering the situation. "I guess we'll have to trade for her."

"What do you think I've been doin'?"

"Great. I'll join you."

Hollis looked Theo over. "I'm fine alone," he said.

But Theo was all business, apparently immune to the sides of their conflict — apparently immune to the apoplectic rage Sonny must have bellowed about Hollis before Theo left.

"Don't be ridiculous. I'm seeing what the big tickets are going for. I saw the tag. Banks just put them on the market, and neither of us will have a chance of affording them alone. Why are they there, anyway? And who's the other girl?"

Hollis didn't want to answer any questions. "Move on, Theo. I got this."

"I keep thinking about what we discovered," Theo continued, undaunted. He was speaking to Hollis as if they were two halves of a research team who'd taken a break, not two quasi-criminals who'd been forced apart by Sonny's desire to string Hollis up by the uvula. "I only saw a tiny bit of what you had, and I get why you wouldn't show us more. But even that much, if the aliens really are using that database as some sort of effort to neuroform the whole—"

"To *what?*"

"Neuroforming," Theo repeated. "It's complicated."

"Well," Hollis said, "that's really amazing. But I'm still not interested in ..."

He trailed off as Theo reached for his neck.

"What's this?" he asked. Before Hollis could pull away, Theo tugged the turtleneck down to reveal the edge of Vika's collar.

"Jewelry."

"Are these explosives?" He was circling its perimeter now and prodding at its every edge, as if Hollis had no shame. "Who put this on you?"

"Sonny's mother."

"You should get this off," Theo said.

"You don't say."

Theo was about to say something stupid again, but a

sound rippled through the arena that shut down every single bit of conversation.

It was a low rumble, almost like a purr.

"Christ," Hollis said.

They both looked.

In the room's corner, the featured auction area was being rearranged, a forklift now pulling an enormous reinforced cage into view.

With one of those black, insect-like aliens inside, thrashing and making its horrid, man-eating noises.

13

Mia perked up.

"Did you hear that?"

"Hear what?" Carol asked.

"I could've sworn someone said 'Hollis.'"

"I didn't hear that."

Mia was scanning the Exchange floor. Their cage's elevated position gave them a wide field of view, but in every other way it was inferior to their last place of confinement. Her idea had sounded so good, and now here they were — inspected, poked through the bars, stared-at, mentally undressed. They were a package deal: two chicks in one, and very valuable as she understood things. She'd meant to convince Brendan that she and Carol had value even without Hollis, and that chain of argument had just made him fed up, just made him toss them right out into the meat market so he could turn a high-maintenance asset into something more liquid. Whereas they might have found a way to break free from the office, getting out unseen from the cage would be impossible.

Good job, girl, she thought. *Your smooth talking made Brendan decide you were more hassle than you were worth.*

Anyone might buy them. Anyone, who might be worse than Brendan.

There was a scuffle. One guy ran into another and papers hit the floor. They picked them up together. Mia stopped paying attention as her eyes were drawn toward activity in the featured area, not far off. When she thought to consider the two men again, they'd moved almost out of sight, now looking like an argument. She hoped they'd fight. Provide a distraction, let her try and gain some room to maneuver.

"That guy's still around," Carol said, pointing.

Mia looked. And tried not to look.

"Who is he, anyway? I'm getting tired of feeling like something hanging in a display window every time he loops by." Which, of course, was exactly what they were.

"That's Thomas."

"Your husband?"

"Yeah."

"What if he's the one who buys us?"

Mia had been thinking about that. Thomas was a fool-me-once sort of guy. Chances weren't good that she'd be able to talk her way out of anything with Thomas after this, especially since he seemed so eager to buy for revenge. She'd been too scared to speak the first time he'd come up. He'd surprised her, throwing her off guard. But now the die had been cast. She'd had her chance to pretend to be happy to see him — to gush in her fake-Mia best and blame the whole thing on a big misunderstanding. But shock had kept her mouth shut, and the second time he'd been glaring, already pre-decided. Now there was no point in denying what she'd done. No point in batting her eyelashes and trying to play innocent. After all that silence, attempts to worm her way out would only make him angrier before he placed his bids, and then the thumbscrews would be turned. Literally, maybe.

"We'll figure it out."

"What if whoever buys us wants us for ... you know ..."

Mia did. She wasn't an idiot. Before putting them out here, Brendan had stuffed Mia into a dress that screamed man-bait. She wasn't being offered for her organizational skills. But that was a problem for later.

"Let's cross that bridge when we come to it."

"Honestly," Carol said, "if he—"

The both stopped talking when they heard the alien's purr. The sound was stranger than it had before — more bass, more echo. It was a canned version of what she'd heard under the Congress Street bridge, and when they brought the big cage around, Mia saw why. They'd somehow gotten a helmet of sorts over its head. It couldn't have been easy. The helmet's matte surface was dark with dried blood.

"What the hell," Carol said.

She was shaking.

"How did they get that thing? Why would they—?"

Their cage started to move. Mia looked back and saw three men shoving from the rear, moving them away from their spot on bottom-mounted casters. That was interesting, but not as interesting as where they were going. What other popular offering they were being placed beside.

The alien, up close, was absolutely terrifying. Somehow, it was even more terrifying than when she'd seen the things before — and that time, they'd been cutting human beings into ribbons. It was still now, but was nowhere near resting. It rocked slowly with the rhythm of what seemed like alien breath, its angular limbs flexing slightly with each cycle. It didn't strike Mia as *dormant* so much as *waiting*. At some point, some fool would let it out of its cage, and that would be bad; she'd seen that their teeth were nowhere near their only dangerous parts. But if that same fool tried to remove its helmet? Well. Mia just hoped he was smart enough to take it home before that happened.

Carol had moved to the opposite side of their cage. Mia was just as scared of the thing — especially given those long legs that, if the thing weren't wearing its helmet and could see them — looked plenty long enough to reach all the way through their bars and through the other side, with room to spare.

Carol's mouth opened, but Mia held a finger over her lips:

Don't make a sound.

Although, might it *smell* them?

The tag on the cage, carefully lettered, read, *REPTAR.*

Was that the name of the person selling it? Or was that what they called these abominations?

She could hear its insides clicking. She could hear the minute ticks of its exoskeleton as the thing shifted, sharp appendages making do on slick metal.

How the hell had they caught the thing? And why?

"Okay, ladies," said a man from Brendan's camp, coming alongside the cage.

Beside them, the alien stirred. The body language, on any species, looked the same. It could hear them, and was considering what lay close — what delicious thing nearby might make its move.

The man, oblivious, kept right on chatting while the big bug oriented itself, trying to find its target.

"You're up," he said.

Mia nodded silently, eyeing the bug as if to say, *Stop talking, dammit. It hears you.*

The thing made a tiny, tentative stab, but struck nothing. It was a violent little prelude that their escort, still, continued to miss.

"Come on," the man said. But not to Mia and Carol; to the men who'd pushed them before.

A few seconds later, they were away from the alien, Mia's heart like thunder in her ears. She didn't want to look back. Didn't want to hear those sounds. Didn't want to see the blue glow, from the spark in its throat, glowing across the inside bottom of the helmet. And most of all, she hoped it wouldn't purr again — not while they were so close. It wasn't quite nails on a chalkboard. More like nails across her very soul.

"Smile," the man said as the cage stopped again at one end of an impromptu stage. "Try and look pretty."

"Go fuck yourself," Mia told him.

And the man said, "That's the spirit."

14

"Hold still," Theo said.

"I'm holdin'," Hollis told him.

"Hold your neck still. You want to get a shock?"

"I ain't movin' my neck."

"You are."

Hollis did move his neck now, fully turning to face Theo and making him drop his little tools he'd been using to tinker with the deadly collar around Hollis's neck.

"What the hell? Do you want help with this or not?" Theo said, stooping for a tiny screwdriver.

"Are you talkin' about my breathing? Is that my 'neck moving'? Cause that's just me trying to stay alive."

Theo pushed Hollis's face back into position and said, "Now don't move. I don't really want to get my hands blown off by these explosives."

"Is that a thing?"

"It is if you make me cut the wrong thing, yes."

"Vika said it'd blow if anyone tried to take it off," Hollis said.

But Theo was back in position again now, again with his

little screwdrivers in-hand, both held delicately where Hollis's peripheral vision couldn't quite see them. He was holding a third tool between his teeth, and replied around it with confidence he didn't normally project, when he wasn't working on something in his zone.

"It will blow," he said, deftly operating his tools, "if it calls back to the base unit and reports that the clasp has been opened. I told you, there's no direct loop here, on this board." He tapped the lock. "If it can't call out, it won't blow. If it can't broadcast or receive, you're in no danger."

Hollis glanced around. They were inside one of Brendan's many supply cages. It looked like a batting cage to Hollis, totally incapable of protecting more than the contents from a thief who didn't have the key. The only reason it had been open when they'd come was because, as Theo had predicted, Sonny had emptied it in prep for the Exchange. All the electronics this place had protected were out on the auction floor.

"Don't look like it's gonna stop anything. It's not like I couldn't hear you when I was in here and you were out there looking for tools."

"That," Theo said, leaning in and working, still with the butt of a third screwdriver in his mouth, "is not how it works, and you're not dumb enough to think it is."

"You don't know how dumb I am."

"Mmm-hmm. Hold still."

Hollis waited, sure that at any minute his head would blow clean off. But then there was a click, and some quick work made, and then his neck could suddenly breathe as Theo carefully raised the thing off of him, a jumper wire spanning the two contacts where the lock had recently been closed. So far, Theo was right. The collar wasn't blowing up, wasn't having a fit, and wasn't calling home to Mommy Vika.

"Move," Theo said. He was holding the thing with two hands, treating it deftly.

"Are you gonna throw it in the corner to blow?"

"I'm going to throw it in the corner ..." Theo said, "... because I don't want to carry it anymore."

Hollis watched as he lifted up half of a stack of rags along one wall, laid the collar on what remained, and then covered it up with the other half. Just like that, the collar was a memory — and Hollis lives to fight another day.

"What, you're just going to leave it there?" Hollis asked, referring to the rag pile.

"Sure. It'll look to the people who put it on you that you just went out of range or something. They can triangulate all they want, but they'll never find it as long as it stays inside the cage. Blocks all signals. Know what I mean?"

Hollis looked at the rags. Had it really been that simple? And the answer was: No, it hadn't been. Theo had been able to open it; Theo had been able to jumper the clasp; Theo had known that Brendan's Faraday structures would keep the thing from going off.

"Well," he said, rubbing his neck. "Thanks."

"No problem."

"Still not sure why you did that."

"Because I need your help."

"I can't help," Hollis said. "Sonny self-destructed the case."

"But you must remember some of what you and the others talked about. You know where to start, if we want to look anew."

Hollis moved through one door of the cage, then the other. Of course Brendan's Faraday cages had airlocks, to make sure the perimeter was never broken. What if an EMP happened while some asshole was holding the door open for a friend?

He looked at Theo, as he emerged.

"What?" Theo asked.

"Why you doin' this?"

"Helping you get your collar off?"

Hollis shook his head. "Goin' after what was in the case. Not Sonny's reason. If you were only here for Sonny, you wouldn'ta bothered with me."

"I told you. Whatever the aliens are doing with that database, it's dangerous. I think they operate in a hive mind. That one we saw out front, in the cage? I've been following ones like it since I started to suspect they were working with a shared brain. Every once in a while you'll see one acting solo — no others around, exploring rather than bold ... almost tentative. I think they're individuals who've been cut off from the collective. Maybe so they can be spies — live embedded among us; know what I mean? The rest, though, work like one big organism. And so I got to wondering: what must they think of us, with all our differences? In their shoes, I'd try to quantify it, then try to pick it apart. See what *makes* us different. Have you heard the rumors about psychic phenomenon around the aliens?"

Hollis thought of what he'd experienced near the big stones — the way his mind and Mia's had connected. "No," he lied.

"What about mind control?"

"They can *control our minds?*"

"Don't act so surprised. We run around mind-controlled all the time. Marketing fills us with subconscious triggers. The people we know and love manipulate us to get their way, even if they don't know we do it. And mothers? Don't even get me started on mothers and mind control."

"That's different," Hollis said.

"It's an earlier stop on a long and well-documented continuum," Theo told him. "That's all."

Hollis thought he was being dramatic, but he also thought back to how many times what Carol or Theo had said about the case had scared the shit out of him. Mind control? Yeah, he sort of bought it.

"You can't sell it, you know, even if you somehow get it."

"Of course not. Sonny will try to sell it. Even if I didn't have to go back with 'bad' news for him, I wish I didn't have to go back. I didn't want to be his guy, you know. He made me an offer I can't refuse, and now that things have changed, I'd really like to."

Hollis studied Theo for a long moment. For some reason, he believed Theo — believed his do-gooder's words. Something primitive told him that trust was a mistake, but ultimately the practical part of Hollis's brain spoke up. Once it did, the arguments ended.

It doesn't matter if you trust him, that voice said. *At this point, there's very few ways to make this worse.*

Which, once he thought about it, was true. If Theo somehow learned all the case's secrets and took them back to Sonny, how would the world be any different tomorrow? The case's value, on the open market, was surely decreasing. Money was already losing its universal value in places like this. And while Hollis liked to fancy himself an optimist and wanted to imagine the traditional economy surviving this invasion, he just didn't think it was likely. *Let* Sonny collapse what was left, if that's what was meant to be.

"You really not going back to Sonny?" Hollis asked. Trying to believe it.

"I'm really not."

"If you could get that case back, what would you do

with it?"

"Figure out what the aliens are doing. Try to stop it, if it's what I think."

"You really think you could do that?"

"Why, do you know something? Do you remember what was on any of the papers?"

"Any. Or all. I took pictures."

"Pictures?" Then he started to get it, and his frenzy built. "Wait. You mean pictures of the contents of the case?"

"Maybe."

"Well ... where are they? Show them to me!"

But Hollis wasn't quite *that* ready to trust.

"When we're done here," Hollis said.

Theo seemed to think. Then he said,. "All right. The woman. You need the woman, who built the shell."

And the lady who was in with her, Hollis supposed. He nodded. "Carol."

"Okay. How do we do that?"

"We pool our assets. You want me to trust you, contribute to the freedom fund, will ya?"

"Of course." He began shoving nondescript papers at Hollis. Presumably they meant something. "When's the auction, anyway?"

"Any time, the way I hear it."

"But they were over by the featured auctions."

"And?"

"Well, they're going to be auctioned off. I thought that was clear."

"Nothing's *clear,*" Hollis said. "When's that happen?"

"Around three?"

Hollis looked at his watch.

Then he ran, Theo taking the hint and running along behind him.

15

THEY ARRIVED JUST as Thomas Davies was raising his hand. He said "fifty AR-15s" after being called on, and Brendan, visible onstage beside the cage containing Mia and Carol, nodded. Apparently this was how it worked: the auctions were conducted with goods instead of currency, and the one offering the auction determined which bid felt bigger than the others, which bids he might be willing to accept.

Right now, the price on Mia and Carol stood at fifty military rifles.

"What you got, Theo?"

"Vehicles."

"*Vehicles?*"

"Sonny collects classic cars. Not just the Chevelle you took. He sent me with a car carrier full of them. All work even after the EMP because they're old enough to be all gears and belts. No computers."

"How many vehicles?" Hollis asked. He still breathing fast from the run here. At least they hadn't missed it. At least there was still a chance.

"Twelve."

"Any Corvettes?"

"Two."

Hollis raised his hand and yelled, "Two Corvettes!"

Brendan and Thomas Davies both turned to look at the new bidder. Both looked like they almost recognized Hollis, but not quite.

"No," Brendan said when the auctioneer looked to him for bid approval.

"That's two Corvettes!" Hollis shouted. "Two whole Corvettes!"

Brendan looked more closely now, probably because when Hollis shouted, it was hard to conceal his voice from anyone who knew it well.

"Who are you?" Brendan asked.

"Ken. Who the fuck are you?" He knew, obviously, it was better to play offense than defense.

"I don't need two Corvettes, *Ken*. I only have one ass to sit in the driver's seat at a time."

"Sell the other?"

"Denied," Brendan told the auctioneer.

"Any more bids?"

More bids came, and more were accepted. A minute later, to get Mia and Carol, they'd need more than a semi truck filled with decent beer.

"What else you got?" Hollis asked.

"More vehicles."

"Ain't working, fella."

"Well, what do *you* have?"

"I got a Mercedes," Hollis said. "Can I put it on your car carrier?"

"You planned to trade a single Mercedes for two healthy people in a featured auction?"

"Hey! I started with a protein bar. I think I done damn good."

Theo took the initiative. He called out to the auctioneer. "Tell us about the lot," he said.

Brendan answered. "Two ladies," he said. "Both smart, both at least reasonably attractive, one a serious pain in the ass."

"Who's the pain in the ass?" Theo asked Hollis from the side of his mouth.

"Guess."

"Ten luxury cars!" Theo called out.

"Denied," Brendan said. "Again. *One* ass."

"We have to trade them separate," Hollis hissed. "Trade out all the cars, get better stuff, then come back. You got all twelve sets of keys?"

"Ten's all I have."

"I thought you had twelve?" Hollis said.

"I bought some videos earlier. I'm bored with everything on my Juke."

Hollis, because he was suddenly so frustrated with Brendan's denials, with the tilt of the auction, and with the fact that more and more intrigued bidders were crowding around licking their lips, ripped all the papers out of Theo's hand. The top one was the inventory of movies he'd bought using his earlier vehicles.

"These are all shitty 90s movies."

"You have your tastes. I have mine."

"What's *Bloodsport?*"

"Oh. It's awesome."

Hollis was still reading the list.

"*Mr. Destiny?* Are you fucking kidding me?"

"It wouldn't have made a difference if I had all twelve! He doesn't want more than one!"

Theo grabbed his papers back. There was a brief, tantrum sort of interaction wherein both held the stack, slapping at each other like kids over a favorite toy. Then Hollis's hand suddenly let go and the recoil on his arm slammed his elbow back into the arm of a man who'd come up beside them.

It was a man in the entourage of the rapper-gangster type with all the gold Hollis had seen earlier. *Bacon?* No: *Beef.*

The bodyguard looked at Hollis, who pulled his arm back and apologize.

The man himself — fat, reeking of cologne, and with a mushmouth that made it sound like he was eating marbles — had pulled up next to Hollis and Theo.

"You want those bitches?" he said. Thanks to his mushmouth, "want" came out sounding like it almost had an F in it. Then, without waiting for a reply, he raised his hand and called out, "One bag of Beaver Nuggets!"

Immediately, Brendan sat up straight. Looking like he didn't believe his fortune, he told the auctioneer, "Accepted."

"Beaver Nuggets?" Hollis said.

Beef nodded smugly. "That's right, playa."

"I had Beaver Nuggets earlier today!"

"And you don't no more?" He laughed and his entourage laughed too, probably because they were being paid to. "You stupid."

Hollis held up his hand and shouted, "A bag of Beaver Nuggets and a Mercedes!"

"Accepted!" Brendan said, now standing, now eager to see how far this crazy train might go.

Theo pulled Hollis's arm down and hissed, "You don't have any Beaver Nuggets!"

"Man, we're gonna lose 'em!"

"Where the hell are you going to get Beaver Nuggets?" Theo demanded.

But Hollis could hardly hear. The auction was spiraling away, and this plan wasn't going to work. Letting anyone else win was unacceptable. Right now, it was impossible to get Mia and Carol and duck away. But once they were taken elsewhere? He'd never find them again. He didn't understand why Theo wasn't more agitated, determined to win.

"You hearing me, Hollis?" Theo whispered.

"I'll figure something out! Bid!"

"*Two* bags of Beaver Nuggets," Beef calmly announced.

The room gasped. Murmurs spread. Brendan looked like he couldn't believe his ears.

"Look," Hollis said to Beef, minding the threatening glares of his bodyguards, "I know those two. The one in the dress is a serious asshole. She'll fuck you up, man!"

"Sit down, bitch!" said one of Beef's men.

"What do you want with them? I'll buy them off you. I got ..."

"What?" Again with the almost-F sound; Hollis could swear the man had a sock in there. "What you gonna pay that I care about?"

"Information about the aliens!"

Everyone laughed. "Like I fuckin' care!" Beef said.

Hollis made his eyes soft. "Please," he said.

Beef seemed to consider. Then, even though he already held the top bid, he turned to the auctioneer and shouted, "*Three* bags!"

Hollis was still staring. "What are you going to do with them? Why do you want them?"

"I got a thing for brunettes," Beef said, picking his teeth with what seemed to be a gold pick.

"You're not her type."

"I buy her," Beef said, "then I'm her type." He ticked his head back at all the others. "Then maybe all of *them* are her type. I like to spread the wealth, *knowwhati'msayin'*?"

"Fuck all y'all with the skinny bitch. I like the older one," said the man Hollis had elbowed. "That's *my* type."

They were all staring at the cage, licking their lips. Only now did Hollis realize just how greasy Beef's fingertips were, between all those gold rings. He looked like he'd just set put a bucket of KFC, and done so with extreme prejudice.

The crowd parted. Thomas Davies stepped between Beef's men. He looked at Hollis again, brow still furrowed, seeming not to understand why this same guy was right in front of him again — and not quite understanding why said guy struck him as familiar. Hollis looked around for Theo. For support. But Theo was no longer at his side.

Thomas turned to Beef. They embraced: big, showy man-hug complete with series of handshake gestures after.

"Hey," Thomas said. "Favor to ask."

"You name it."

"Let me win this auction."

"No can do."

"I'll make it up to you."

"So *you* gonna suck my dick, then?"

"That's my wife up there," Thomas said.

"So, what, you want her back or something?"

"Yeah. So I can kill her." Now Thomas was studying Hollis. Part was probably this casual talk of rape and murder in front of strangers, but on the Exchange floor, such things weren't all that unusual. The look was more about a missed connection — a recognition Thomas's brain wanted to have, but that he couldn't quite see.

"You just gonna kill her?" Beef said, looking at Mia. "What a waste."

"She's a pain in the ass, Beef. She'll trick you, then rob you blind."

"Exactly! She's a pain in the ass!" Hollis blurted. They all looked at him. *Oops.* He'd already been telling Beef about Mia's personality, but he forgot with all these nerves that Thomas might find it strange that some random guy would know his wife's ways.

"What's your name again?" Thomas asked.

"You know this guy?" Beef said before Hollis could answer. "He's been tryin' to talk me out of buying."

Thomas's scrutiny doubled. Hollis stood still, feeling transparent, clueless what to do. He wasn't wearing a false nose and makeup; his "disguise" was simply being beat to shit. Anyone could look at him as he was, then extrapolate what he might look at without the bruises and blood. Thomas seemed right on the edge. Any second, his eyes would change, his small mouth would form a smile, and he'd poke Hollis in the ribs: *You. It's you, Hollis Parker. And where's my sixty million bucks?*

But he wasn't getting it yet. Hollis had his attention — not good attention, either — but Thomas hadn't figured it out just yet.

"How about," Thomas said sidelong to Beef, keeping his eye on Hollis, "you buy her, do whatever you want, *then* sell her to me when you get bored? I don't care what you do with the other lady. Use her for target practice, if you want." His head tipped and he said to Hollis, "How's *that* deal strike you, Friend?"

Unsure what else to say, Hollis replied with, "Can I get in on that?"

Thomas laughed. Beef's entourage laughed. They turned toward each other, shutting Hollis out.

"Three bags of Nuggets!" the auctioneer called. "Going once ... going twice ..."

Hollis retreated, finding Theo, grabbing his shoulder.

"Where'd you go?" Hollis asked.

"I wanted to get some information. About the trades. About what happens *after* a trade is made on the main auction floor. You with me?"

Theo raised his eyebrows and waited for acknowledgement. That's when Hollis realized that he must look like he was starting to feel. Somewhere between the beatings, the no-sleep, and the other beatings, he must have lost his rascal's luster. The look Theo was giving him was one that tries to bring a wayward brain back from the clouds: *You with me, man? Are you picking up what I'm putting down, or are you just blitzed?*

"What happens?" Hollis asked, blinking himself back to center.

"Workers prepare the sold goods, then transfer them out the back door." He pointed, past what looked like a holding area. The area was cordoned off with hung drapes, leaving them to guess what was behind. But from here Hollis could at least see the door in the wall beyond: double-tall, wide, and rolling on overhead tracks, just like the front. "I have no idea how many people are back there and who might be guarding the door, but I do know something else ..."

"What?"

"That guy. Beef? He lives near Houston and has a compound twice as fortified as this one. So while trying to grab the women now might not be exactly ideal, I'd say it's a whole lot more ideal than it'll be if you let Beef take them home."

Hollis considered. He used to be better at infiltrating, but all signs lately said he was losing his edge. He'd been part of Thomas's staff, but even if he hadn't run, *Mia* would have run with a whole lot of Thomas's stuff and framed Hollis for it. His attempt to get inside the Banks household the first time had nearly ended in skinning, and this latest infiltration of the Exchange was inches from blowing up in his face. Trying to do the same at Beef's wouldn't be a good idea. Especially since, judging by Beef's current entourage, his staff had a few things in common that Hollis did not have. He'd stick out a little, with his skinny white body.

"All right," Hollis said, moving fast as the auction concluded — as Mia and Carol were rolled offstage and toward the area Theo had indicated. "You stand guard, and I'll go in and see what I can do."

16

Mia made her body language scared until the kid in fatigues had parked their cage between a stack of 1-gross boxes of toilet paper and something that looked like a James Bond weapon. Then, when he was gone, she sighed and got to business.

"Thank God," she said.

Carol was backing up, putting her strap-bound hands against Mia's — also strap-bound. Wrapping their wrists in plastic zip ties had been the first order of business after they'd been wheeled off the stage. After, there'd been paperwork. The guy had bound them way too tight for transport, and Mia felt her hands going numb. She fumbled the nail clipper out of her panties — a maneuver that required hiking the dress all the way up with locked hands and that in the end, Carol had to help her with. Using the clipper was even harder, but she managed to get Carol's wrists snipped. Then Carol snipped hers.

Rubbing wrists, trying to restore circulation, Mia surveyed their surroundings. She'd been watching the earlier auctions from their old crow's nest office, and now that they were sold, they'd ended up right where she'd seen assistants taking the other sold lots. She wasn't positive of what came next, but had a pretty good guess.

"I thought your husband might win us," Carol said.

"Yeah. That would have been bad. Thomas knows me too well."

"But that gangster guy ..."

Mia laughed. "Don't worry. I know the type. All we have to do is tell him how fly he is. Over and over and over again. And if you can stomach it, definitely beg to suck his cock."

Carol made a face.

"We don't have to do it, you know. It's just playing a card."

"I know. Just ... gross."

Now Carol was unbuttoning her jeans. Both of them began unpacking. Before calling Brendan in and picking that last fight, they'd spent a lot of time on an office scavenger hunt. There'd been no weapons, conventional or improvisable, but they'd found and packed a bevy of smaller items with specific purposes. The nail clipper, for snipping ties. A paperclip for picking the lock on the cage, which Mia was working on now, unsure what she was doing but encouraged by the cage's animal smell: What was usually locked in here, she'd decided, wasn't the kind of prisoner that merited pick-proof locks. Mia had a small ring of keys, which could be clenched in a fist to use as improvised brass knuckles. Most interestingly, they'd found an operational cell phone in one of the desk drawers. It didn't have service, of course, but it did have an app on it called DRONE. Whether it turned out to be a control program for the compound's security drones or not, Mia didn't yet know. But it looked custom from the icon, and any chance was better than staying where they were and just hoping for the best. Especially considering Beef's reputation.

"You remember what to do, right?" Mia asked.

She nodded. "If you get that lock open, I go first, and hold the cage door like it's still closed. Then, when anyone with a gun gets close enough, I slam it into his face."

"Then I go for the gun," Mia said.

"Are you sure this is going to work?"

"No. Not at all. Not even *close*. But I know we weren't going to get out while Brendan was watching us. It's personal with him. Even if we can't get away now — even if we try and they catch us and then suddenly their defenses are up — it's still a better chance than we had if we'd stayed here."

"I wish that other bidder had won," Carol said. "The one with the cars. He looked beat to crap already. It'd be easy to get away."

"This is fine. We'll make do. As long as anyone other than Thomas won the auction, it was going to be an improvement. Here. Can you try this?"

Mia stood. Carol, giving a shrug that indicated she had no clue about picking locks either but was game to try, knelt in her place. Mia handed her the bent paperclip. Mia had given this part 20/80. If they couldn't unlock the cage door, they'd just wait and leap on the person who did. They'd lose surprise, but it was still a better chance than staying still.

Mia took in their surroundings. The storage and holding area was about like she'd imagined it after spying it from above — packed with goods, tight aisles, not a ton of room to move. If the Exchange survived another few years, it might learn the logistics chain of a grocery super-store, but for now it was just a bunch of goobers trying to figure things out as they went. From above, she'd watched the unnecessary shifting and re-shifting of goods, because nobody had established an intake and check-out order and lined the packages up to make it all easy. Nope, they just sort of shoved stuff in and then did whatever acrobatics were required to take it out the other end when the buying party was ready to pull up and take it home. That, more than anything, had attracted Mia to this idea. Disorganization could be exploited. Confusion could be exploited. All that really needed to happen was for them to be auctioned off to anyone (other than Thomas) at any price. All that needed to happen, in Mia's mind, was for them to get here. Even if they ended up being securely transported to Beef's place, they'd have better escape chances than here.

Luckily, Brendan was easy to goad into arguments.

Luckily, Brendan was already fed up enough with Mia and Hollis that convincing him to say *Fuck it* on the whole affair was pretty easy. One fight and one nudge later, he'd given up on Hollis and on exacting revenge. The world was changing, and Brendan was a warlord with things to do — especially since that chicken-shit governor had left him in the lurch. Why should he waste any more time with the likes of Mia? He'd lost out on the case. Time to move on.

"Do you hear that?" Carol said from her crouch.

Carol listened.

"It sounds like a convention of people wearing high heels."

Mia would have said it differently. To her, it sounded like teeth.

"Oh, *hell yeah*," Carol whispered, suddenly beaming. Fuckin-a-*CAROL!*"

Mia looked. She'd gotten the door open. It opened outward. The perfect iron thing to brain someone with, after playing possum with hands pretend-bound behind their backs.

"You see anyone coming?"

"Not yet. But I hear them. Three or four people over there."

And they'd be armed, Mia reminded herself. There were only a few people on the Exchange floor with working weapons, but the guards were those people.

"Keep the door closed, then," Mia said. "And let me know if anyone comes around a corner. I want to check out this Drone app."

And she did.

"Oh, *Carol,*" she said a few minutes later. "We really are a good team. After we get out of here, what do you say to starting the new A-Team? I call Mr. T."

Carol, keeping an eye toward the sounds, stepped back to look at what Mia had in her hands.

"What happened?"

"I may have just gained access to all of the drones watching the place and told them to mind their own business."

"It can't be that easy."

"Real people don't think like movies," Mia said, still tapping around in the app, making sure. "I think it's that easy."

A cough came from where they'd heard human feet, as if to remind them that "easy" was relative. They still had guards to contend with. A few. With guns.

Carol was readying herself, taking her place, holding the door in preparation.

But Mia was getting another idea.

"Hang on," she said. "Maybe we try something different."

And yes, that seemed sensible. When she'd planned this, they'd been in the crow's nest, not even part of the crowd yet. There'd been things she could guess and things she couldn't. Up there, she'd assumed they'd be watched more closely, and a dramatic smash-and-grab escape, dodging bullets, might be necessary. Now that they were here, reality was different.

They'd cut their restraints.

The door was open.

As far as Mia could tell, the drones were off-patrol, on standby.

There'd be humans and razor wire yet to get past, but right here and now there seemed to be literally nothing between them and the door.

"Carol."

Carol looked up.

"Let's just go."

"Just ... *go?*" She indicated the door, as if Mia might have meant another kind of "going."

"Yes. Look where the cage is. Nobody's going to see we're not in it until they specifically come to take us away. This is as good a time to try and sneak away as any."

"Your first plan had us getting a gun before setting out."

"My first plan also had a maybe 50/50 chance that one of us would die trying to *get* that gun."

"Fair point."

They stepped out. Slowly. The cage's door was squeaky, and Mia clenched her teeth as they sneaked through. But nobody heard; nobody came.

"Here," Mia said. Not far off was a long rack of automatic rifles. She took one for each of them.

After taking hers, Carol said, "How do I shoot it?"

"You don't. They're not loaded."

"Then why are we taking them?"

"Point it like it's loaded," Mia said. "I'll bet you can make some people think twice about treading on you."

"If nothing else, it's a bludgeon."

"A *hell* of a bludgeon," Mia agreed. "Except ..." She sighed, looking at Carol. "You're right-handed, aren't you?"

"Yeah?"

Mia took the gun from Carol, then reversed the strap so she was holding it the other way.

"Try to be cooler, Carol."

"I'm sorry." Then, pointing the thing an imaginary enemy: *"Hasta la vista, baby."*

"Come on." Her heart was pounding. They'd seen this area from above and now on the ground, and its construction made it a maze. People were selling a lot of stuff, but the buyers were waiting until they left to load up what they'd gotten, and sticking around all day before leaving. The exit traffic jam when the Exchange ended would be a nightmare ... and maybe a means of escape from the premises, Mia considered.

But until then, the Exchange's logistical failures would be a mixed blessing. On the pro side, the maze of goods would make it easy to stay hidden. But on the con side, they might run into anyone at any time, without any warning.

They moved away from their cage. Almost immediately, Mia lost track of where it was. She was keeping her eyes high, tracking the back door they were trying to reach. She had to assume there'd be guards by the door, but maybe the guards would take breaks; maybe they could sneak past. They could also point the weapons they held and hope the guards would believe they were loaded, or engage and attack using them as clubs. The last option was the worst. It sounded good, but in reality they'd almost for-sure be mobbed the second they swung at anyone — and Mia didn't think that Carol, confident as she was, would be much good in an honest-to-God fight for their lives. Almost nobody was.

After a few turns, Mia stopped like she'd been shot. She went board-stiff, hand up for Carol, face unable to move.

Carol was about to speak, but then she saw and went just as stiff as Mia. There was a trio of armed guards right in front of them, not six feet away, facing the other direction. If Mia breathed wrong, they'd hear her.

She pushed backward, her palm pressing Carol's thigh.

Back up. Slowly.

Carol did. Mia followed, both of them still looking forward.

They hit an interior wall. There was a cluster of rooms that abutted the wall. But now to one side was a stack of boxes, and the other side quite nakedly led to the open trading floor. It was packed, and at any minute any of the traders might turn to look and see prizes walking free. What's more, the end of the passage was flanked by two guards.

"Around this way," Mia said.

Which wasn't any better. Now they were beside a rolling garage door that covered most of the wall of one of the rooms, looking like targets. There was a man door to the left, no windows. It didn't matter. That wasn't the way out; that was just one more level in.

The guards they'd just walked away from were coming this way. Mia could hear their voices, growing louder. They wouldn't see the guards' backs this time; this time they'd see their faces. And then it would all be over.

Carol had moved to the side. Toward the man-door to the interior room. Her hand was on the knob when Mia turned to look.

"It's unlocked," she whispered.

Mia looked around. She wanted out, but right now she'd settle for staying free, staying alive.

"Mia!" Carol said.

Mia moved to the door as the voices approached the nearest corner, ducking inside.

They closed the door behind them before realizing what the room was for. What was being kept here.

"Shit," Carol said.

In Mia's opinion, that was an understatement.

17

HOLLIS WAITED until the cage containing Mia and Carol went behind the curtains, then followed it with his eyes as best he could. The holding area was large and seemed full, but the riffling of hanging partitions — visible from the outside, given how far they hung from the tall ceiling — suggested where it went. A while after Mia and Carol were wheeled in, the partitions stopped moving. Hollis went close, listened, and distantly heard the walking-away of footsteps.

He looked back at where Theo had stationed himself, trying and failing to look casual. Dammit if Theo wasn't going to give them away.

What are you doing here, sir?

Just being casual. Yep. Super casual. Nothing to see here. In fact, I think I'll whistle.

While shaking, eyes darting, like a spaz.

Come with us, sir, for your beating.

And then they'd catch Hollis, too, and it'd all be over. Fucked because bro couldn't just relax.

In his nervous, spaz-like way, Theo tipped him a miniature nod.

Hollis wanted to give him a look back that said a thing or two, but there wasn't a point. All things considered, Theo was doing pretty well. Hollis — who had a finely tuned bullshit detector — thought he was sincere about wanting to help, sincere about leaving Sonny now that Sonny was a state away and with such divergent desires, sincere about getting Mia and Carol out of hock so the four of them could start hacking. He hadn't gotten a chance to tell Theo that the photos he'd mentioned taking, of the attaché case's contents, were on a phone that might not still be where he'd left it. Probably for the best. Theo was uneasy enough.

Feeling charitable and uncharacteristically thankful, Hollis decided on impulse to give Theo a thumbs-up.

Good intentions. Somehow, it just made Theo look more nervous. He looked away, trying harder to seem casual, failing miserably.

"You better be worth this, ladies," Hollis mumbled to himself.

Then, with one more quick glance around, he dropped to the floor and crawled under the curtain separating the main floor from the closed-auction layaway. He'd noticed the way Brendan had posted guards at the gaps in the curtains, and almost wanted to see the bastard again just so he could laugh. In some ways, Brendan was brilliant, and paranoid, and brilliant in his paranoia. In other ways, he was a motherfucking moron. *Curtains aren't walls, bitch. You can just go under them.* Brendan struck Hollis as the kind of guy who'd lock his car with a drink inside to prevent covert poisonings, then lose a week's worth of work because he'd turned off Dropbox sync and forgotten to turn it back on.

Once inside, Hollis immediately felt claustrophobic.

He'd heard mumbles about the Exchange and its history, from Vika's brainchild to the abortion Brendan and his people had turned it into. Here and now — standing in a forest of disorganized-but-already-traded-for merchandise — Hollis saw how fine a line the whole thing balanced upon. There was a ton of stuff in here, and it was hurriedly labeled. He could do anything he wanted in here. He could swap all the tags, poop in someone's new boat, whatever. The options were limitless.

He heard voices. Coming.

He ducked down.

Feet approached. Hollis could see them, from where he was hiding. And of course that's where they stopped. Hollis couldn't see their faces or hands, but he could hear a muted *tap-tap-tap* that seemed unmistakably to be the sound of typing on a touchscreen. He'd seen that Brendan's crew, disproportionately, had electronics — probably due to the EMP-proof cage in which he'd so recently left his death collar. The cell network and internet were off far more often than they were on, so far as Hollis had seen, but Brendan's men seemed to be communicating anyway. Maybe some sort of closed messaging app, workable through proximity and Bluetooth?

"Gives me the willies, man," said the owner of one of the pairs of feet. A woman.

"Did you really just say 'willies'?" Her partner, a man.

"Yeah." Almost defensive. "You know. *Willies.* What do *you* feel when you're around it?"

"The Reptar?"

"No. Brendan's mother."

"I don't know. Freaked out?"

"Like you've *got the willies,*" said the woman, *Q.E.D.*

"I feel like it sees me."

"It's wearing a helmet."

"That's not the kind of seeing I mean. It's like it's inside my head, looking out."

The woman didn't reply to that. Hollis was guessing, but the silence she returned struck him as agreement.

"Did you lock the door?" the man asked.

"No, I didn't *lock the door*. I don't have the keys to open it again."

"Don't you think we should have locked the door?"

"Why?"

"Well ... you know."

The woman laughed a little. "It's in a cage, Curt."

"I just know I like as many locks between me and that thing as possible. Why the hell did Brendan allow them to bring it? I heard those things talk to each other with their minds. What if it's calling its buddies?"

"Supposedly this one is different."

"Or lying."

"It doesn't talk, Curt."

"Let's just get out of here."

"It purrs. Like a big friendly kitty."

"Fuck you," said the man. "'*Willies.*'"

"It's out of sight. It won't freak out every worker who walks by. That's enough. Nobody has to see it again until they drag it out for auction."

"What's anyone going to do with a reptar, anyway? I mean ... shit, Lily."

"Not your business. Not mine, either."

Something blipped, probably from the cell phone one of them had been typing on.

"Wyclef wants us. Come on."

The feet moved away. Hollis stood. Standing was hard, coming from a crouch. Everything — and he did mean *everything* — hurt. His joints were taffy gone stiff. It'd been a thousand years since he'd slept.

Come on, come on, he told himself.

He moved in the direction he thought he'd seen the cage move, finding the back area more labyrinthine than he'd expected. There was a direct line toward the last curtain he'd seen move, but getting to it took some doing. He didn't hear any other guards, but was no wondering how exactly he was going to pull this off. They were in a cage, after all, and might even be bound, now that they'd been sold. Was he planning to get behind the cage and push until someone asked him where he was going?

Just take one step at a time.

He could do that. It was kind of his life's mission. Taking one step at a time and never bothering to figure out what lay beyond had gotten him out of Vika's collar, had brought him an apparent and unlikely ally in Theo, and was about to put him in front of Mia and Carol despite all odds. He'd figure out how to extricate them and open the cage later. The answers, he told himself, would come.

But when he arrived and found the cage right where he'd expected it, it was empty. The door was open, nobody home.

Motherfucker. I missed it. That fat little bastard already claimed them.

He moved forward, then found something that confirmed his theory. Yep: two sets of zip-tie restraints, recently cut. The cage was now just a cage. What Beef had really bought had already been removed, then marched out to whatever blinged-out pimpmobile he'd driven here.

He wanted to punch something, but then his internal voice spoke up.

What, you think that guy moves fast? How far could they

have gotten? His eyes moved up, spied the top of the big back door, halfway open. *Haul ass, dumbshit. You can still catch them.*

But before Hollis could so much as take a step, he heard a distinctive noise behind him: the *chick-chick!* of a semiautomatic pistol's slide being racked.

Then someone began laughing.

Behind him were six armed guards, and Brendan was in the middle.

"You're almost unrecognizable, looking that fucked up," Brendan said, smiling. "*Almost.*"

Hollis, for once, found himself at a total loss for words.

"But when Thomas Davies told me that some weird, beat-up stranger looked familiar, I only had to ask my guys one question to figure out it was you. Would you like to guess the question?"

Brendan's eyes moved down. All the way down, to the floor. And Hollis, when he realized what Brendan was looking at, wanted to kick himself.

"'Is he wearing alligator boots?'" Hollis recited. He scuffed one of said boots against the floor, hating the mistake, wishing he was able — just once — to be less cool than he naturally was.

"Welcome back, Hollis," Brendan said.

18

MIA PAWED and pawed before understanding what was wrong. Turned out, she wasn't reaching for the door latch as she'd thought. She was reaching for Carol, who was between Mia and the door.

She didn't think she could speak, until she could. Everything other than her hands was paralyzed.

"We have to ..."

"I know."

"I need to ..."

"I know."

Mia wasn't even sure which person she was, in that conversation. Was she the one making the panicky half-demands, or the one calmly stating that she knew? She'd seen it from the outside, as an observer. Because absolutely all of her attention, right now, was focused on the black thing moving through the room's heavy shadows.

The *room's* shadows, not just those of the cage it was supposed to be in.

"Why is it ... ?"

And apparently Mia was the one who kept trailing off

because this time nobody answered. The latch was behind Carol, closed the second they were both inside on a heavy pneumatic hinge. Her hands were searching for it, but she had reach for it as blindly as Mia had. The room had just one window, and it'd looked out on the rest of the floor before someone had piled merchandise against it, blocking all but a hint of illumination. The air was thick, all sights just suggestions. And Carol's attention wasn't on her hands, anyway.

Neither one of them could take their eyes off the alien. The way it moved — the very way it took up space — was so ... *foreign*. But wasn't that what "alien," at its root, truly meant?

Reptar, they'd called the thing.

Carol, still not looking where her hands were working, pushed the latch too far down its end. It had an L-shaped bar you needed to rotate a quarter-circle downward to exit, and this time Carol only caught its end. It went halfway down, then sprung back up when Carol's hand slipped away.

The hard, mechanical noise startled Mia, who hadn't seen it coming — but startled the alien, too.

It lurched forward, toward them from the left.

Dodging, they skirted right.

Mia had seen before; they moved in bursts studded with pauses. After its lunge, the big black thing stopped. Mia held her breath. She tried to remember that it was wearing a helmet, and that its yellow eyes couldn't see her. Both inside the cage and out, it'd been reacting as something truly blind: feeling its way, perhaps scenting the air. But it wasn't sensing them through X-rays or psychic hints; that much was clear. Even just a foot from the thing's long, matte-black leg, Mia was invisible. As long as she didn't make any more sound, it seemed not to know where to find her.

But now it was between them and the door.

In front of the door now, its many-jointed, exoskeleton-covered body flexing but still. One handless appendage was up, now touching the lock, now tugging it a fractional inch before letting it go to rebound. Each time it did, a miniature version of the noise Carol had made to spook it filled the little room.

The room seemed around 24x24, the size of a generous garage. In one corner, where someone had parked, was the cage in which they'd seen the alien — the "*reptar*"? — Earlier. Most of the cage was like the one they'd so recently occupied, surrounded by bars like something out of an old-timey circus. But unlike their cage, the alien's now-empty cage had one solid wall: a metal ramp, it seemed, that could be lowered on a hinge to allow keepers to herd the contents in and out.

Right now, one of the top latches holding the ramp in place as a wall was broken, the ramp itself twisted and thrashed as if by invisible knives — or *claws*, as felt more likely. The metal was thick, but thinner than the bars. For some reason the alien hadn't been able to thrash its way through the bars, but had had no problem with the metal plate.

Although — and this really freaked Mia out — it had known to wait until it was alone to escape. She'd heard the commotion it'd been causing amongst Exchange workers and patrons alike, and that's probably why they'd put it in here in the first place. There was storage within the storage, where troublesome lots could be hidden from virgin eyes. Watching the thing, Mia found a strange kinship forming.

They'd all been captives; they'd all made a plan and bidden their time.

Carol backed away. So did Mia. But on a whim, Mia whispered, *"We're like you."*

The thing immediately lashed out, almost opening Mia's chest with its razor-sharp claw. She inhaled, startled, then wondered how close her shave had been as the claw nicked the fabric of her dress — if the half-inch her body compressed when she gasped had saved her life

Carol dragged Mia back. Now they were getting further and further from the latch.

They moved to beside the cage, on the side the thing had opened like a can of sardines. It didn't look like it'd been hard to do. For some reason, when Mia imagined the scene in her mind, she imagined the alien opening the metal slowly, not in big, violent thrashes.

It puts its claw against the metal.

Then it pushes, just a little.

And opens it like cutting hot butter.

She felt a shiver. Her breath came faster, her heartbeat harder.

But the alien hadn't followed them. It was hard to see with just the one stuffed-up window for light, but Mia and Carol could see that plainly enough. It either didn't want them or didn't want them badly enough to try — as if they were an inconvenience, nothing more. It knew there were humans in the room; Mia's impulse to speak had made sure of that. But it was making no effort to get at them.

Mia watched, fascinated, as it remained where it was.

It couldn't operate the door latch.

Carol caught Mia's attention. Then she shrugged and pretended to rake invisible claws down the wall. She was asking a question: *Why doesn't it rip through the walls like it ripped through the walls of its cage?*

Mia shook her head. She had no idea. There was exposed electrical conduit running circuits around the walls, so maybe it feared getting an electric shock. But even that didn't truly make sense; there was a large corrugated metal door to one side that the handlers had probably used to put the thing, still in its cage, inside. Mia had seen that the big door was padlocked from the outside, but couldn't its claws go through the door itself and make the lock irrelevant? Was it possible the thing didn't know the big metal door was there? She didn't think so, so there must be another reason. Too much stuff piled up outside the door now? Or was it an alloy that the aliens were allergic to — a weakness humanity could mass-produce and exploit later, like the Red Dust in the old series *V*?

No clue. It only underscored the raw, unfiltered *newness* of all that Earth was facing. Here was something wholly different. Wholly unknown. Who knew how they might live, how they might think, how they might be able to enter and exit rooms like this one?

But she could feel something coming from it.

Like an energy.

And it was clear, from looking at Carol, that she was feeling nothing but terror.

Her impulse to speak to the thing hadn't been pure, unadulterated crazy. It had gone nowhere, but the idea wasn't nuts. Because the more she crouched behind the ruined cage, the more she thought she understood. The more of the aliens' movements made sense. The more, somehow, she began to understand its thinking. Its plan. Its frustration, of all things, with the door.

And even without knowing or understanding or seeing

details, she could tell that for reasons unknown, the room frustrated the reptar in a way the cage hadn't. Mia tried to remember what they'd seen, outside. The room was dual-layered, for one; she'd seen the wall-inside-wall construction when they'd stepped through the door. Outside, it'd also been covered in conduit. And most interestingly, the room's corner had been marked by a large steel pole, at the conduit's apex, that pierced the concrete and plunged into the ground beneath.

She looked more closely, straining in the low light.

Racks along the far wall. Marks on the floor where heavy equipment, until recently, had been stored.

Was this one of the rooms in which Brendan had stored what he wanted protected from things like that alien shockwave? Was this one of the places he'd kept electronics that somehow still worked? Was that part of the reason the alien seemed so reluctant to rip through it? Or was it unable?

It didn't matter.

The alien was still trying to work the latch. It was odd to watch: such a powerful thing, uselessly flicking at a stubborn latch. Sight-unseen, thanks to the helmet still fastened over the thing's lozenge-shaped head.

She watched its movements. Sensed its frustration, as if it were her own.

Why? How?

Carol was tugging at her sleeve. Pointing at the alien. Gesturing vaguely, still making herself understood, referring to the door.

We have to get out of here.

And the door, of course, was their only way out. They couldn't rip through walls with sharp claws, and the garage-style door, even if it wouldn't be loud as hell to raise (not to mention loosing the alien, which so far was still nicely contained), was locked from the outside.

Mia settled into the haze above the pall. That sense of understanding, somehow, the alien's thinking.

We're both alone.

She didn't know why she thought it, but she did. She thought it, and she knew it, and she knew that the thought was only half hers, agreed-to by an animal anger. There was a connection here, somehow. Only, instead of making Mia feel better, it scared her more.

She felt fear that came out as deadly determination.

She felt separation that, instead of feeling lonely, felt furious. It was a desperate, violent thrum in the air: the need to find something missing, then rejoin it or die trying.

The stones, Mia thought.

Yes. Maybe. The last time she'd run across aliens, they'd been planting tall stones in the ground. Weird stones, that did something to send you on a head trip. Last time she'd been near those stones, she'd *sworn* she could hear Hollis's mind even from a full state away. That had happened right around the time that the aliens she'd encountered had turned a whole group of soldiers to meat ribbons.

They didn't attack us because we weren't armed.

She knew it wasn't that simple. She'd seen footage, on the internet, when the internet sparked and refilled browser caches, of these things ripping up innocents like sushi. But the cousin of the thought still felt right. There was still something here. Something to this.

The alien still hadn't left the door.

Mia stood. Carol grabbed her arm.

Mia shook her off. Carol tried again, making a scuffing sound, causing the alien to whip its big head around, more staring them down through its helmet than legitimately meaning to strike. Or so Mia thought; anyway. Just looking at Carol, it seemed clear she'd expected it to cut them open.

Mia held up both hands: *Let me be.*

She moved up beside it. Definitely within striking distance. She could hear the thing breathing now — a low sound she'd missed before, like a tire losing air from millions of tiny holes rather than through one big one. Warmth seemed to sigh from beneath its carapace. At the same time, she could smell the thing. Clean and hard — offensive in the way aromatic chemicals are offensive, not in the way a body's odors can be. But even the scent was subtle. If Mia closed her eyes, she could almost imagine the scent was a pile of pennies covered in motor oil. It was metallic, with a hard tang that touched the back of the tongue.

Be a hole in the world, something inside Mia told her — the voice of her more intelligent self, perhaps. *Don't be nonviolent. Instead, be an instrument. Be a thing that thought uses rather than a thinker of thought, the way they are. The way this one should be — and would be, if it hadn't been severed.*

Because she was quite sure this one wasn't thinking the way the others thought. Hadn't someone told her that this specific alien was separated from the group mind the others seemed to share? She could've sworn she'd overheard someone saying that not far from here, but she'd be damned if she could remember when, where, or why.

Be unnoticed. Be a void that's decided precisely nothing.

Inside her mind, Mia pictured a moon eclipsing the daytime sun. The moon didn't move the sun, yet blacked out the planet anyway. All the moon did was to get in the way.

She took another step, ignoring Carol's visual gasps. She moved until she was almost entirely in front of the door, putting the alien so close, she could hear the idle ticking of its mouth over her shoulder, moving beneath its helmet.

This is stupid, the terrified part of her mind thought. As her hands wanted to shake, as her heart wanted to accelerate, as her legs wanted to wobble and drop her to the ground.

Tick. Tick-tick. And beneath it, a sigh that could become a whisper, a whisper that could become a purr.

But then another part of Mia's mind said, *It's not stupid. It's not anything at all.*

She pushed closer. Now the alien was actually touching her back. And it was touching her mind, too. She could feel it, like a distant whisper. She let her thoughts reach out in tendrils, then waited as the desperate, cut-off mind of the separated alien sniffed them in the darkness, like a dog sniffing a stranger's hand.

"Mia!" Carol hissed. The black reptar was now fully between the women, around Mia like a shroud.

This time, the alien did not respond. It didn't hear Carol. No, wait: It *chose* not to hear her.

The alien's appendage had sagged. Mia's hand wrapped the door latch.

There was no room to open it. Breathing deep, she pushed backward. Gentle pressure against the heavy metal helmet, against the front legs with their heavy claws on the ends.

Be nothing. Be the lack of decision. Be part of a whole, insignificant without the others.

Mia arched her back. Applied pressure.

The alien, legs clicking on concrete, retreated obediently.

We're not here to harm you. We're not here to fight you, Mia's mind told the void. *We're not even here. We are* you. *We are all of* you.

She didn't even know where this stuff was coming from.

Maybe those weird psychic rocks had infected her, and maybe she was about to be julienned. But wrapped inside the alien's space as she was, she'd gone too far to stop.

The door, now, had room to open. She waved Carol forward.

But Carol wouldn't move.

Couldn't.

Mia crouched. Looked under the alien's legs — the shortest and easiest way to go.

Carol shook her head — voilent, like a child's denial.

"It's okay," Mia whispered.

Carol firmed her chin. Hardened her eyes.

"I swear," Mia told her.

So Carol got on all fours. Shaking almost uncontrollably, she shambled forward. It didn't take long to pass the reptar's pointed legs, with their many jagged barbs. She was clearly ripping off a bandage, going as far as she could before the thing ended them both.

But it didn't end them. Or move. It backed up another step.

"*Go,*" Mia said, opening the door.

Carol did.

Mia, when she was most of the way out, turned to look at the insect. It was shifting slightly here and there, as if uncertain.

"Thank you," Mia whispered to it.

The reptar did not respond.

19

HOLLIS AND HIS STUPID, tattle-tale alligator boots were marched unceremoniously out of the holding area, two of the largest of Brendan's men on his arms. Both were wearing uniforms. Seeing this, Hollis wondered whether Brendan had bought all the uniforms in advance the way he'd bought Panzers and Howitzers, or whether he had some sort of on-site sweat shop to make them for him. Both of the men holding him were big, like Big-and-Tall-Store big. Did their uniforms need to be made custom? The new world was so full of interesting mysteries.

On the way out, amidst all the staring eyes of the Exchangers, Hollis spied Theo. Without giving himself away, he did his best to stare hard at Theo and say, *What the hell, man? You were supposed to be standing guard!*

Theo's shoulders rose and fell. It was a dumb, halfway gesture full of befuddlement more than apology. It was a shrug that didn't say, *They bested me* so much as it said, *Sorry, bro ... my bad.* Then probably: *Duh.*

He turned you in, dumbass, Hollis thought.

But did he? Trapped as he was — and having played so many of his aces already, so not a lot of hope about getting free — Hollis honestly wasn't sure. Logically and on a gut level, Hollis believed Theo's sincerity. But then there was the fact that Hollis was in custody and Theo was free, and the fact that Theo hadn't remotely done his job as lookout, and the final fact that Theo, let's not forget, had come here on behalf of Sonny Malone. Maybe, halfway through their caper, it'd dawned on Theo that he had nothing to gain by helping Hollis and had everything to lose. Right now, he was protected. He was also a state away and should be able to give Sonny the slip ... but maybe he'd lost his nerve? Wouldn't be such a bad idea for Theo to have Brendan on his side, either. Maybe he'd finked in exchange for a better trade. Information was information on this floor, after all.

Within seconds it didn't matter. There was a set of stairs and a ramshackle elevator — possibly for hay or equipment meant for the loft — past the holding area. Brendan and his bouncer duo led Hollis into the elevator, rose, and seconds later entered his office. It had a window at one end that lined up within the roofline, looking half out onto the Exchange below and half across the metal roof. And there was a strange scent inside. Something slight but familiar — almost decipherable by his deeper mind. It was a pleasant scent. Floral? It was hard to scent through all the body spray the bouncer-types had doused themselves in.

"Brendan," Hollis said when the door closed, the henchmen left, and they were alone. "It's good I found you. I actually have—"

He stopped speaking when Brendan hit him impossibly hard with a fist. The room went dark, filled with stars. For a few seconds Hollis didn't know where he was, and it took him time to again find the walls, find the ceiling fan, find that slight feminine scent, and find the blood wad on the floor Hollis could only assume he'd made.

He spat again. Yep, that blood was his.

"I don't want to hear anything you have to say," Brendan told him.

Hollis was still wincing. That had really, really hurt.

"Fuck! You hit me right where it's already bruised!"

Brendan was pacing. Hollis was still on his knees, mostly doubled, body tense as he waited for the pain to pass.

"Everywhere on you is already bruised, idiot. Like ... *HERE!*"

He kicked Hollis hard in the ribs. And yes, that had indeed been a bruised spot.

Hollis's knees and hands slipped. He hit the ground, writhing and holding on as best he could. A cough began, trying to realign shattered muscles. Each cough hurt more than the one before, and it went on for a long time. He didn't spit again, but the force of his diaphragmatic contractions coated the floor in fine spray of red droplets.

"What the hell, Brendan? You invited me!"

"I didn't invite you, Hollis. I gave you an ultimatum, and you decided it'd be more fun to fuck me. Well, tell you what, champ? You thought it'd be more fun to screw me over than to play fair, which I guess means that an attache case is worth more to you than those two women, even after I told you what I'd do to them. And do you know what *that* means, Hollis?"

Ordinarily, Hollis would have a witty response to a question like that, but he stuffed it down. Getting hit again did not feel like an option.

"It means," Brendan went on, "that you're more of a

piece of shit than I thought you were. Was I really that wrong? I figured you were a human being, in the end. But look what happened? You really *do* value money over human life — even of people I had pegged as your friends. Congratulations, Hollis. Even *I'm* not that big of an asshole."

"I don't have the case," Hollis said, back on his knees.

"I know you don't. You thought you'd try to have your cake and eat it too, so you either hid it or sold it to someone else. Why trade me when you can just come up here and seal what's mine? Well, the joke's on you, fucker. The guy who bought your girls? He might actually do worse things to them than I would have. Only, you're not going to be able to trade anything for them to Beef like you could have with me. They're gone, and all you've got, wherever you stuck it, is your goddamn case. Well, you know what, smart guy? I don't even want it anymore. I could demand that you tell me where it is, then try to beat the information out of you. But what fun is that? If you confess, I'd have to stop. And after knowing you for as long as I have, I've realized something." He smacked one fist into the palm of the other hand. "When it comes to you, I don't *want* to stop anymore, whether you have something I want or not."

"I do! I have what you need!"

Brendan had been about to kick him again, but he paused.

"Bullshit."

"It's not bullshit! The case was destroyed. Do you have a working phone? Or a walkie? I can prove it! Do you remember Sonny Malone?"

Brendan set his foot back down from kicking posture, but didn't look happy about it.

"Yeah?"

"I took it to him. But after that I learned enough to know

I didn't want the wrong person to have it. The case had a self-destruct combination, for emergencies. That's the combination I gave Sonny before I left. And the next day, when texts were still coming, he sent me a lot of threats, because the case was gone."

Brendan looked surprised by this, but then a decidedly insane grin crept onto his face.

"Well. That's even better. Say 'when,' Hollis."

Hollis didn't understand, but then Brendan kicked him again, and again. Finally Hollis croaked, "WHEN!"

"I'm sorry. I can't hear you."

Kick. Kick.

Pain like bombs now. He held his hand out, sure Brendan would kick again and probably break a few of his fingers, but then he stopped.

"I made copies," Hollis said.

"What copies." A statement, not a question. Not believing even a little.

Hollis tried to sit up, failed, then tried harder for credibility. Nobody believed a sad sack bleeding on the ground.

With his hand still out, Hollis said through what felt like broken ribs, "I took pictures. Of everything in the case." *Wheeze.* "Front and back. I've got copies of everything, Brendan!"

"Oh yeah? Where." Still not actually asking. Still challenging.

"On my phone."

"We searched you. You didn't have a phone."

"It's not here. I hid it."

"Like the case?"

"The case isn't hidden. It's destroyed."

"If I ask you the same questions enough times in enough different ways, eventually you'll screw up."

"I'm not lying! The case is destroyed; the phone is hidden!"

"Convenient. Where's it hidden, Hollis?"

"I don't know!"

Brendan knelt on one knee. Looked Hollis in the eye from close up, seeming to study whatever was inside his gaze. Then, without warning, he punched him hard across the jaw. Again Hollis spat blood.

"I'm telling you the truth!"

"No you're not. You've never told the truth. To anyone."

"I had a car! The phone is—"

"The EMP fried the cars. That's why so many of the Exchange crowd arrived in so many different and interesting ways."

"It was an old one. No computer. On electronics, other than the solenoid. It was a Chevelle. *Sonny's* Chevelle. He gave it to me so I could get back to Austin!"

"Sonny's. The guy you screwed by giving the self-destruct combination. He just ... gave you his car."

"I left the car, with my bag inside, parked in a subdivision. I was just checking out something I saw by the side of the road, but then noticed a bar with a bunch of motorcycles outside, most with the keys right there in the ignition. I needed a more nimble form of transportation. So I took it, and the Flesh Eaters caught me and chased me, and—"

"So you just *left* your bag. With this valuable phone inside."

"I was going to take the motorcycle back to it."

"Ah. But they chased you instead."

"Right!"

"I understand now. And do you know what I like to do to celebrate, when I finally understand things?"

"Umm ..." That didn't sound like a question he should answer.

He was still thinking when Brendan pulled the heavy fire extinguisher off the wall and hit him with it, aiming low to bash his chest in the world's most aggressive golf swing. It hit his probably-broken ribs and sent a rocket of blinding agony through him, complete with actual visible phenomena: a bright arc of fire and shooting sparks, roaring behind his clenched eyelids.

Now, while Hollis lost all dignity and rolled on the floor clutching himself and waiting for the worst to end, Brendan squatted low, ass on heels.

"I don't like that you lie," Brendan said.

"I'm not lying!" Saying it took wind he didn't have and effort he could barely muster.

"But actually, I'm finding that I don't mind that you don't have anything for me. It makes my decision easy."

"I'm telling you the truth. This time, it's all true. I swear, Brendan. I swear!"

But Brendan was shaking his head. This time, it was true. But this time was the first time.

He opened the door. The bouncer-types were still outside. To the one on the right, Brendan said, "Call the doctor for Mr. Palmer."

Hollis couldn't believe his ears. He said, "Thank you. Thank you. I swear, if you send someone out to look for Sonny's car, the bag might still even be—"

Brendan cut him off. "Oh. Just go out and look for Sonny's car? And what will *you* do, Hollis, with the time that takes? What will you do when we can't find it?"

Hollis's brow furrowed. "But you just said ..."

"You misunderstood. This is the same doctor as I was

going to have meet with your girlfriends, before I sold them."

The one who did unnecessary surgery, just for fun. The maniac.

"Brendan ... I ..."

But Hollis found he didn't have any words left.

The door to the little office space closed, and he was alone.

20

Mia and Carol were successfully out of the building, sure they'd gone as far as they could. And the clock was ticking.

The tall back doors they'd seen the tops of from inside turned out to be the contact spot for a kind of layaway pickup line. When they'd rounded the final corner, hearts still thumping (and shocked to still be alive) after their strange encounter with the alien, they'd discovered a little administrative setup at the door's opening: two of Brendan's people, a man and a woman, with a desk beside them. On the desk were a few piles of paperwork. While they watched, several people came and went — checking in with the two at the desk, then going into the held goods maze to locate whatever was called for. Beyond the doors was a line of vehicles: some older cars, a few electrics that must have been stored in protective garages, and a whole lot of improvised transportation right out of a madcap chase movie. From their hiding spot, lined up to receive the goods they'd traded for from the clerks at the desk, Mia saw a bicycle with a hacked-on engine, two bikes welded in side-by-side tandem with a sidecar (or storage compartment) between them, two go-karts pulling trailers, and a handful of ancient cars and trucks held together with duct tape.

They ducked back.

"I guess this is where people pick up," Carol said.

"Yeah."

"And the only exit."

"Well, not exactly." Mia was thinking of the main entrance, also an exit, that they could reach by crossing the Exchange floor. Given how popular their auction had been, the two women's chances of walking through the crowd unseen seemed remote. They could dress down, pull up hoods, and sneak around the edges, but they found no caches of clothes to wear. There must be some, but if so, it was all boxed. Unless they wanted to start opening all the sealed vessels at random, what they saw was what they got.

"There's the front, then this," Carol said. "I've been looking around the whole time."

Mia didn't reply. She'd been looking, too. Unfortunately, neither exit looked very good right now.

Then she said, "We could stow away. We could get inside a box and let someone else take us through the gate."

"If we're going to do that, we might as well get back inside our cage. Let that Beef guy take us."

"Except that we weren't going in the cage."

"Oh," Carol said. "Right." They'd probably be stuffed into the back of Beef's limo, which rumor said had survived the EMP just fine. Of course, that would let him touch them inappropriately during the trip, and dribble through those fat lips of his. Not a good recipe for an easy escape.

"Look," Mia said. She touched a massive metal object to the side of one aisle. "Gun safe." She opened it.

"We can't both squeeze in there," Carol said.

"Sure we can."

"And then there's the matter of air."

"Oh. Air. Yes. Let's find something with air."

But there was nothing that would work. As heavy as gun safes were, the additional weight of two stowaways wouldn't have been noticed, but most modes weren't as forgiving. Together they weighed nearly 300 pounds. Only wheeled objects might hide them, and everything with wheels in here was either open or would need to be driven. A driver would probably see them.

That's when Mia noticed the grenades.

They were in a helpfully labeled wooden box, the cover of which lifted right off. Mia picked one from the cluster of others, like an orange with behavioral problems. It wasn't covered with the waffle-iron surface she'd expected, and instead was oval, smooth, and heavy.

Carol only saw once Mia was holding the grenade.

"Woah. Put that down."

"Do you just pull this?" she asked, pointing at the pin.

"Very funny."

"I think you hold this," she said, indicating the long thing down one side, "and pull the pin. I'm pretty sure that until you let the lever thingy go, it's safe."

"The fact that you just called it a 'lever thingy' should make you think twice," Carol said. "Come on, Mia. Put it down."

But Mia wasn't just getting an idea. She was also becoming very interested in throwing the grenade. She'd gone shooting, once or twice, and had to admit she'd liked the power of it. This was a few levels up. And why should men have all the fun?

"I've got it," Mia said.

"You don't have it. Put that thing down."

But Mia was shaking her head. "No, I've really got it. We just need a distraction."

"And when you leap out into the open to create it?"

"I won't have to leap out into the open. Look." She pointed, using her grenade hand, at an open window. It was too small to climb through, but would work for grenade-hurling. Unless, of course, her throwing hand hit the edge in her rush to throw as far as possible, causing her to drop it on the floor. And she'd need to stand atop some rickety boxes to throw at all, in plain sight. Lots of potential for trouble there, once the clock was ticking.

She moved toward the boxes, started to climb.

Carol rushed to her. "Wait. Now I think you're actually serious."

"Of course I'm serious."

"That's a *grenade*, Mia."

"Thanks. You're always helpful."

"Well ..." Helpless, looking around, realizing Mia was going to do what Mia was going to do. "What's the plan?"

"'Run away from the explosion.'"

"They'll see us!"

"No they won't. Check it."

She was up on the boxes, seeing her target. Carol was still at the bottom, unable to see a thing.

"Check it, Carol." Waving for her to climb.

"I don't want to check it."

"Check it!"

Carol climbed up, but only halfway. High enough to see. Then: "You're kidding."

"Oh, come on. I'd be stupid *not* to do this!"

She was referring to an outhouse. Ramshackle, clearly disused, probably on the property for a century and rotting where it stood for twenty years. The barn's addition, to turn it into a full-on arena, had simply been built beside it. Mia would have knocked it down during construction, but maybe things were more complicated than that. There was a hole filled with poop under the thing. Maybe it needed to be filled with concrete, like sealing a nuclear waste site.

"Look," Mia said when Carol put on her doubting face. "It's real simple. I played basketball in high school. If I can't get this thing through that hole in the roof from here, I should just retire."

"That doesn't even make sense. You 'retired' by graduating high school."

"I'll toss, then jump down from here," Mia went on. You should be ready right ... there. Duck low and be ready to run. Wait until the guard runs toward the outhouse, then we run the other direction."

Except that the guards would *have* to cross their loading dock space to reach the outhouse from where they were, and if they didn't (say, if they simply gawked instead of running toward danger), Mia and Carol wouldn't be able to run at all. Someone would probably start looking for folks throwing grenades after that, and things would get worse. But Mia didn't feel like pointing that out, if Carol hadn't yet thought to raise it.

"And if they see us?"

"We run faster."

"This is crazy."

"The alternative is to stay where we are. We can't cross the floor and we can't get outside through this door unless everyone's attention is elsewhere."

"We could hide," Carol said. "Wait until the Exchange is over and sneak out then."

"Uh-huh. And nobody will look for us? Nobody will

check all of the security footage, decide we're still on the grounds, and then double-down?"

"It's better than *this* idea!"

Mia, now that Carol was climbing down, decided she was sick of this waffling. So she pulled the grenade's pin. Carol startled immediately, actually moving arms to cover her head.

"It won't blow until I let go of the lever thingy."

"Put the pin back!" They'd been whispering, and this came out as a shouted hiss.

"I'm telling you. Two points."

Mia threw the grenade. Carol ducked immediately. Mia held her spot just long enough to see the grenade hit the edge of the enormous hole in the outhouse's roof, bounce off, and begin its disobedient trip toward wherever it wasn't supposed to end up. That's when Mia jumped down, slamming the empty automatic rifle into her thighs.

"Don't say you told me so," Mia said.

"What?"

There was a deafening report. The explosion was at once sharp and deep, like a jackhammer used to unearth an old tree's roots. Heads turned immediately. Mia was able to peak around the corner and saw that instead of nailing the outhouse's center, she must have blown up the back of it. She saw smoke and still-raining debris. She watched as the outhouse, its rear foundation sundered, began to lean drunkenly backwards. The motion was slow and pointed, as if the thing were embarrassed.

The people in the eclectic line of vehicles looked. Many stepped forward. The female guard rushed ahead, weapon at the ready. But the man stayed right where he was, looking like he didn't understand.

If he doesn't move, we're trapped.

Mia, adrenaline surging, made a split-second call. It wasn't thought out. She only knew that their window was seconds, not minutes, and that they wouldn't get another.

So, dragging Carol because there was no time to explain, she rushed behind the unseeing back of the female guard and right up to the man. They must have looked interesting, in full makeup with hair styled, wearing dresses and holding machine guns. *These bitches are bad, mister.*

Too many stimuli at once. The poor bastard had no idea where to focus, what was going on. He probably should have raised his weapon at their approach, but instead seemed unseated. The others were still moving toward the outhouse, nobody seeing.

Striding purposefully, as if she had every right to be here. Dragging Carol, who was projecting far less no-bull-shit confidence.

"Do you have the time?" Mia asked the guard.

"I ... Are ..."

These were great points. But Mia hit him in the face with the butt of her rifle anyway. He collapsed like someone had pulled his plug.

Mia was already marching on, but now Carol was gaining her wits. At most, six seconds had passed since the grenade had blown. Time was moving that slowly. So now Carol, glancing around, woke and pulled her hand from Mia's. She grabbed a hand of the unconscious guard instead. Mia, understanding, took the other hand. No more than ten seconds later, he was out of sight around the door's corner. There was a drainage ditch, like a moat, around the arena on this side. Mia rolled the guard untidily into it, eliciting a splash at the bottom.

"He's swimming," Mia announced.

But Carol, because she was Carol, scampered to where

the guard was and, before Mia got what she was doing, had turned the guy over so he wouldn't be face down in rainwater. It was Carol, then, on her way back up, who grabbed Mia by the sleeve and pulled. Another three seconds and they were crouched beneath a bush, sheltered from the pickup line.

There was already shouting. The remaining guard was yelling for reinforcements, telling the people in line to get back. She, unlike her partner, was at least efficient. They'd probably assume he ran off. Seemed like the vacant-brained type, from what Mia had seen.

"You increased security," Carol said.

"Yeah, well. One step at a time. Come on."

She was mentally channeling herself from the past, when they'd been here before, looking at those aerial photos of the property. Brendan, like any good isolationist, knew exactly what he owned and guarded his property jealously. The photos and maps had all been marked: borders here — *what's mine* versus what might fall to enemies.

Away from the arena, their angle oblique, avoiding the gravel road and the footpath Brendan used between here and the house. If memory served, the margin between structure and boundary was thin here. Just over a shallow hill and there should be ...

Yes, of course, there it was: the fence in all its glory, topped with an open V guiding several lines' worth of barbed wire, the whole works topped with the deadly Slinky of rolled razor wire. It wasn't a welcoming border, but it was a border nonetheless.

"How are we going to get over—" Carol began.

But as they got closer, Mia slowed her feet. She'd been crunching underbrush but now didn't want to. She shouldn't make a sound.

Because beyond the gate, perhaps fifty yards out in a slight clearing, were three of the small alien ships. She'd seen their sizes vary, but these were barely anything. Perhaps fifteen feet through the center, maybe enough for three or four passengers and no cargo.

Like a patrol car, guarding a perimeter.

"Are they watching Brendan's property? Are they here to—?"

This time, Mia didn't drag Carol. She simply marched away, her feet moving fast to stop her brain from its worrying objections.

"We'll follow the fence," she said, "and find a spot they aren't guarding."

There might not be such a spot, of course.

But that was a thought for later.

21

"HEY!"

Mia didn't even look back. She didn't want to see who'd yelled after them. There was no good answer. Frankly, she was getting tired of this shit. Every situation was supposed to have a weakness begging to be exploited. *Every* situation. This one, however, was proving to be obnoxiously ignorant of the rules. At first, she'd done everything right. She'd manipulated Brendan into thinking that trading them away was a good idea, then gotten traded to the one man she gathered they wouldn't easily be able to give the slip. So they'd gotten out of the cage only to find themselves still trapped in the building, then gotten out of the building only to be stymied by aliens at the gate. Now they were free again, but the aliens seemed to have the place (rather politely and quietly) surrounded. If the people inside weren't freaking out, that probably meant nobody had noticed, and *that* probably meant that the front gate was clear. The front gate, which Mia and Carol couldn't use to exit for other reasons.

So they'd just kept running, kept trying to find a spot

that was both alien- and soldier-free. So far they hadn't seen any drones, but that had to be luck that could break at any moment. She'd dropped the phone with the DRONE app on it at some point, never having learned whether it did what she'd hoped.

And now here this asshole was, chasing them down.

"I told you not to throw that grenade."

Fucking Carol. Hadn't Mia just told her not to say I told you so?

"They must have noticed we're gone by now," Carol went on. "They know it's us."

"Knock it off, Carol. You don't know that," Mia said, fear and stress coming out as annoyance — seeing as that was the only emotion that wasn't nebulous, that actually had an outlet.

But they were running harder now, not wanting to admit they'd been made even to themselves. Soon it would be hard to talk for all the exertion, and *then* who would chastise Carol for her constant lack of faith?

"HEY!"

"This way."

They almost didn't see the man come over the hill before cutting behind the tree row. *Almost*. But they did see him, and that meant he saw them, and followed.

Mia's mind was already considering Plan B. He wasn't carrying a big gun, and that meant he'd only be carrying a small one. A pistol. The kind of thing that a wily dame, if she could schmooze close enough, might be able to knock out of his hand. She'd have to try. At this point, they couldn't cooperate and hope for the best. She'd played all her cards, and all stops after the Exchange were about rape and/or murder. Maybe both, maybe simultaneously.

So, yeah. She'd grab his gun hand, try to get her torso

out of the muzzle's way, and kick him in the nuts. If she could pull him around like in those online self-defense videos, she might be able to use his momentum against him and bring her elbow up to break his jaw. But probably not, so testicles it was.

Not that she was ready to give up running yet.

"Mia! Carol!"

The use of names disarmed them both. Guards were seldom so familiar.

"Could it ... be ... Hollis?" Carol panted.

Mia frowned even in her near-sprint, wishing she'd get off of it. Hollis wasn't coming. Why did Carol seem so determined to believe he was? *That*, she had faith in? What a crock of gullible horseshit.

"Hollis is white. Remember?"

"That guy's not?" Of course. Carol hadn't looked back, or hadn't seen. Never mind the rest of the evidence: Hollis's distinctive Alpha drawl, versus this guy's nasal voice. Or the fact that Hollis could easily overtake them on foot unless he was injured. Or the fact that ... *No*. Just ... *No*. Hollis was gone, sunning with his millions down on Loyola Beach.

Mia ran faster. Carol turned on the afterburners and kept up. The voice fell farther back.

"Mia! ... Carol!" Huge puffs between words, like the guy was having an asthma attack. *"Hollis ... Hollis ..."*

Then a *Fwumph!* sound, like a sack of grain hitting the floor, or possibly something catching on fire.

Carol stopped. "He said 'Hollis.'"

Mia stopped too, hating the delay. "No he didn't."

"He said it twice."

"He said something else."

Carol was watching the path behind them, seeing nothing. The guy should have caught up by now, or at least be visible. She started walking, moving in the wrong direction.

"Carol!"

Carol's composure broke. Mia wasn't the only one, it seemed, who'd had enough of the other's attitude.

"What do *you* think he said?" Carol snapped. "'Ho-ho-ho'? He's not Santa."

"Where do you think you're going?" Mia realized she was talking to nobody. She could honor her implied threat and run off solo, but now that they were right down to it, she didn't want to go anywhere without Carol.

"To see if he brought me any presents," Carol said, already fifteen feet back up the path. "I've been *really fucking good* this year."

"Carol. *Carol!*"

Now trotting to catch her, irritated beyond belief.

"Are you crazy?" Mia asked.

"Are *you?*"

"We have to go!"

"Actually, we don't. There are aliens outside the gate. Exploring options that don't get us fried by lasers just seems smart to me."

"I'll leave you! I'll get out of here on my own!"

"Go ahead."

Carol didn't even slow. She wasn't running, just walking with purpose. Mia didn't slow, either. She paced along, two steps back, wanting to pout.

They found the guy who'd been chasing them lying on the ground, on his back, hand on chest, heaving to catch his breath.

Carol stepped forward.

"Careful," Mia said.

Carol looked back, said nothing, and stepped forward again.

She came astride. The guy's hands were empty. He was a thin black man with black-frame glasses and a dress shirt buckled into jeans with a belt.

He hadn't seen or heard them. Now he did.

"Mia," he panted. "Carol."

And Mia said, "Who the hell are you?"

He extended a hand, but seemed to lack the stamina to sit up or come forward.

"I'm Theo," he said.

22

THEO SAID he was with Hollis, which Mia didn't believe. Then he said Hollis had come to the Exchange to save them, which she *really* didn't believe.

"*He* came to save *us,*" Mia said. Not a question.

"Yes. He had a plan to break you out."

"I had my own plan."

"Well, he had one, too."

"What was Hollis's plan?"

"I think he was playing it by ear."

"So, no plan."

"He wanted to bid on you. He would have won, too."

That's when Mia, now having context-corrected from Exchange floor to running in the woods, realized she'd seen Theo before. He'd been in the crowd, near the guy who kept bidding with ...

Wait.

"That wasn't Hollis," Mia said.

"Who?" Carol asked.

"The guy with the beat-up face. That was *Hollis?*"

"Yeah," Theo said.

"What happened to him?"

"Several people, I think. He didn't tell me the whole story."

"But you came together."

"I was sent by my employer."

"Yeah, who's that?"

"Sonny Malone."

"Sonny ..." Mia knew that name. "Oh, so you're a bad guy."

Theo's eyes kept going to the weapon Mia still had slung over her shoulder. He didn't know it wasn't loaded, and right now she wasn't sure she wanted to tell him.

"I left Sonny."

"To come here."

"No, I mean I *left* Sonny. I guess I'm one of the good guys now."

"Convenient."

"Wouldn't I just have killed you if I wasn't?"

Mia laughed in his face. Theo, still trying to catch his breath, seemed slightly offended.

"So ... what? You and Hollis just happened to run into each other here and decided to play some reindeer games?"

"We were after the same things. Well ... the same types of things."

"So you were there to buy women, too."

"I was there for information. Hollis showed me his attache case, when he went to see Sonny in Louisiana. What I saw bothered me, so I let Sonny send me back for more. But I'm not going back. I'm through with Sonny."

"Oh ... *I* know who you are," Carol said, perking up. "You're the one with the theory about why the aliens attack groups of humans who fight in too big of ways. Turned out to be right, you know. They dropped a bomb in Austin, and we had to—"

"We should really keep trying to find a way out of here," Mia interrupted.

But she'd already lost her battle of wills against Carol — rightly, as things turned out — and was working from a disadvantage. Carol ignored her and Theo, caught up as he regained his breath and moved to sitting, ignored her, too.

Isolated as they were in the backlot of Brendan's property, they fell into conversation as if nothing else mattered. Mia learned a lot she didn't care about anymore, like what the aliens might be trying to do with the database Thomas's case gave its owner access to and what sinister (but ultimately *who-gives-a-shit*, in Mia's opinion) things that seemed to point to. She also learned that the case had been destroyed, that Sonny was, like everyone, after Hollis's ass, and a whole bunch of techno-geek-speak about computer systems that didn't remotely matter. Among the was the tidbit that with the internet unreliable and electronics disrupted, the only real way to get back into the database would probably require going to where the machines were held and hacking in manually. Mia found it three shades of irrelevant. First, the case apparently didn't exist anymore. Second, they had no way to get out of this compound, let alone to some mysterious datacenter. And third, *who gave a shit?* Certainly not Mia Davies.

"This is fascinating," Mia said, now tugging at them, "but right now, we have to go."

"Then look at the data again," Theo said.

Carol nodded. Obnoxious. *Great*, Mia thought. *Now there's two of them.*

"We can't get at it. You said yourself, the case was destroyed."

"Which is why Hollis didn't come earlier," Carol said. "Not because he didn't want to."

Mia scoffed.

"Hey. He came for you."

"For both of us," Mia said. Then: "If that."

Carol and Theo exchanged a glance. Mia saw the look and wanted to punch them both.

"Regardless ..." she gestured back the way they'd been headed.

"We have to go back," Theo said. It was presumed, as if they'd all discussed this, all decided.

"Why?"

"Because they got Hollis."

"What? When?"

"When he went into the holding area after you. I was standing guard, but they must've gone in another way. I saw Brendan Banks and some other guys taking him away. I think they went up to the office way above the ... *What?*"

"Jesus Christ," Mia said.

"What's wrong?"

"Tell me again why Hollis came to the Exchange?"

"To save you."

"Where are we, right now?"

"Forest?"

"And where is Hollis?"

"Captured."

"I see. Because he's saving us."

"Saving *you*," Carol insisted.

"I'm flattered." She put her hands on her hips, head shaking, and began to walk a small loop.

"*What,* Mia?" Carol demanded.

"That dumb shit got himself caught. That's what. But he didn't just *get caught;* he got himself thrown in *exactly the place we were when this whole thing started.* He's in the crow's nest. You remember — where we were, before we made a plan to *save ourselves*?"

"We can still get him," Carol said. Mia felt her cheeks reddening with blood flow and anger at the bold, ball-out proclamation with absolutely no thought behind it. *We can still get him.* Oh. Right. No big deal.

"I don't think they know we're gone," Carol said. "If they did, they'd have sent people out after us. We'd have seen it back at the building and we'd hear and see it now. But ... look."

Carol pointed. The arena was a good bit away now, but they could see it through all the trees. And, to Carol's point, there was no activity around it at all.

"We've gotten lucky so far," Mia said. "He's got drones everywhere."

"Actually," Theo said. He held up a mobile phone, and Mia realized it was the same phone she'd dropped at some point. He explained about the DRONE app she'd noticed, and remarked that it seemed to do what they'd all figured. "How else did you think you were getting away so easy?" he asked, showing them the phone's screen, where he'd turned surveillance off.

"Guards, then," Mia said.

But she was losing steam, and Carol and Theo had both moved from active arguing to something far more passive-aggressive. Worse, it seemed to be working. It didn't matter whether Hollis's dumb ass had gotten caught or whether his aims, in coming here, had been just as commercial as they'd been personal. The truth was that he'd come, to save the girl, when she'd been sure he wouldn't. He'd apparently

come without even the case to trade. Blind stupidity, as
adorable as it was infuriating, had to account for something.

"Oh ... *fine*," she said.

Theo and Carol smiled. But then again, they were
stupid, too.

23

HOLLIS CONSIDERED ALL POSSIBILITIES, but before Brendan left him to wait for the torture doctor, he seemed to have thought of all Hollis had thought of. He opened the desk and removed two knives, then cut the cord on the anti- quated desk phone even though the lines were dead, just in case. He sent someone in within seconds to screw the windows closed, then used zip ties to bind Hollis to the wheeled chair. Because nobody had done *that* to anyone recently, with embarrassing results.

He did, at least, find his restraints positioned such that he could stand up with the chair hanging behind his ass, still tethered to his wrists. If he hunched just so, he could walk around with it — more to appease stir-craziness than anything else.

But then something beyond the window caught his attention, and he found himself transfixed. He even lowered the awkward chair and sat back down, to watch it.

Brendan entered, without anyone in scrubs, wielding scalpels.

"He's on his way," Brendan said. Meaning the torture doctor, Hollis supposed.

"Do you expect me to talk or somethin'?"

"No, Mr. Bond. I expect you to die!"

Hollis stared.

"You know. That line from *Goldfinger*."

Hollis said nothing.

"The James Bond movie. When Bond is strapped to that table and—"

"I caught the reference. I was just marveling your failure to intimidate me. It's stunning, really."

Brendan's face twisted, but Hollis had already noticed that his right fist was wrapped in an Ace bandage, bleeding through, and that whoever had done the bandage job had wrapped an ice pack right into the mix. Hitting a person, folks always forgot, hurt the person hitting almost as much as it hurt the victim.

It was a dumb game to play, but Hollis had to have some dignity. Brendan wouldn't hit him now, probably, and wouldn't pick something up to hit him with, probably, either. He'd be jerking off lefty for a while.

Brendan moved to go.

"Have you seen this?" Hollis asked.

"I'm not falling for another one of your—"

"Shut up, Brendan. I ain't gonna try nothin'. If you're so scared, stand back there and look. You can see just as well from your desk as I can see here."

Brendan moved, then looked. And saw.

Alien ships beyond the fence. Blocking the gate, now. No actual beings, just the moveless ships. They were about ten feet apart, hovering a few feet above the ground. Waiting, with a hum that it'd taken Hollis most of an hour to recognize. Then he couldn't unhear it.

"How long have they been there?" Brendan asked, forgetting all the rules about captor/prisoner power dynamics.

"Ten, twenty minutes? They came from yonder." He pointed. Brendan looked, as Hollis had looked. And had the same satisfying reaction as Hollis had had, when he'd first seen it.

There was a cluster of the alien shuttles hovering just beyond Brendan's property, maybe fifty feet above the ground. They were in a rough circle, the round silver orbs together looking like the many holes in a lotus.

"What?" Hollis asked. "Am I tellin' you something you don't know? This place really is Fort Knox."

Brendan slipped a phone from his pocket, poked around, then swore.

"Problems?"

"Surveillance is out. Something's wrong with the drones." He squinted at Hollis. "Did you do this?"

"How could I do this? I'm up here, ready for your closeted sexual whims."

Brendan pocketed the phone, then went to the window. This time he wasn't cautious about Hollis at all. If Hollis weren't mostly dead and not tied to a chair, he'd be kicking some ass.

"What are they doing?"

"Maybe they want to trade. Maybe you offended them, by not inviting them."

He pulled a walkie from his belt and spoke into it.

"Richards."

Crackle. A woman's voice. "Yeah, boss."

"You still on that explosion?"

Hollis had heard something earlier, but was intrigued by the mention of an explosion. Had that somehow been Mia, on her way out the door? Sounded like something she'd do. To bad he'd probably never see her again, because that shit deserved a high-five.

"No. All clear. It was a grenade by the outhouse."

"Who threw it?"

"As best we can tell, it was just an accident," said the voice on the walkie. "A prior client in line had been loading some ordinances, plus grenades. Must've dropped one."

"Without the pin? All the way over by the outhouse?"

"Maybe someone was using the outhouse," Hollis said. "Maybe they had the chili."

"I'm not sure, boss. Asher walked off somewhere, too, so I'm light-handed down here. You want me to look more into it?"

Brendan shook his head, attention fixed on the ships beyond the fence. "No. Do me a favor. Look south."

Pause. "Okay."

"Do you see the fence?"

"Not from here."

"Who can you spare?"

"Me? Nobody. But I'm sure there's someone inside who can handle whatever you need. What's up?"

Brendan considered, then must have decided it was too much to explain. "Never mind. Who inside has a walkie?"

"We only had a few. Vince has one, but he's in transport. Aaaaand ..."

"It's fine. I'll go down myself. Faster that way."

"All right. Let me know if you need anything."

After Brendan put the walkie back on his belt, Hollis said, "You know, you're supposed to say 'over' when you're done talking on those things."

"Why?"

"So the person you're talking to knows you're done for now."

Brendan walked in front of Hollis, between him and the window. Past Brendan, Hollis could see the ships beginning to move, subtly shifting their positions along the perimeter. They really did look as if they were after something — as if they were merely lining up now, preparing to make their move later.

"Hollis," Brendan said.

Hollis looked up. Brendan raised one foot, then stomped hard on Hollis's balls. Which, for the record, had already been repeatedly abused.

"Over," Brendan said.

And then Brendan, done for now, left the room while Hollis clenched his teeth, fighting for breath.

24

THEY WERE CROUCHED behind a low shrubbery, pretending to be a battle troupe that knew what it was doing. Mia, Theo, and Carol very much did not. Without a plan or knowledge or training, they really at least needed a set of binoculars or night vision goggles to be posing like they were. It would have made the whole thing look a little less embarrassing, a little less unprepared.

They watched as the guard outside picked up a walkie talkie and spoke to someone. They watched as, sometime after, guards began to shuffle and scramble, assembling in some unseen way for some unknown purpose.

"They realized we're gone," Carol said.

But Mia didn't think so. This didn't look like a search party. And although Theo had already assured them that he'd found a geeky way to keep the drones grounded and the security cameras blind — "using their own app against them," he'd said with something like a supervillain's laugh — Mia still thought that a guy as prepared and resourceful as Brendan Banks would have redundancies for situation like this. For instance: Can't find the girls that had netted top bid at today's Exchange using the drones? Send up a helicopter instead.

"Maybe, and maybe not," Mia said. "Either way, it just got a whole lot harder to operate." She pointed, noted a group of guards leaving, heading somewhere unknown — but not toward them, at least. "See? Sneaking in is easy, since nobody cares if people sneak *in*. But getting to Hollis all the way up in the crow's nest?" She shook her head. She didn't want to say that she had no clue what came next, because it was so obvious to all of them.

"Maybe we can make a distraction," Carol said.

"Oh. *Now* you're for me throwing grenades."

"If you go in brandishing that thing," Theo said, pointing at the empty gun around Mia's neck and shoulder, "do you think you can bluff like it's loaded?"

"What good would that do?"

"Maybe we can figure out where Brendan is. Get close and put the gun up to his head, threaten to blow his brains out."

That was the worst idea of all. Brendan lived with tigers and slept with guns. Mia didn't know enough about such things to have any idea how Brendan would know the thing wasn't loaded, but she was positive he would. Smell the lack of gunpowder on the far end of the barrel, for all she knew.

They were thinking, with no ideas in sight, when a tremendous thumping sound came from behind them.

They all looked at each other.

"Don't ask what that was," Mia said, eyes wide, frightened for a reson she couldn't name. "It's a cliche."

The other two were already moving. The perimeter fence wasn't far behind them, and the sound had come from the fence.

"Holy shit," said Carol.

The alien ships they'd seen earlier were still there, but now there were a lot more of them — including a round cluster, like a patten made with black pepper — maybe a half-mile off in the sky. Mia couldn't see the mothership from here, but her mind showed it to her instead: the giant mother orb streaming out its many little babies, swarming around a place whose ass they planned to kick.

The sound had been a giant slab of rock slamming itself a third of the way into the ground. That much was clear, because as they watched, it happened again, then again. The rocks were flying in, just like the shuttles. Where they came from, Mia didn't know — but as they arrived, each slab floated, then slammed straight down. Making a line, like she'd seen before under the Congress Street bridge, along the bike-and-run path.

"What are they doing?" Carol asked.

"Thinking," Theo said.

They both looked at him. He turned from assured to sheepish.

"That's my theory, anyway. If they think in a collective and expect us to think in a collective, it makes sense they'd treat us as-if. I did some research on those stones, before Hollis came to visit, because they'd been showing up around Lafayette."

"How was there research already?" Carol asked.

"Not new research. *Old* research. Like ... old Ancient Aliens theories. There were rocks just like this in France, presumably left by alien visitors, called the Carnac Stones. I ... I think they might be like an antenna."

"Why do you think that?"

"Because when I walked past a line of them," Theo said, "I found myself thinking my brother's thoughts."

Mia didn't ask what that meant, though her question

would have been obvious. She didn't need to ask. She'd experienced it. They *were* an antenna, somehow. But not *just* an antenna. More like an amplifier, turning on psychic circuitry.

"Do you think they're going to attack the compound? Like happened downtown?"

"Maybe," Carol said. "There's a lot of weaponry inside that building." She looked at Mia. "And you set off a grenade."

Theo considered, then shook his head. "They can't police everything. We know that people can fight all they want if they keep the fights small. It's only big, city-sized battles they seem to get involved with."

"Then it's not about humans fighting humans. Maybe they just want to kick some ass."

But Theo was still thinking, lips pressed, shaking his head slowly. "Not with the stones. This suggests consideration. Pondering. Maybe searching."

"'Searching'?" Carol said.

"The way you search for a solution to a problem," Theo explained.

But something inside Mia's head was turning on as she watched more of the stones fall, one after the other. Each impact was bone-jarring, like a tiny, high-intensity earthquake. She'd felt the stones' effect, too — and some part of that, she thought, had stuck with her.

Theo was wrong. Just a little, but wrong nonetheless.

"It's literal," she said.

Carol and Theo turned their heads toward her.

"Literal searching," she said.

"For what?"

"For the man they left behind."

25

THE CHAIR SHOOK. The desk shook. There was a half-full mug of coffee on the desk, and the impacts — like someone punching the Earth with extreme prejudice — made the mug jump, spilling, almost leaping onto its side.

A picture fell from the wall. Hollis's bones, bruised and battered, felt each impact like a hard shake. It burned with dull agony, a break between each impact so he could wonder how long he had before it hurt again.

The door opened. The guard Brendan had stationed outside poked his head in.

"What are you doing in here?" he demanded.

"Listen, G.I. Joe, if you think *I'm* big and bad enough to—"

Another thud. A glass vase fell from a filing cabinet and detonated. Hollis, even bound, watched it go. It mostly became rounded-off cubes — very few sharp shards for the taking. So much for using one to cut his bindings. So much for using one to shiv the guard, or the so-called doctor, if he was really on his way.

"What the hell *is* that?" the guard asked.

"You wanna come in, sit a spell, and we can discuss it?"

The door slammed. Apparently the guard was not interested in tea. Hollis rolled to the window and looked out where the impacts seemed to be coming from, seeing nothing. Nothing but the ships, some of which were glowing slightly. But if they were doing something — causing the whole building to shake, somehow — it wasn't something Hollis could see.

He wheeled the chair toward the opposite wall, toward the broken vase. He'd already reconsidered on the glass shards. Truth was, it didn't look like there was anything sharp enough in the glass pile to cause damage, but the impacts were too scary to just sit by and ignore, hoping everything would work out.

Hell. He'd rather slit his wrists than wait around for the crazy surgeon and an alien ass-probing that was feeling increasingly imminent.

He positioned himself as best as he could, then threw his weight hard against the chair's armrest on one side. He wobbled, settled upright, then swore and tried again. This time he went over, hitting the unforgiving ground hard enough to make him shout. He did his best to keep his head tilted away from the floor so as not to rack it, but of course the recoil of falling over while strapped to a chair just whipped his skull into it anyway. It was only marginally better than going limp and letting his head take the full brunt. Hollis saw stars, indignant over just how many times he'd been beaten lately, and waited for reality come back around.

This was when the door opened again — with Hollis on his side, still bound to the chair, blinking to make invisible little birdies stop circling his head.

And look who it was: Doctor Mengele, in the flesh.

Although he didn't look scary. He was at least six-four, taller than Hollis even when he wasn't horizontal, and couldn't weigh more than a buck thirty. He was that breed of emaciated where you see every tendon and ligament, every striation in every muscle. The look where they seem as starved of water as they are of food, as if they've been bottled with a desiccant, then left to dry in the sun.

Wearing light blue scrubs, top only, over skinny jeans that, due to the man's frame, looked as large as bell bottoms. Hollis felt sure that the scrubs top was being worn only for effect. It still had crease marks in it from where he'd taken it out of the bag. Probably at Brendan's suggestion, seeing as Brendan was the one trying to freak him out.

"Well then," said the man, coming forward and kneeling before Hollis. "What are you doing down there?"

"Catching a nap."

"My name is Dr. Greensward. I thought we could get acquainted."

"Cool. Get on down here, Hopalong. Got your favorite blankie?"

Greensward grabbed the back of the chair Hollis was sitting in, then embarrassed himself trying to pull the whole works upright. He didn't have nearly the ass in him to heft Hollis's 185, let alone the chair he was fixed to. The flex of his arm muscles beneath the short-sleeved scrubs looked like slugs trying to mate. Unsuccessfully, but graphically.

"I've put on some holiday weight," Hollis said as the halfhearted attempt to lift him died. "Don't judge."

The doctor sat, cross-legged, in front of Hollis. Right on top of the shattered, but rounded, glass fragments from the detonated vase. His manner was stunted, like he'd never grown up, or learned the subtle social cues that normal, non-vivisecting adults used day to day.

"Do you like puzzles?" he asked.

"Why? Did you used to work as one?"

Greensward ignored him. Hollis noticed a small black bag he'd missed before, which the man now set before him and opened. He didn't pull out the predictable scalpel or bone saw. Instead, he removed a speculum.

"Gonna check my vaginer, huh?"

"Not quite that. A puzzle that preoccupies me lately is the passage of food through the body." He held up the first finger on his right hand, then made knowing face before wagging the finger. "You'd think it'd be an impossible process to follow, seeing as food in the system isn't visible unless the subject is opened up. And that, you'd further think, might cause a little bit of an oopsie. Good luck seeing where things go next if a person dies, am I right?"

Hollis thought, with that "am I right?" that the doctor might ask for a high five. Who didn't suffer such problems?

"They're wrong, though. So, tell me, Mr. Palmer. Or Hollis. Can I call you Hollis? Have you eaten recently?"

"Had a sandwich earlier. Got a sesame seed stuck between my teeth." Then he looked at Greensward with inspiration. "Hey, think you can slip into the gap and grab it out for me?"

But the mood was flagging. Hollis, for his usual wiseassery to work, needed a reaction from his conversational partner that was, say, "on the human spectrum." Irritation would do, as would anger, frustration, eye-rolling, or even sometimes complicit humor. But Greensward was none of that. It wasn't that he truly didn't respond to Hollis's smart remarks — more that he responded like something not human that was trying its best to approximate humanity. He displayed what normal behavior would look like if it were written into and then read out of a manual: technically correct, yet not quite right.

He didn't really want to keep sparing with Dr. Greensward. It wasn't funny, it wasn't distracting him from the fear he was increasingly convinced he should be feeling, and he was surer with each passing minute that Greensward genuinely didn't get it. And he should. These were some clever lines. Mia would be in stitches.

The doctor reached into his bag and pulled out a set of needle-nosed pliers.

"Going to do some home wiring?"

Greensward gave an approximate smile. Then he set the pliers down and said simply, "No."

He reached in again, came out with a scalpel. Hollis wanted to make a joke about how the doctor was being predictable, but things had very suddenly stopped being funny. He didn't want to show fear; that's how they got to you. But seeing that blade — and especially Greensward's not-quite-right body language — made fear inevitable, its avoidance impossible.

"This," he said, "I like to use for peeling."

"I thought you liked to do puzzles."

"Yes. And like any puzzle, a person must start at the edges." He stood, then looked down at Hollis.

"You can stand with that chair attached to you," he said. "Don't pretend you can't."

Hollis didn't remotely consider it. Obedience had arrived like a train with no stops. Quite suddenly and completely, Hollis wanted to do everything this man said, forever.

His heart had started to beat harder. His skin kept tingling, and not in a good way. Fatigue had finally caught him, mixed together with hyper-awareness, like that of an animal being hunted.

So he said, as earnest as he can, "I can stand from sitting. The zip ties are loose enough for that. But from here ..."

Because the chair was wedged into a corner, nixing all his leverage. Because he had no way to get his legs under him, despite their being free. It was, truthfully, an impossible task.

Instead of truly replying or even helping, Greensward moved to the desk, climbed onto its top, and again sat cross-legged. He was still holding the scalpel, and once he'd sat, he began to pick his thumbnail with it. The thing must have been sharp, because almost immediately he started to bleed. And, it seemed, didn't even notice.

"I'll tell you what," he said. "I want to see if you can get up without help. If you can, you'll get a reward."

"Oh yeah? What reward?"

Freedom. Time away from this freak show, no matter how brief.

"The reward of avoiding punishment."

Hollis thought that was pretty shitty reward as rewards went, but opted not to say so.

"If you fail, however, I can only assist you by lightening your load."

Hollis didn't know what that meant, either. Or rather, he was pretty sure he knew what it meant and didn't want to think it.

Legs were heavy. Arms were heavy. Maybe a guy tied to a chair, if he could be secured in new ways, would be more mobile without so many heavy parts.

"Tick-tock," Greensward said, still picking and cutting his thumb.

26

"I DON'T UNDERSTAND," said Carol.

Theo didn't say anything, but he looked closer to understanding than Carol. Maybe because he'd studied the aliens, maybe because he had this theory about collective consciousness and the artificial brain they seemed to be building from human thoughts in database form, or maybe just because his personality struck her as intuitive and good with data. Whatever it was, it was okay. Because Mia, who'd said the words, didn't understand them either.

Except that she kind of did. And the more stones they dropped, the stronger her hunch became.

Searching ... for the man they left behind.

Not a man. Not literally. But a member of their group nonetheless.

She felt herself back in that little dark room, with only the muted light from a blocked window by which to see the captive reptar. She remembered what that had felt like, because she felt a cousin of the same thing now. The thing had gotten into her head, just like those rocks, now, kept sending new visions into her head.

The separated.

A phrase without meaning, except that it had all the meaning in the world.

"Theo," she said. "You mentioned that some of the aliens seem not to be as connected to their 'hive mind' as the others."

"It's just a theory. I have no evidence either way to suggest whether they *actually* think via a—"

"But good enough, right?" Mia interrupted. He'd already told them about his academic background, and how he'd done his doctoral thesis on neural networks and quantum computing — the kind that could be applied to minds as well as machines, and did a hell of a lot more to explain souls than any dualist view of the mind and body. Right now, on this particular subject, she'd trust Theo's guesses more than she'd trust anyone else's banks. Good enough, she felt, was plenty good enough.

"I suppose," he said.

"And what about those who *aren't* as connected?"

"Well," he said, still hedging, having trouble accepting that Mia and Carol weren't going to peer-review his every statement, raking him across the coals of academic literature. "According to reports, there are some of both types of aliens who seem to respond differently than their masses. From what I've heard, people have spotted a very few individuals of both types off on their own, appearing to make decisions autonomously. Seemingly isolated. Maybe even *outside of* the group mind."

"How could you tell whether or not they were connected to a group mind?" Carol asked.

"Like I said, it's just a theory. But if beings with human-or-above levels of intelligence thought collectively, you'd expect the individuals within that group to work with extreme coordination." He seemed to think of how to make the idea relatable, then shifted before going on, addressing Carol directly. "Take yourself for example. If you want to pick something up with two hands, your right hand doesn't have a different mind than the left. You, as the single intelligence that runs your body, just think, 'I want to pick that up,' and your right and left hands fall into line. Your right and left hand don't have to shout back and forth to each other to let the other know that they've got a grip and it's safe to lift now. Your right and left hand don't send messages back and forth saying, 'Okay to let go now? Ready? On the count of three!' That'd be true of the Astrals, too, if they share one mind. One would see something and the others would know it. You'd see flock behavior when they moved *en masse* — surges and waves and ebbs and flows. Maybe they'd even make formations like birds flying south. But if they *do* share a hive mind and if a few of them *are* somehow disconnected from that mind, those individuals wouldn't exhibit those behaviors. Not as fluidly, anyway."

"Meaning?"

"They'd be more like us," Theo said. "I don't know that it's in them to develop truly individual personalities, but they'd definitely move the way we move, as beings who know that all we 'are' is contained in the literal radius we can see. They'd lack the assurance that comes with knowing almost everything about their surroundings, like a mind with many eyes to map those surroundings would do. They might attack as individuals, flee as individuals ...."

"*Why* would any be separate, though?"

"Who knows? Maybe there are accidents. Maybe it's something like a birth defect, and they're born that way. Or maybe it's something they can turn on and off because sometimes they *need* individuals. To immerse with us and learn our ways, maybe. To go deep cover and stalk around in the shadows, the way a group could never do."

Carol was taking it all in. She looked from Theo to Mia, her eyes asking if Mia, who'd started this, agreed with what Theo was saying. Mia, in reality, wasn't sure. Whatever she was aware of — whatever a deeper part of her mind seemed to *know* — wasn't happening at the top level of her consciousness. It was like grasping in the dark for something she'd never seen and knew nothing about, yet would somehow recognize by touch. Things either felt right or wrong, with no context or support. And this, so far, felt right.

"So you think ... ?" Carol began. But she didn't try to finish the sentence, and instead left it for Mia to fill in.

"All I know is that there's one of them in there," she said, pointing at the building. Theo must have heard the rumors, too, or maybe even seen the thing, because he didn't react. "And a lot of them waiting out here. But not just waiting. Theo said they were *thinking*. That's what the stones are doing to me, anyway. I don't know about you guys, but I'm remembering things I was sure I'd forgotten. I keep thinking my mother is right behind me, because it's like I was just talking to her. I get this feeling of Hollis, like I've had before. Somehow, I know he's in danger, and not just because Brendan has him. *Immediate* danger. Something I can't see or guess, but that right now is making my skin crawl."

Subtly, Theo and even Carol nodded. They weren't feeling all that Mia was, but they were for-sure feeling something.

Mia pointed at the ships. She pointed at a bare area where, as if on cue, another of the hugs stones plunked into the ground.

"If their rocks are doing that to *us*," she said. "Imagine what they must be doing to *them*." She nodded, feeling this.

"If they wanted to attack, why not just attack? I don't see why they'd surround a place with thinking rocks if not to *think really hard at it*. The way this feels to me? It's like they're scratching their heads. Rubbing their chins. Concentrating really hard, on whatever's inside that building. Like one of their 'Separated' who needs the collective. Like a soldier captured behind enemy lines."

"That's awfully altruistic for an advanced species," Theo said. "Compassion is inefficient. Assuming they think like us — that they'd care about 'someone left behind' enough to risk others — might be a mistake."

"It's only more compassionate than practical," she said, "if there's a risk."

Because based on what Mia had seen, was seeing, and what she felt, there was no risk here. If what seemed to be brewing actually happened, it wouldn't be a brave mission to rescue a comrade. It would be no more dramatic than peeking under the couch to find a dropped coin.

She stood. In plain view of the alien ships, if they cared to look in their direction, she stood.

"I know how to get Hollis back," she said.

"How?"

"By giving them what they want."

27

HOLLIS MANAGED to get to his feet. It was a supremely difficult move, like something a great athlete would have trouble doing while climbing rocks. Standing, with the chair behind him and cuffed to his wrists, with the chair's bulk at the backs of his legs and making them bend, required simultaneous use of one wall, another wall, and the floor. When he got upright, he was covered in sweat. Oh, the things a man could accomplish when sufficiently motivated.

Dr. Greensward, who'd been unpacking his little black medical bag while Hollis had been wrestling the chair gauntlet, looked disappointed. He'd stopped picking at his fingernails with sharp objects, and all the time Hollis had taken had given his thumb wound time to scab over and dry. He didn't wash it off, though — just kept right on unpacking his horror show with blood across his palm and wrist.

The doctor unpacked:

A surgical steel device that looked like a round spur on a boot, or perhaps a pastry scorer. It rolled on a central bearing with spikes coming from the center, and while

Hollis watched he'd tested it, rolling it back and forth on the desk as if cutting (or at least wounding) a very small pizza.

A thing that looked like a finger with three joints, operated from the base to curve and curl — also like a finger, beckoning someone forward. It was overly elaborate, like art more than equipment. Its workings recalled the machines of Da Vinci — a mechanism as fantastical as practical, bound by many wires that acted as wire tendons. On the end was a sharp point, like a claw.

An instrument that reminded Hollis of a tiny battle axe: a central steel shaft flanked by two outward-curving semicircular blades.

And lastly, what looked like a circular saw in miniature, which the Good Doctor operated by holding the shaft between his first and second finger, pushing a plunger beneath using his thumb. This one reminded Hollis of toys from long ago, which moved or made noise when you pumped them so. And when Greensward did, the little blade spun and it made a noise, like the grinding of stone parts.

"Look," Hollis said, finally at his limit, unable to even point out a rather obvious pop culture reference about the doc's tools that kept springing to mind, "I'll do whatever you say."

"*Good,*" said the doctor. It was a horrible sound, coming out like a purr.

"What does Brendan want? Information? I told him, I have pictures of information he wants. I just need to find it. And I get it; he thinks I'm crying wolf. He thinks it's a scam. I've certainly pulled my share of scams before, including on Brendan. But this time it's real. He doesn't need to send me. He can send someone else. I'll tell them where it is." He'd been watching Greensward's hands the entire time, seeing how he was playing with the finger-and-claw tool, pressing something, making it curl in a hideous come-hither. Hollis lowered his head, did his best to wipe away forehead sweat on his already-soaked shirt. "Look. I'll do anything. Tell me what it is, and I'll do it."

The doctor said, "The things I want you do, say, and feel, you won't need instruction to do."

He set down the finger. Picked up the mini buzzsaw.

"All I want," he said, "will come quite automatically."

"I need to talk to Brendan," Hollis tried.

"Mr. Banks is occupied."

"I don't give a shit. I need to talk to him. This is something he'll want to hear."

Greensward, not looking up, slowly shook his head.

Hollis considered his options. He wasn't on the floor anymore; he *must* have options. The doctor was still cross-legged on the desk. Hollis might be able to get close, then pivot hard and thrown the chair beneath his ass into him. But what would be the point? It wasn't a light little camp chair behind him; it was a forty-pound luxury office chair. Just standing with it was so hard as to be unsustainable, let alone swinging it as a weapon. Hollis, if he was lucky, might be able to bang Greensward's shins. Leave a nasty bruise, maybe some light abrasions.

"Get me the guard," Hollis said, trying again.

"No thank you."

"It's not a request."

"It is very much a request."

"You aren't in charge here. On this property, Brendan is the boss."

The doctor nodded, still not meeting Hollis's eye. "Correct. And he asked me to deal with you."

"Things have changed. I have new information."

"To deal with you," Greensward elaborated, "and to 'leave him the hell alone until it was done.'"

Hollis didn't know what to say. It was like talking to a human doll, not a real thing.

Finally Greensward met Hollis's gaze.

"You seem tired."

"But I did it. I did what you asked."

"Have a seat. Can I get you a chair?"

Hollis stared. Then he realized that was probably supposed to be a joke. Told by someone who'd read about jokes and perhaps studied them like Goodall studied apes, but never encountered one in the wild.

Hollis sat. Between his fatigue and the accumulated weight of standing so long with the chair. It was more collapse and less voluntary lowering. The chair's wheels hit the ground with a crunch sufficient to crack them.

Then the doctor came to Hollis — sidelong, probably because he was smart enough to see a nuts-kick coming — and plucked at the black Wal-Mart turtleneck as if curious about its make. Then he retrieved a folding knife from his pocket and cut it open: a long vertical slit, then two angled slits at the top. A big Y shape, like an autopsy.

The air was cool against Hollis's exposed chest.

"Please," Hollis said.

But the doctor was already reaching for his instruments.

28

GETTING IN WAS EASY. With the distraction of the dropping stones, not a single person Mia saw was paying complete attention. Even those with guns and marching orders — those whose job it was, specifically, to keep an eye out — were distracted. The thumping sound of dropping rocks jarred them all, and only finally stopped when, by Mia's estimation, they'd made a 360-degree circuit. The Brendan's property was now surrounded by the giant stones. It made Mia feel walled in without any walls at all.

And, as she'd seen before ducking back inside the building, the round silver ships kept arriving too, each hovering a few feet above the ground and not doing anything at all.

So yes, sneaking in was easy. She didn't even have to throw a grenade. This time, all she had to do was throw a rock. The poor soldier who heard it land was so amped up, she almost blew half of a hillside away before realizing it was nothing. By then, Mia was inside.

She glanced back at open air before slipping around the corner. Moving in felt claustrophobic — especially now, especially with their entire compound surrounded by the city's most unmotivated occupying army. Theo and Carol had stayed outside, ready to act as support whenever they were needed. Without walkies (none available, and they'd be overheard anyway), contacting them again might be tricky. But right now, Mia trusted her ability to find them anyway. There was something in the air. Something moving *through* the air, by the feel of things.

Her nerves built. The fear percolating through everyone inside the Exchange — seeing as none yet had had the guts to challenge the barricade and try to leave — was palpable and infectious. Hadn't she *just* escaped this place? Going back in, frankly, was bullshit. She'd gotten them traded; she'd gotten them out of the cage; she'd even managed to snag a phone that (in Theo's hands, but whatever) had quite handily shut down drones and surveillance to let them escape the grounds. Even with the aliens arriving, they could have been outta here by now, if they'd moved fast enough to break the perimeter before it fully formed.

Stupid Hollis. Why had he come to save her? She didn't need saving. She'd been just fine, either with Carol or on her own. Now, thanks to his macho bullshit — because he'd gotten himself caught, proving himself less nimble than her — she was right back in danger. But what was she supposed to do? He'd already done the right thing, as misguided as it was. She could have left him to rot before, but not after he'd failed to leave her to rot. Goddamn Hollis, putting the onus on Mia to prove she wasn't the asshole.

She wiped at her brow. She was starting to sweat. There was no reason. It wasn't hot inside the building and she hadn't been particularly exerting. This was a fear sweat, and yet she wasn't particularly afraid. Should be, but wasn't. And yet, the feeling now creeping up from deep inside her was primal — a fear no rational person should ever have occasion to feel.

And her legs were sore.

And her back.

And her wrists, for reasons unknown.

She felt stooped, unable to straighten up, like there was a weight dragging her down.

Around the corner. Leaning on a partition wall, sliding down it to sit on the concrete floor. She was still well-hidden, a few turns into the layaway labyrinth. She could hear all the Exchange floor activity — trades and auctions still in full bloom — but the area was dark, like a dream. When she'd fallen, it'd almost been like a slump. Like she'd fallen more than sat, and now she wondered if she could get up.

Shake it off, girl, she told herself. *You're letting it get to you.*

But it wasn't just fatigue; it wasn't just nerves. Somehow, it wasn't. She knew, in that way she knew but didn't truly know, that this had something to do with the occupation. Specifically, with the ring of stones around the property. In some way, they were dragging her down.

Absurd.

Except that her heart was hammering way too fast. Except that it wasn't absurd at all, and the danger she felt nipping at her neck wasn't entirely her own.

Someone was coming.

"Intolerable," said a voice. The voice had a somewhat soft palate. Or a fullness, perhaps, as if the speaker's tongue was too large.

She knew that voice. She'd heard it before, during the auction.

"Insufferable, incorrigible, unbelievable, unacceptable,"

the voice went on. "I demand restitution. I demand reparations."

It was that gangster who'd bought her and Carol. He'd had an odd name. Beef. That was it: *Beef*. She knew from his mushmouth and wordmongering. Half of what he was saying didn't make sense, using big words for the sound of them, rather than their meaning.

Now another voice Mia knew: Brendan Banks.

"We'll find them."

"How you gonna find 'em, bitch?" Beef demanded. "You got three bags of my very best, and now I've got nothing new for my crew to play with."

Mia made a face.

"We'll of course refund you," Brendan said.

"I don't want a refund," Beef said. "I want my merchandise. It's the principle. I live large, with exuberance. With grand salutations! People know my sit'chation, y'know what I'm sayin'?"

Brendan paused, because *nobody* could understand a sit'chation of livin' large with grand salutations and exuberance ... know what I'm sayin'? But Brendan covered well, playing VIP customer service to the hilt.

"Nobody can leave the grounds," Brendan said. "They probably haven't even left the building. We'll seal down and search every corner. Believe me, Mr. ... Believe me, Beef," he tried again. "We'll find your property."

"You betta swear, bitch."

"I swear."

Bitch.

They moved away, never fully seen. Mia was left alone again, ironically aware that she'd experienced liberation, escape, and now a near miss with exactly no change in her station. It was curious to hear how close she apparently was to caught (her absence discovered, those looking for her not twenty feet away) so long after she'd realized she was fine. It was strange to be closer to peril now than when she'd just been following her nose.

More specifically, it didn't feel like peril at all. Her nerves — on that matter, anyway — were nonexistent.

I'm not hiding and waiting to be caught, assholes, she thought. *I'm sneaking in, on purpose, right under your big fat nose.*

That made her stand up not with worry that they'd find her, but with intention to evade them further. It didn't make her retreat so she wouldn't be found. Instead, it made her advance, because her plan was working perfectly.

First of all, she was too conspicuous in this dress. So she hunted the aisles, quickly finding a cache of clothing that she'd missed before. It felt like a sign. So she quickly slipped out of the dress and into pants that were too baggy and an anonymous dress shirt that was the opposite of flattering. Farther in she found hats, so she tucked her hair up and wore one of them, too. There were no reflective surfaces in which to check her reflection, but she didn't need one to know she looked ridiculous. But it was okay. It was the kind of ridiculous that blends in, and that's what mattered most.

The only thing she couldn't find were shoes or boots. But because she couldn't wear her new ensemble with the high heels they'd given her (and which she'd been carrying tied to her gun strap, because maybe any shoes would prove to be better than none), she opted to go barefoot as the least of evils. It's not like she still had the unloaded gun — that was outside with the others, so she'd have to ditch them or keep carrying them in her hand.

She tucked them away, with the dress. Other than her

exposed feet, she supposed she looked entirely unre-
markable.

And now for the next phase.

She slipped out, into the crowd, and eventually found a
pile of fliers she'd seen circulating earlier. It was dead
simple and without frills: a list of key auctions and times.
She and Carol weren't actually on it; they'd been a last-
minute addition. But the alien was, and a quick check of a
wall clock told her that it was only a half-hour away.

She needed to make sure Brendan bought it. He'd be
able to afford it. Not only did he have the best cache and
biggest army around; he also had electronics, which few
others had and everyone wanted. If Brendan bought the
alien, she'd be able to control him — to get the thing out of
confinement and into some cage or another in Brendan's
weird zoo. Maybe it could even sleep with the tigers, if it
wouldn't eat them.

The aliens would know. The reptar, once relocated,
would tell them — through the stones.

There'd be chaos.

And? Carol had asked. *After there's chaos, what exactly is
the plan to get Hollis?*

I'll figure it out, Mia had responded.

Which meant that here and now, she had no idea.

And in fact, now that Mia was on the Exchange floor in
frumpy disguise and surrounded by exactly the type of people
she'd so recently risked life and death to escape from, she had
even less of an idea. Her idea-making muscle had gone limp.
This had all sounded like a grand idea in the safety of the
woods, but now it just felt stupid. Who did she think she was?
The energy she felt from the alien rocks, outside, had felt like
a superpower. Now it felt like a liability at best. Not only was

she completely vulnerable (unarmed and without contingency, exposed in the middle of the arena floor), but she couldn't believe she'd put so much faith in "somehow."

Somehow, it'll work.

Somehow, helping the aliens will make them want to help us.

Somehow, showing the occupying ships where they could find their missing soldier would ingratiate them to the rogue humans and ...

... and *what*?

This was stupid. So, so stupid.

She turned. Time to regroup. Carol had pressed her outside, and Mia had waved it all away. The bravado had been intoxicating out there; she'd felt planning was for pussies. Now it was clear that Carol was right, and about something so obvious: Of course she needed strategy. Of course she couldn't just *somehow* find Brendan, *somehow* manipulate him into bidding on the reptar and winning it without him catching her, and then *somehow* counting on the aliens to ... well ... to *somehow* help in a totally undefined way.

The stones were making her stupid. Making her drunk. She thought she knew why: What Theo had said about collective intelligence was true, and the combined voices of all those different brains (if the aliens had them) was unduly persuasive. She felt like she was on a lectern, pitching her proposal to thunderous cheers of support. Only, that wasn't really the way it was, was it? She was hearing and feeling them, but what they thought and felt in return had nothing to do with Mia. They thought, and she listened in on that thought. They weren't with her, or for her, or likely even knew about her.

So. Yeah. With the intoxication drained away, the point-less of this winging-it plan was fully apparent.

"Excuse me."

Mia looked halfway up, then immediately away. Her pulse beat so hard, she was sure it was visible in her neck and forehead. Her hands shook, from steady a second earlier.

Because the man beside her was Thomas Davies, her estranged husband.

Mia lowered her head, putting more of the hat's brim between her face and his eyes. She was as tall as him and wore loose, unisex clothing that did nothing to flatter the bosom. With luck, maybe he'd think she was a man.

Making her voice as low as possible and coughing to disguise it further, she said, "Yeah."

"Do you know how many more main-stage auctions are left?"

Mia kept her head down and handed him the flier. But of course, dammit, they'd painted her nails when they'd done her hair for auction. She shoved the flier toward him more than handing it delicately, then retracted her hand before (hopefully) he'd looked down to notice.

He looked the paper over. She wondered if they were through. If she could exit, or doing so at the wrong time might attract his attention. If he had reason to look, he'd see something wrong — or, perhaps, just something familiar. Even walking might give her away. Nobody else here was barefoot — and fewer still with toenails painted bright red.

"Hmm," Thomas said. "So they're really auctioning off an alien. That's pretty freaky, right?"

Mia mumbled.

"Not that the time matters. Did you hear all those heavy slamming sounds earlier?"

Stupid small talk. Of course she'd heard, like everyone had heard. They'd been impossible to miss.

Mia mumbled again.

"I heard someone saying there are aliens outside the fence. Dropping rocks. That's what the booms were: rocks dropping."

Tired of mumbling, Mia murmured.

"I know," Thomas said, taking this for conversation. "But whatever. Those ships have been all over town. Then they occupied downtown. In fact, from what I hear, they almost *destroyed* downtown. But they didn't, now, did they? I think they just see human commerce and maybe are curious about it. I'd be curious about us, if I were them. Just because we don't understand something — or a whole race — is no reason to be afraid. They might be like us. The biggest fears create the best opportunities. That's the way I see it, anyway."

My god, she thought. *Is he honestly talking about trying to find ways to partner up with them?*

But still Mia shrugged and nodded along, falling back now into Thomas's rhythm. He didn't really talk *with* people so much as *at* them. In the later years of their marriage, Mia had learned the best way to give Thomas the sense of a fulfilling conversation was to just let him talk. He made points, then agreed with them, then laughed about how well the agreements happened. She became a bystander, while he amused himself. Honestly, it wasn't that different in bed. Thomas, like so many people, was involved enough in his own affairs that if nobody interrupted, it didn't really matter if anyone else was there.

But now he was looking at her. Waiting, finally, for her to really join the conversation.

It might be dawning on him that he'd yet to see the face

of the person he was talking to. Dawning that something about this exchange was odd. Not everyone wanted to chat and not everyone was friendly, but in just about any meeting people at least *saw* each other. And right about now, Thomas might be realizing that, if only at a subconscious level.

She could feel his eyes on her. Not in the way his eyes used to be on her, but in this new, curious way.

The plain, nondescript body presented by her ugly clothes.

The feminine hands, which she'd now stuck in her pockets.

The bare feet, which she tried to keep hidden without exactly hiding. If she stayed close, he might not be able to easily look down.

But it was a balance, because if she was too close, he might smell her. They'd given her a good shot of perfume to go with her makeover, knowing how much the kind of men who bought women at auctions liked their perfume. Although, maybe the perfume was a blessing? She and Thomas had lain together countless times. Supposedly women had the superior sense of smell, but wasn't it possible that he'd recognize her natural scent beneath it all?

His eyes. On her. Perhaps noting that she wasn't the man he seemed to have supposed, and curious. He'd have noted her smooth, sweeping jawline. Her bunched dark-brown hair, long but not man-long, beneath the ballcap.

All he needed to do was wonder, and things would unravel from there.

"Say," Thomas said, "are you here for the—?"

"MOTHERFUCKER, I SAID *WE GOT A PROBLEM!*"

Mia startled. Thomas did, too. Their heads turned to see Chapter 2 of the Brendan and Beef show, now playing out loudly to the side of the makeshift stage. Beef was the loud one; Brendan was the rep trying to calm an irate customer down. From appearances, they'd been arguing for at least the last few beats of her one-sided chat with her husband, but only now had something happened that had set Beef off. She'd been watching him earlier, during the bidding, and seen the body language between him and a beat-up guy she'd since realized was Hollis. He had the swagger of someone who'd been down and out once, then had clawed his way up and earned his due. Everything about him screamed, *I only settle for the best and only accept respect.* Everything beneath that, in Mia's mind, screamed *something to prove.*

Brendan's attempts to quell him were futile. That much was obvious. Whatever wrong Brendan had perpetuated on the man — whether it was loss of his property or something new — it wouldn't be resolved with talk. It wouldn't, she thought, be resolved at all. This was a tantrum. This was a show. This was Beef having his say, now solely for the sake of showing the world that he didn't take any shit from no one.

Hushing, pacifying gestures from Brendan. As ineffectual as Mia's assessment of the man predicted.

"NO. NO. YOU GET ME MY SHIT AND YOU GIVE ME MY SHIT. EITHER WAY, IT'S ALL MINE. BECAUSE FUCK YOU!"

Every word projected. Every word a shout. Brendan stood before him, stooped the way the powerless were stooped, eager to give him whatever he wanted, so long as it'd calm him down.

Mia let her attention flag. As riveted to their argument as she was (Beef's intention, for all to hear and care), this was a better opportunity to slip away than it was to gawk. So she stepped back from Thomas, and when he didn't notice, she stepped back again.

And back. And back, as the shouting resumed.

Into the corner, farthest from the back door.

Where, she saw now, the entire holding area staff was busy scrambling, trying to deliver whatever unreasonable thing The Remonstrating Mr. Beef was demanding.

You can't get out that way anymore, lady, said a voice in her head.

But that much, she'd already figured out.

29

THIS IS GOING to be a problem.

Mia thought this as she leaned against the side wall, beyond a drape meant to conceal an electric panel, hidden from view without looking like she meant to hide. Not far off was Brendan and Beef, who'd at least quieted, if still weren't in agreement. That would go on for a while, Mia decided, because Brendan was solving for the wrong problem. He was trying to address what Beef was saying, while the true problem was what Beef was feeling but would never admit. All Brendan needed to do was to keep saying and doing whatever told Beef, *I respect you. You are better than me. You are amazing, and everyone thinks so.* But he was too blind, too dumb, or too stubborn to see it, and so the argument raged on.

Mia, hearing the hole dig deeper, could only think about herself and Hollis.

I need him to bid on the alien. That's the only way to get it transferred out onto his grounds quickly. That's the only way to occupy him, please the aliens, and show them who's on whose side.

Not that solved anything. She was steering toward granting the occupying alien spheres a modicum of success, for reasons consciously unknown. Some part of Mia insisted that if the reptar was at least visible to the spheres, they'd stop whatever they were doing, stop guarding the gates, and let the building empty. Or, alternatively, they'd exact revenge and come storming in, killing everyone. Or perhaps there'd be something in the middle — a dash through the fences, perhaps, to snatch the reptar back from whatever external pen Brendan's people moved it to. The specifics didn't matter. Somehow, however it happened, Mia felt sure it was the right move. Part of the vaguely psychic monkey on her back, she supposed.

But that wouldn't happen if Brendan didn't bid.

If someone else won the alien, it'd stay in the storage area for a while longer — too long, probably, for Hollis — and none of the scenarios she imagined would play out.

It doesn't matter, she thought, turning cynical. *Because how the hell would Brendan even want to win that thing?*

But some part of her had already figured that out. The answer was simple: it wasn't just a zoological curiosity like his three tigers, nor was it just a really clear token to mark Brendan Banks as the ultimate outsider badass. It was, she thought, also a weapon. A weapon that nobody else had — and from that perspective, it didn't even matter that anyone could control it.

Listen, Brendan, she could imagine herself saying. *Just think how terrified people would be if you threatened to throw them into the pen with it.*

Yes. Easy to sell. She'd even begun to figure out *how* she could sell it without doing so personally. She wasn't proud of her forming plan, but it involved seduction of men close to Brendan, perhaps nudity, perhaps implied handjobs for a job well done. She didn't intend to follow through on the handjobs, of course, but promising them was still gross. She wanted to rise above, but the guys in this crowd were just so predictable. If you wanted a solution fast, you went for dick. Was it dignified? Not exactly. But it got the job done, no pun intended.

But as she listened, Brendan capitulated in exactly the wrong way.

"Of course," she heard him say to Beef. *"Of course* I'll give you back your Beaver Nuggets, whether we find your items or not."

Items. That was as insulting as a reneged handjob. She wasn't an item and neither was Carol. Hearing it made her want to give those handjobs after all, while holding razor blades and salt.

But she couldn't stay angry about her objectification, because something more dire had just been said. And the die, once cast, couldn't be taken away.

Of course I'll give you back your Beaver Nuggets.

And Mia, hearing this, thought:

What the fuck, Brendan. Grow a spine. Have some balls, because I'm going to want to cup them while I've still got blades and salt in my hands. Three bags. Three whole bags, you asshole, and you're still going to give us to him if you catch us? Give him one back, for his trouble. Two if you're a coward. But never, never all three.

Because fucking hell ... three bags of Beaver Nuggets was a fortune. Even *one* was a fortune. If he really meant to refund all three, that might make him hesitant to bid on the alien no matter how cool she made it sound — no matter how many handjob-hypnotized men she sent to convince him.

The irony deepened. Her plan to rescue Hollis — who'd

come here to rescue her — had been foiled by Mia herself, just by escaping. Thinking out the possible outcomes was like solving the twisted dimensions of an Escher drawing.

She moved away, keeping to the edges, keeping her hat low.

Then, she felt cold.

Cold on her chest. Cold, as if someone had cut her shirt open, even though she was wearing two layers. And with the cold came fear. Deep, instinctual, primal fear. The fear of a trapped animal who'd do anything to escape, including chewing off a limb.

Hollis.

He was in trouble. Deep, *deep*, no-bullshit trouble. This new problem with Beef and Brendan barely mattered. The auction was too far off. Too far away.

She felt a sliding, etching sensation, as if someone was dragging a hard fingernail up a chest that still felt exposed, bare to the world.

He's going to kill him.

Who was going to do the killing, Mia had no idea. Nor did she know where, or how, or why. But she knew it would happen, and soon. She felt it. She was more certain than certain — the way she was certain that sky was up and ground was down. It was the most curious sensation. It didn't feel like looking forward to something that was *going* to happen. It was more like she'd leapt forward in time and was looking back on something that had *already* happened. That's how sure it was.

Done.

Complete.

Yet to happen, but more than certain.

Think. Think, *Mia!*

But the pressure was on her. She was having a hard time

differentiating her own thoughts from whatever this cold knowledge was, invading from the outside. She could still feel the thing tracing up and down her chest, her heart hammering, knowing that the sensation was only a prelude — only playing. For now. And with that cold finger on her and that cold surety inside her, it was hard to think. It was hard to be herself, with part of her mind an unknown elsewhere.

Deep breaths.

She forced herself.

One,

Two,

Three.

Eyes closed.

Then they opened, that phantom sensation barely at bay.

Motherfucker.

She knew.

It was time for Plan B, and Plan Be was bound to be a bitch.

30

INTO THE DARK.

It was still undisturbed. Of course it was. If anyone had been in here, they would have noticed. There would have been a problem. A panic. It was smart enough, Mia felt sure, to not waste a second chance. When she and Carol had been here, they'd fooled it. It wouldn't be fooled again.

Whoever opened the door to the interior space, to find the reptar out of its cage yet unable to escape the room, would have gotten a nasty surprise.

Mia thought this as she opened the door, saw it like a giant spider in the corner, and forced herself to go on anyway.

It can't see you. It can't see you.

A refrain, repeated like a mantra. But she knew that didn't matter, didn't she? She'd seen into it before, and she'd be a fool to think it hadn't seen her.

Just not with its eyes. Not with those horrid, yellow eyes above its many-toothed mouth, a blue spark burning in its gut.

You don't need to go inside. Just open the door. Just open it and step back.

But Mia knew that wasn't true. She remembered the sensation of reaching out to the thing with her mind, using mental muscles she'd never used before. It had happened by reflex, but happened in a way that had let them live. It had been like extending her hand for a dog to smell it. That, she'd done many times in her life. Most times, interested dogs sniffed and let you pet them. But every once in a while, they bit.

"Don't bite me," she whispered to the thing as she closed the door, shutting herself inside.

Its head turned, still inside its heavy helmet. But it hadn't needed to hear, to know she was there. She'd felt its attention right away. Powerful black attention, like intelligent oil. It wasn't like a human, but wasn't like an animal, either. This was something new.

It came forward. Close. She could hear it breathe. She could *feel* it breathe.

She reached out a mental hand. Again.

Let it smell you. Let it know you're not afraid.

But she was afraid. So very, very afraid.

She felt its thoughts reach inside her. And as it did — and this was something she'd lose when it was over, and never be able to explain despite hard trying — she was sure that Theo was right: This was one of the Separated. One who, despite being of a group that shared a singular mind, was not part of that mind. One who had, she felt sure in the moment, cut itself off. She could feel its singularity. She could feel the non-plurality of thought. It was sharp-edged, like an individual, not rounded like an average.

"Good boy," she said.

Letting it sense her. Letting it explore her. Letting it

know — through psychic potential it had despite its separation, made stronger by the stones — that its goals and her own were not dissimilar.

It meant, but did not say in anything like language: *I will destroy.*

Mia, similarly outside of language, felt back at it: *Do not destroy me.*

The monster seemed to say something else. Indecipherable. Foreign.

And Mia, obeying mixed impulse and instinct, reached out.

Touched its skin. Its black scales, with their odd almost-leather texture, with their curious mix of cold and heat. Not warm. Distinct sensations of hot and cold, separated by space.

The mental tendrils retracted. Mia felt suddenly empty — singular in a way she'd been all her life, but that now felt strange, almost lonely. Then the feeling passed and her fear returned, and she stood before the mammoth black thing.

They'd made an agreement. It would, she thought, honor it.

Help me and do not harm me, and I will free you.

She didn't realize she was reaching for the helmet's clasp until her fingers were on it. But then she pulled away thinking, *No, they should have a fighting chance.* It would not need its teeth, she felt sure, to do what it meant to do.

Aloud, she said, knowing it would never understand, "Remember. You promised."

Hand on the handle.

She turned it and opened the door.

Then the big black alien bug — its horror now illuminated by the light, far more terrifying than she'd realized —

squeezed its way out, clattering exoskeleton denting the frame.

Then it stopped and seemed to regard her.

And just as Mia had spoken to the thing knowing it wouldn't understand, so was it speaking to her, now, in ways she couldn't understand. Yet the message was clear:

If I meant not to honor our deal, its quiet presence beside her seemed to say, *you would be dead already.*

Then, in a single bound far more elegant than its shape seemed to portend, the reptar leapt above the drapery partitions and onto the Exchange floor, among all the people, and the terror began.

31

THE DOCTOR, tracing lines up and down Hollis's chest with the articulating metal finger, stopped when a crash came from the window, from the Exchange floor below. Hollis was sideways to it and, despite seeing some species of chaos, was unable to see exactly what it was without turning his head. Which he wouldn't do because ...

"What the hell was *that?*" the doctor said, turning to look.

... because when dumbasses were distracted, dumbasses stopped paying enough attention. Luckily Hollis, who'd lived by wits and impulse for his entire adult life, didn't have that problem.

He lunged forward, hard, knowing that for this to work he'd need to extend his arms and let the chair come with him, at least for a few inches. So he felt the rip on his wrists, from the zip ties, followed by the lurching bulk of the chair trying to drag him back. But he'd thrusted enough and immediately after there was blinding pain and blackness as his forehead struck the doctor's nose just as he was turning back to center.

The crunch of cartilage as it folded like thick plastic. The sickening give of the bones beneath the cartilage, altering the doctor's appearance forever.

Then the blood, pouring rather than dripping. A burst water balloon filled with gore, drenching Greensward's scrubs and spattering Hollis's pants and bared chest.

The doctor backed off, out of range. His hand went to his nose, cupping it. The blood welled and spilled as if he was squeezing a sponge, and then his eyes went hard. Furious.

There was something happening below — for sure now. From the corners of his eyes — and with the doctor staring at him like this, it would remain only the corners — he could see what looked like a spinning blade scattering the floor and turning the crowd to chaos. He could hear screams, too, and shouts, and a few gunshots. But none of that mattered. What mattered, right now, was inside the room.

"You'll pay for that," Greensward said.

He picked up the scalpel — the most pedestrian of his House of Horrors toolkit, but the most reliable. He brandished it like a surgeon would in a fight: overly aggressive, too high, fussy delicate fingers ill-suited for battle. Hollis would normally be able to take him easy, but he was still bound. His eyes went wide and made to dodge and evade, but his body could only rattle the chair.

Greensward had let go of his shattered nose. It ran freely, turning his face to a monster mask. He looked, quite simply, completely and totally insane.

Hollis expected more banter and bargaining — from either of them — but instead the doctor just came at him. He stabbed instead of swiped, neglecting the scalpel's razor edge in favor of its rounded point. It did the job, though, because even as Hollis tried to shrink back, Greensward

impaled him in the side. Hollis screamed out, sure his opponent had punctured something necessary. But it wasn't a
lung and it wasn't his heart, and that meant he had to keep
right on going.

Bound. Motherfucker.

The doctor lunged again, but this time Hollis scooted
hard right. Then, using the wall against his shoulder as
leverage, he wobbled onto his feet and, knowing what it
might cost him, aimed a kick. The kick landed well in
Greensward's stomach and caused him to drop the scalpel,
and that was the good news. But then the inevitable
happened and Hollis, unable to balance on one foot given
his current situation, fell heavily back to the ground. Luckily
the chair caught him; he fell upright rather than onto the
floor. If *that* had happened, he'd be sunk. He'd seen how
hard it'd been to rise from fallen, and how long it'd take. By
the time he moved, the doctor would have him in slivers.

Get up, he told himself.

But he didn't have the muscle. Or the time. And that
chair ... man, it was *heavy*.

GET THE FUCK UP!

Greensward stabbed again. Hollis moved inside his
lunge, half-tripping him, taking a scalpel slash across the
clavicle — the bare part, where his shirt had been cut away.
Hollis cried out, but the pain was nothing compared to the
adrenaline.

Just keep moving. Keep him on his toes.

Which sounded great, until he remembered he was
lashed to a chair. He could kick and he could roll. Given the
rare chance that the doctor got very close again, he could
maybe head-butt. That was the limit of his repertoire, and a
total gyp. It was like playing a 1990s fighting game with half

the buttons broken. The joystick, too, shit. It's not like he could rush like Ryu, jump like Chun Li.

Use what you've got.

Which was nothing. Again: *motherfucker*.

Come on, asshole. Nobody fights in a chair like you. Other bitches should be so lucky as to have a chair!

It was a shitty reframe. There was no way to see the desk chair as an advantage. Greensward came again, slashed his upper arm. Through the fabric this time, so not as bad. Why wasn't he coming in for the kill?

Your feet. Keep him in front of you, and you can kick.

Until he got around one side, which was inevitable and easy, and just cut him open to start unrolling intestine.

Then get out.

I can't *get out.*

But ... that wasn't exactly true.

Hollis remembered his father, telling him the difference between *possible* and *willing*. Usually, people said, "I can't" when what they meant was, "I'm not willing." Sure, you can buy that car you want ... if you let your wife divorce you and sell everything you own.

But don't let the crazy ideas fool you, Hollis, the old man had said. There come times when "What am I willing to do" is the only thing that saves you.

Hollis looked at the window. Dumb little half-thing, with a long drop below. Locked, of course — screwed shut by Brendan's people before Hollis had been brought here. Two thirds of the big frame were below the roof and one third was above.

Definitely not enough to squeeze through, even if it were unlocked.

But that wasn't remotely true. That was Hollis deciding

that something wasn't possible just because he wasn't willing.

In those times, my boy, Hollis's father's voice whispered, *you have no choice but to be brave.*

The Exchange had to be twelve feet down, floored with hard concrete. The window was closed and locked, and Hollis was bound to a chair.

He'd die. If he tried what he was thinking, he'd probably die.

But, he thought looking at Greensward, if he stayed here, he was dead for sure.

He rolled to the room's center, kicking at the doctor.

Then he pushed back, very hard. The impact cracked the window glass but did not break it, and Hollis thought, *Well, now I'm fucked.*

Greensward came at him. Hollis kicked.

Again!

He rotated as he retreated, again to the room's center, using his feet to keep the doctor at bay.

Then, with the mightiest lurch he could summon, Hollis pushed back, and pushed back.

And the glass, this time, offered no resistance.

He fell, ass over teakettle, to the concrete below, dragging his sitable burden behind.

32

TWELVE FEET DOESN'T SOUND TERRIBLY FAR from the ground. Two tall men standing on each other's heads. But it's a lot farther when that's how far you're about to fall, or have to jump, or spill out a window tied to a chair.

Hollis made the short trip in just under one second, but during what passed for free-fall it felt like closer to a minute.

Hollis saw the glass shards, displaced from the window, spilling weightless around him, dropping as he dropped. He noted the subtle pitch, yaw, and roll of the Hollis/chair combined system, flagging like a pilot who's lost control of her plane. He had time to consider the floor below, consider what he was about to flatten (in a convenient tale it'd be a wagon full of pillows, but in Hollis's it was a tipped-over weathervane someone had dropped during the melee, that might impale him if he landed soft-side first), and who, if they didn't haul ass, was about to be squashed. Luckily, in that very long falling time, the square below him was crossed and then cleared entirely by the time glass began to fall. Except for that weathervane, of course. Who goes to a black market traders' exchange and buys a weathervane? Nice, soft dildos. That's what he wished they'd bought.

And lastly, as he kicked back and got used to his long/slow journey between the crow's nest office and the trading floor, Hollis got his first real glimpse of the chaos.

People running. People screaming. Some sort of kerfuffle by the rear door, merchandise tipping over and flying as if some big kid was having a tantrum. A really good place to land in the middle of with a chair stuck to you, basically.

Then the floor rose up, like an asshole, and knocked his teeth halfway out of his head.

He hit that asshole floor from behind, managing a last-minute roll correction accomplished either by skill (the controls were sluggish, requiring full-body momentum to shift) or pure dumb luck. The impact came barely off-square, like a car rear-ended just south of the left-side quar-terpanel. It rattled and bruised Hollis's spine, but the shock cracked the plastic chair apart at its joints. When reflex caused Hollis to try and cover his face, he was shocked to find he could do it.

He had an oval section of hardened plastic — what used to be the chair's left side, armrest on top — still hanging from his wrist, but it was mobile, at least.

Someone ran by him. He heard shots. Typically when you drop a chair into the middle of a room, people look and often have issues with it. That didn't happen at the Exchange. Nobody noticed. Everyone freaking out about whatever-it-was was far too cool to care.

Hollis stood, finding with surprise that he could. He was beat-up, but he'd been beat-up before he'd fallen. He felt mildly concussed, but he'd felt that way for days. His leg muscles protested, but they weren't union. They had to work or else their asses would be fired, said firing to be accomplished by murdering the host.

Speaking of that ...

Hollis looked up. He saw Dr. Greensward's face ten feet above his own, looking down. Finally, the man was registering emotion. It was a half-lost, half-indignant look. It said, *Someone took my toy!* But not in a way he was going to let go without a tantrum.

Hollis — despite the pain, despite the fear on the floor, despite the moment, and despite the pieces of broken chair still hanging from both wrists like enormous earrings — found himself grinning.

Greensward vanished. One moment he was leaning out the broken window with one hand on the frame, and the next he was gone like something deleted.

Running, surely, for the stairs.

Hollis got to work, ignoring the running and shouting people all around him, aware more than ever that he needed to tackle just one thing at a time. Both of the armrest pieces had broken from the frame, but the right-side break was only partial. Hollis shook it, stomped it, and bent it back and forth, trying to weaken the plastic still holding it to the seat and back. As he looked down, concentrating and feeling liquid seconds tick in accelerated time, something black shot through his peripheral vision. He looked up, startled, but did so too slowly. He'd heard a scream; he'd heard something break and fall. But now he saw nothing.

"Come on, fucker," Hollis told the chair.

Far end, in a little hallway where Brendan had added semi-public restrooms. The face of a psychotic surgeon appears. His posture is like a joke: legs wide and bent as he rounds the corner from the stairwell, one arm still holding a railing against the centripetal force of rounding his last corner and the other out, hand open, fingers spread. He's practically giving jazz hands. It'd be musically delightful, if his entire front wasn't covered in blood.

Hollis yanked harder.

The surgeon sees him. Pivots, again as if he's on a Broadway stage. This could honestly be a production. A real Bob Fosse number, with fabulous costumes. Pitch it as Cabaret, *with aliens and dickbags. The tickets sell themselves.*

Hollis, deciding the chair wanted to play rough and his arms were too pussy to deal with it alone, raised one foot and stomped down hard on the seat piece still attached to his armrest. The maneuver worked, but came at a price. The stubborn plastic bit finally broke, but not until the whole works — still bound to Hollis's wrist — yanked his arm halfway out of socket.

But there was no time to worry about that. Greensward, done being showy and now back to business, had spotted him and was sprinting. He moved pretty well for a stick bug, except that his arms didn't know to stay at their sides. Instead, they flailed, tinging Hollis's nerves with bizarre amusement. It was like being shaken down by Elmo.

Hollis ran, with two enormous armrest pieces — each the size of a steering wheel — pulling on his wrists and banging his thighs. After the first few lunging paces, he decided to stop treating them like dingleberries and pretend he'd snatched them on purpose. So, with an upward swing of each arm in turn, Hollis caught the big ovals and made like a running back with two footballs tucked instead of just one.

And he'd be damned if he was going to be robbed of this particular touchdown by the likes of Skeletor.

Who, as it turned out, had some ass under the hood. Arms finally coming down from Muppet pose, Greensward became a big ugly bullet. Hollis's bedraggled state began to catch up with him as the good doctor turned up the throttle.

The gap narrowed.

Hollis evaded, dodging, finding obstacles and groups and improvised corners to duck around.

That bought him some time; Greensward cornered like a school bus. But it wasn't long, still, until Hollis found himself facing the man across a round, 8-foot-diameter table that had until recently (judging by the smashed crap at their feet) hosted a collection of ... *What?* ... butter dishes? Hollis could see nothing in the debris that looked remotely valuable in an alien apocalypse. Antique dealers — at the Exchange, anyway — need not apply.

"You can't run from me," Greensward said, satisfyingly out of breath.

"Tell me more things I can't do," Hollis said. "Go on, now — I'm taking notes."

Saying this, right now, took maximum exercise of his smartass muscle. He felt sharp, glassy pain from the places the scalpel had kissed him and knew without question that he was on his final fumes. The best thing to hope for here, if he couldn't escape, was quick death. Either way left room for sarcasm, if you were as determined to seize the moment as Hollis typically was.

Greensward lunged. Hollis lunged better. Hollis had been totally prepared for a comic standoff of who's-going-to-flinch-first around the table, but there was no need. One flinch and Greensward went the wrong way — and then Hollis, who was apparently still in better shape than the surgeon even injured and exhausted, was away.

Into a crowd that was running away from ... something. Hollis went the wrong direction, on purpose, figuring it was the best way to lose his tail. Because right now, things were getting ridiculous. Whatever had happened down here had, without compromise, ended the trading day. The floor was in shambles; things were broken and spilled everywhere. The curtains covering the layaway area where Hollis had found the women's empty cage had been raked aside, revealing a whole lot of weapons that nobody could use because they weren't loaded. A rack of brown coats had tipped over, and running feet had scattered them like mud dragged inside after a rainstorm.

He looked back. He didn't see the doctor. Maybe he'd gotten away. Because — let's face it — he should. He didn't have a longstanding feud with Greensward; they'd just met a bit ago. There was no reason for the man to keep chasing. Hollis, at elaborate personal risk, had earned his freedom by now.

Still, Hollis's eyes were drawn to the pulled-back curtain. He couldn't see the cage, but his mind's eye pictured it. Open. Mia and Carol gone. But at least, on the bright side, they were away from all of this.

That's when Hollis stopped.

Enough. You don't run just because everyone else is running. That's dumb. That's what the brainless do, and then they cause problems.

So he listened for a gunshot and heard none. The last gun, maybe, had been fired for the day.

Instead, he peeked.

Saw.

And then, finally, began to fear on a whole new level.

33

MIA — not gone, not away from all of this — crouched in a corner. The problem, at this point, wasn't the reptar. It was mob mentality.

Luckily, Mia saw as she laid low, the crowd was singularly focused on getting away. That was a problem, though. The first place the alien had gone was to the front door, where she'd watched the only people in the building — Brendan's guards — shoot at it. But the guards were grown-up rent-a-cops, given weapons and taught to shoot, but expecting human targets if any targets at all. Mia had watched as they'd panicked and fired with admirable precision that wasn't nearly precise enough. Then she'd watched as the alien dodged, *Matrix*-like, whipping its narrow thorax and many limbs above, below, and laterally out of the spray of bullets. She thought a few shells hit it; she saw sparks on its carapace where, she imagined, ricochets were going awry. But either the bullets could actually harm it or the bug at least thought so, because it had limboed, leapt, and skewered the guards with its pointed front legs as if it hadn't just been able to see them, but had been able to see them the way a hawk spies field mice from a hundred feet up.

But of course, it couldn't see them.

Mia, who'd spent the past few terrifying minutes trying to get her head straight enough to sift and sort and get the fuck out when an opening occurred, thought she could hear the reptar inside her head. It wasn't talking to her — in part because as far as she'd seen, it didn't "talk" in a way she could understand anyway — but seemed more to be ... say ... *thinking in her direction*. It felt unintentional. It felt like a quickly formed habit, like it'd latched onto her mind because it had been cleaved from the rest of its kind.

And in those almost-thoughts — that black, viscous hate-think — she could almost "see" the guards the way the alien had "seen" them.

As thoughts. As fear. As things with bioelectric pulses in their heads that ceased the second the alien stabbed in that direction.

When it was through with the guards, it had struck both of the overhead rolling door tracks very hard with its rearmost set of legs, rising on its forelegs like a horse to kick. It had hit both squarely, buckling the track. And now the front doors were unopenable, yet that's where half the crowd kept going.

It had known where the door track was because the people surrounding it had seen where the track was.

Mia knew this without any idea how. But knowing it felt sure, and knowing it made her think: *How can they fight a thing that's using all their own senses against it?*

This threw her into a loop. Because what she saw before her was so macabre, her mind tried to slip out the rear — analyzing the things she knew and didn't know as if they mattered in the moment.

Can it read minds, or just thoughts that come out loud?

Can it see, despite the helmet?

She didn't know, she didn't technically think so (a few people, if they moved quickly and quietly, had passed right in front of it without harm), and ultimately it didn't matter. She was evading, trying not to be here. Because here was far too terrible.

The impaled guards, tossed aside — but into the same place as the rest of the impaled dead, as if the alien was trying to establish a dedicated slaughtered zone, keep the room tidy.

The many others, murdered casually in their place, left to die is a much more messy fashion.

The blood. Not just on the floor and on the alien's legs and the other people's bodies or even on the walls, but also high up into the corners in Jackson Pollack spatters that were, in some strange way, the most horrible of all.

The body parts — which, after what felt like an hour but was probably closer to three minutes, began to salt the open floor like scattered autumn leaves.

And to think: They'd given in a helmet. What a joke. It didn't need its mouth, now that it had a captive audience.

The rear door — the only other in the place — was still open. And the alien, sensing prey, had figured that out. So it went there after slaughtering the guards who'd been shooting at it, after ripping their guns apart with surprisingly dextrous front legs as if they'd been made of nothing more substantial than spun sugar. The guards at the rear had had guns too, when they'd still been breathing, still been intact. They no longer had guns. Or heads. Or bodies without holes in them beyond the ones Nature had given them. The guns were similarly shrapnel, and the alien kept returning to that sole remaining exit, so shoo the other players in its game away from it.

Some people — mainly those who'd been near the rear exit when the reptar had visited the front — had gotten away. Or, Mia corrected herself, they'd gotten out of the building. *Away* was an entirely different concept, likely feeling like Everest once they reached the fence and saw all the alien ships waiting to block them. Would the ships fry the refugees as they came? Or were they as uninterested in killing as Mia's gut said they were, at the compound more to find their missing soldier than to punish those who'd captured it?

Not that the reptar would need any help in punishing.

Mia spied the exit, saw a few people sneaking through it. The rushing crowd had felled more of the curtains by now, giving her unfettered view of the entire labyrinth. She could see her old cage now, still empty with the door open. But she could also see other cages filled with other trafficked slaves (mostly women, because what the fuck, you animals) ... and curiously, beside being captive prey, all were unharmed. Terrified, but unarmed. Their shrieks pierced Mia's eardrums, but twice she'd seen the alien cross right before them, looking in that helmeted-and-unseeing way it had, and then moving on.

These survive.

Mia's thought? Or the reptar's? Or a stray thought she was somehow picking up from the ships at the perimeter, their strange stones-fueled intelligence above Mia's mind like a thin and insubstantial cloud? Mia didn't know. It was all happening too fast. Out of time.

Hollis.

That, at least, had been her own thought. Or so it seemed.

Her eyes scanned. She hadn't thought this far. She'd told herself there'd be a way, that the way would show itself, that she'd never see Step 2 until Step 1 was underway. Now, she waited. Waited, and thought. Or had she been duped? Had the alien, having touched her mind before, slipped inside it and made promises that no one could keep?

No. She wouldn't believe that. She *couldn't* believe that. She'd killed those that were dying or dead right now, and telling herself that they were bad people did nothing to assuage the looming threat of guilt. Right now, high-octane nerves held her attention, but that wouldn't last. Eventually, if she lived, this would end. If all she left with was the memory of carnage, there'd be karmic hell to pay. Or at least a nighttime of nightmares, in need of therapy that the new world could no longer provide.

As if to mollify her, she spied a body beside a tipped-over display table. It was large and strangely shiny, its color a mix of brown and red. A big man with a big stomach and fat hands, covered in diamonds and gold. And, because it seemed a fuck-you message from the universe, a smashed bag filled with neon yellow corn puffs partially beneath him.

Beef. Her old would-be owner, may his elegant ass rest in peace.

Only it wasn't Beef, now that she looked more closely. It was his right-hand man, who always walked beside him, copied his fashion and his diet, and seemed to be trying to be his mentor's clone. What was this disappointment she felt? It wasn't cool. It was okay, wasn't it, that she wanted to see Beef dead? He'd have raped them both, passed them around, then killed them ... if they were lucky.

She looked, with *schadenfreude*, for Thomas's body in the mess. *He* had to be dead, right? So many people had been slaughtered; some of them had to be people against whom Mia and/or Carol and/or Hollis had held a grudge. Seeing Thomas's body, at least, would make it all right. Unlike the other vaguely evil people here, she'd actually seen Thomas kill people, then cleaned its aftermath.

Or Brendan. *For the love of God, please let me see Brendan.*

But she saw none of them.

So, yeah. She couldn't believe the situation had merely been using her — that there was no Hollis-shaped pot of gold at the end of this hemoglobin rainbow.

Think, Mia. Think!

Then: *Hey, stupid. You* do *know where he is, remember?*

She looked up. Toward the office she'd occupied with Carol, before she'd conned Brendan into trading her for Beaver Nuggets. She saw the window that she herself had looked down through, what felt like six weeks ago.

Just in time to see the window break explosively, a chair flying out as if someone had pitched it in anger when the Exchange's day of business had gone bad.

Except ... No. There was some poor bastard *in* that falling chair.

She watched, wincing, as the thing hit the ground and turned to plastic kindling. Some terrible part of her waited for the impact of skull-to-concrete most of all — wondering, amidst all this blood that frankly was here already anyway, if it'd pop like a dropped watermelon. But the chair landed mostly back-first, wheels to the left side from her point of view, and must have broken the fall because the poor bastard strapped to the thing rose and ...

"You've *gotta* be kidding me."

Hollis. Beaten even worse than she'd seen him last, bleeding from three or four places as if the splintering chair had cut him on impact. His face was a pulp with two black eyes. If she hadn't figured out that the Quasimodo fella who'd been bidding on her earlier had been Hollis, she'd never have had the missing-link reference to join the smooth Hollis she knew to this sack of tenderized meat. Good thing she wasn't into appearances. Or, what the hell? At least she wasn't into Hollis at all.

Hollis, trying to free himself from the chair (he seemed to be tied to it?) darted a sudden look toward the back stairwell, near the bathrooms.

A skinny guy in blue scrubs stood there, frozen for a second. He had the body type that vanished if it turned sideways, and right now his face looked worse than Hollis's. Hollis looked worse-for-wear, but this guy looked like a skeleton with a skull's protruding-bone nose. His mouth was flanked by a crusted-blood goatee, his shirt a bib used by cannibals.

Hollis, beating the chair until it mostly let him go, running off with the armrests as if he meant to steal them.

The guy in scrubs, running after him.

And finally Mia, her waiting broken, rising to give chase.

34

RUNNING ACROSS THE OPEN FLOOR, her attention split between Hollis, the general confusion, and the tap-tap dance she had to do to avoid all sorts of broken crap on the ground.

Mia had run trails before, in her college days: technical routes, made complicated by protruding roots and rocks the pierced the surface. Navigating those trails had taken both endurance and agility, and as she danced after Hollis and his pursuer now, she remembered how like an obstacle course those trails had been. You had to watch ahead, watch limbs above, and most of all watch the path at your feet.

This was like that, owing to her stupid lack of shoes — a liability she should perhaps have considered more fully before setting the reptar loose. Shoelessness had been a problem for John McClain when he'd fought Hans Gruber inside Nakatomi Tower, and now it was a problem for Mia as she lost ground to the pair she was chasing. She kept having to be delicate, lest she skewer herself. And to think: Even if *Die Hard* hadn't been Thomas's favorite movie, she was such a faithful student of pop culture.

Dumbass, she thought, tiptoe-running after them.

But there was no point in self-hate. At least she was alive, and at least Hollis had the sense to run toward the layaway labyrinth, away from attractive groups of alien snacks. There would be a time, Mia knew, when they'd be forced take their chances getting through the back door. But for now, the alien was too volatile, far too fast. It kept leaping to that back exit, slaughtering a few partygoers too rude to stick around for last call, then leaping away. It covered all the ground, all the time. So far, those who escaped just had lucky timing.

Hollis and his suitor played out a tropey *you-go-or-I-go* scene on opposite sides of a round table just outside the maze-like storage area for a few seconds, each flinching one way and then the other. Mia thought she might be able to catch up, then. Although she no longer had her gun for a bludgeon, she was pretty sure she could take Slenderman down using just her own muscle. She'd leap on his back, pin him down, then make him give her his lunch money. She'd dispatched bigger geeks in high school, when they'd gotten fresh.

But then Hollis faked a breakaway and the other man — proving he sucked — bit line and sinker. Hollis was poised to move the other way, which he immediately did, and blue-shirt almost fell on his ass correcting to follow. Then he *did* fall, and the only thing stopping it from being hilarious was the fact that what'd he'd slipped in might (Mia wasn't sure) have been a crudely autopsied torso.

She could still get Dr. Skinny. She could still do that, and solve at least the first of many problems.

But the man, righting himself quickly, at least wore shoes. He ran off after Hollis, who Mia had seen disappear the wrong way into a surging group passing a spilled rack of coats. Although Hollis's lead was growing, the other — who she now saw was holding a small knife of some kind — was still pursuing. They were both headed for the merchandise area, Hollis still very much in trouble.

If you can take him, Hollis can take him, she thought.

But could he? Hollis struck her as a teddy bear with all the stuffing beaten from it. He was running on adrenaline, his efforts both admirable and unsustainable. He was also cut — victim, perhaps, now that she thought about it, of the small silver knife in his chaser's hand. Hollis's shirt was also ripped and hanging in flaps — also cut, maybe. The thought was jarring enough that it made her look back up at the broken window he'd fallen through. The stairs the other had come down led up there, too. What had they been doing up there, with Hollis tied to a chair?

Yes. He needed her help — still and for sure. So far her rather dramatic distraction had given the others in the building a good reason to disregard him, but he was far from saved.

She caught a glimpse of Hollis now: the only person in the room with two awkward armrest structures cradled under his arms. And ... yeah. That was a problem, too. Not easy to fight with big wheels tied to your wrists, unless you were a ninja and using them was your specialty. Which, honestly, would be pretty cool.

Katana blades, sais, nunchucks, and armrests. Batman, eat your heart out.

As if he'd heard this, the blood-covered man picked up a ninja weapon of his own: a sword that had been someone's lot to change, now garbage on the trading floor.

This wasn't about capture. This was about something far more personal, far more deadly.

As she followed, feeling time on some unknown hour-glass running thin, Mia could see both men: Hollis on one side of the crowd, ready to dive into the maze, and his pursuer, far behind on its other side. She just had to get to them before they clashed — and either would do.

She was far enough back, she realized, to cut the corner. She'd have a hard time catching Hollis if he ran flat-out (especially in bare feet), but now that he was at his new destination she didn't think he'd need to.

She could do this. She could get to him, and together two people would be a match for one with a sword.

All Hollis had to do was to maintain his lead, and she'd reach them in time.

Mia ran, guardedly hopeful.

But then — just now, and fuck him for missing it before — Mia saw Hollis's head turn to see the reptar. It wasn't near him, but still it stopped him in his tracks.

She saw his mouth open. Saw his jaw — and his previously-running legs — go slack.

The man in scrubs, who'd either seen it already or was too psycho to care, slowed not a whit.

"Dammit, Hollis," Mia muttered to herself as she turned on the afterburners, and damn the sharp litter that might fall beneath her.

35

Go.

But Hollis couldn't go.

GO!

And still his body wouldn't cooperate. It was as if, quite suddenly and at the least appropriate time in human history, he'd decided to take a nap. All at once, he felt days' worth of fatigue. All at once he felt every punch, every bludgeon, every cut, every bruise and bump and perhaps broken bone, every cheap shot in the nuts. He'd been running on high-test ether until now, the blower atop the hood of Hot Rod Hollis Palmer shooting blue flame. But now his tank was dry, and all that sexy speed machinery was just dead metal. His cells were depleted, his glycogen gone, his fat spare and useless. He could fall over — and, in fact, that sounded goddamn spectacular right about now.

That thing.

It wasn't an alien.

It couldn't be an alien.

Because that didn't make sense. No; more than that: *It wasn't fucking fair!*

Self pity threatened to boil. He'd been so *good* through all of this. So forward-thinking. So balls-out, heroically driven. He'd even planned, if he could get out of here, to try and stop whatever the aliens were up to in Austin. That's why he'd started this: to get back Carol, who understood at least a bit of what they were facing. And that's what he'd more or less told Theo, and a hundred percent of the reason he'd confessed to Theo he had photos of every document in Thomas Davies's late attache case. He hadn't gotten a chance to tell Theo *where* he'd abandoned the car with the phone in it, if it was somehow untouched, but he'd declared everything else. Maybe Theo could find it, alone, but he shouldn't have to. This was *Hollis's* quest ... and dammit, he'd paid for it with blood. It wasn't fair, that he should have to face an alien after facing *so much* else. A man wasn't make to take this much without breaking. Dammit, it just wasn't fair!

"Hollis!"

Or so it had sounded. His attention wouldn't leave the alien — the one he'd heard was here, but had assumed was duly secured. If someone was calling for him — a woman, by the sound — then good for her. He was done. *DONE.*

"*HOLLIS!*"

He was about to turn his head to look anyway when something struck him very hard. Something bony, like a doctor with a torture fetish.

Hollis hit the ground (again), smacked his head (again) on an upright pole for a rack of something-or-other, and then found himself pinned down (again) and punched in the already-bleeding wound (new, at least, but excruciatingly painful).

Then Dr. Greensward was above him, sitting on his chest, Hollis's superior mass too beaten to budge him.

"Thought you could get away from me," Greensward said.

"I guess I did," Hollis replied, giving a fractional shit. Or actually, less than a fractional shit. More like a negative shit. Or some obscure mathematical amount of shit. If someone took a shit, divided it into pieces, took the square root of one of the pieces and then its inverse cosine, then divided the whole fucking works by zero, that's how much of a shit Hollis felt ready to give.

Something new and uninteresting appeared. It was a sword of all things, in both of Greensward's hands, one on the handle and the other carefully palming the blade. He pressed it against Hollis's neck like a two-handled cleaver.

"I'm going to cut your fucking head off," the doctor told him.

"Go ahead."

"Then I'm going to stick my cock in your neck hole."

"Oh. Okay, you went there."

"Got any last words?"

"'Remember the Alamo.'"

"What, no witty remarks?"

"'Remember the Alamo' isn't witty? Okay. 'Fuck your hamster.'"

"I don't even have a hamster."

"Because *that's* what we should be arguing about now."

Greensward pressed harder, but didn't do what he'd promised. Asshole.

"Come on, Sport. Don't you have a neck hole to fuck?"

Greensward didn't understand his lack of squirming, lack of groveling ... frankly, his lack of respect for the guy about to separate him from his cranium. Or was it the other way around — him from his torso? Hollis wasn't sure. Over the course of his life, he'd fastened his identity in equal parts to his brain and his dick. It was all very interesting: an ontological question for a whole new age.

"Are you up to something?" the doctor asked. "What's your angle?"

"I don't know. The perpendicular one? How many degrees are in a triangle, anyway?"

"A HUNDRED AND EIGHTY!"

A challenger, arriving from the rear. Swinging a big red thing that, presently, swung into play like a pushy pendulum.

The big red thing (a fire extinguisher, as it turned out) hit Greensward's head like Gallagher's Sledge-o-Matic. It was a very angry fire extinguisher — perhaps one that thought the good doctor had shot its pa. In a video game the impact would have blown Greensward's head apart in a gaudy anime explosion, but in life it merely split his scalp, spraying Hollis (again) with a mist of blood.

Mia stood above them both — Greensward, bleeding and dead, and Hollis, merely feeling dead and ready for Jesus to give him a piggyback ride — with her chest rising and falling in gigantic heaves. She was dirty, sweaty, pit-stained, and sexy as hell.

"You're still here?" Hollis asked, not rising.

She extended a hand. He didn't take it. So she said, "Apparently I'm still here."

"Leave me."

"No."

"I'm dying."

"You're too much of a pain in the ass to die."

"And so many of my final thoughts are about math."

"They aren't your final thoughts, Hollis."

He rolled his head. "Your feet are bleeding."

"I had to ditch my shoes."

"It's not hot. I'm usually into feet, but holy shit."

"Get your ass up. We have to get out of here. "

"Tell you what," Hollis said, still looking at her feet. "If you can get some ointment on them pronto, I'll consider it."

"I *should* just leave you. You got ugly."

"Hey, baby. Even my blood is beautiful."

He tried his rascal's grin. Judging by Mia's wince, it was no longer attractive.

Mia picked up the doctor's sword, then used it to cut his wrists free of the broken-off armrests. Dammit, he was just getting used to those.

Then she kicked him. Gently, in deference to his injuries. It was both adorable and bitchy, just like Hollis liked it. Maybe her gross feet weren't deal-breakers after all.

"No," he said again. "There's an alien out there. I'm done. I ain't leavin' this spot. You hear me? I done enough, and now fuck the world."

Mia crouched, took hold of one of his wrists in both hands, and began to drag. To his shock, she made decent headway even with him playing dead weight. Either Greensward's blood had lubricated the floor or she was just scary-strong. Also hot.

"Damn, woman."

"If you make me drag you all the way, when we get out I'll punch your balls until they're blue."

"Give me blue balls, huh?"

"You're a pig." And yet, she kept dragging.

"Anyone ever tell you you're a stubborn bitch?"

"I had it embroidered on my backpack in grade school."

The doctor, either not dead or just very good at post-mortem reflexes, sat up and grabbed for his sword. He was trumped in the moment by Hollis's reflexes, which turned out to be a whole lot better than he'd figured. His foot came up and, in one fluid motion, made alligator-boot waffle marks across his cheeks and broken nose.

Greensward shouted, swore, and began getting to his feet. That broke Hollis's self-pity or flirtation (he wasn't sure which, and was just a tad aroused), and with a second wind surging, he leapt to his feet. Mia still had his wrist with one of her hands, but this time he was the one to provide the impetus.

Behind them, the doctor grabbed the sword Hollis was already kicking himself for not taking the time to grab.

And then they rushed, into the layaway labyrinth, together.

36

MIA FOUND Hollis's second wind to be quite good, once he was motivated to start moving again. Which was interesting, because when she'd come across the creepy guy kneeling on Hollis's chest, it had sure sounded like he was ready to give up and let him win. Strange, then, that the exact same guy chasing them had gotten him off his ass.

Through boxes and racks filled with clothing, food, weapons, and stacks of books and (probably useless, now) electronic media filled with information, they ran side by side. Mia kept hold of his wrist. Not for affection, though she was finding she'd missed his obnoxious behavior (Stockholm syndrome, perhaps). No, this was more because if she let go, she thought he might drag back, decide again to surrender, or go to sleep.

But, honestly ... surrender to *that* guy? If Hollis meant to surrender to anyone, it should be someone impressive. Someone with six arms and an equal number of striated pectoral muscles, perhaps, or arms the size of small foreign vehicles.

Behind them, the guy in scrubs was screaming. Not shouting. *Screaming.*

Hollis, even at full steam, was well below Mia's top-end. They'd beaten him up pretty bad — bad enough, she thought, that she might even feel sorry for him. They'd have to rely on cleverness and stealth if they meant to evade him, since raw speed wouldn't do it. In the end, it was fine. You couldn't haul through this claustrophobic place at full speed anyway.

Rushing but nowhere near out of breath, Mia said, "Who is that guy, anyway?"

"Doctor."

"No, seriously."

"I'm *being* serious. Shit. Nobody believes me anymore. He's a doctor."

That didn't make a lot of sense, but it wasn't a thread Mia was interested in pulling.

"Where's Brendan?"

"Who cares?"

"I figured he'd be the one holding you."

"Well, lucky you."

She could still hear the guy behind them. Dr. Crazy, at your service.

"Why is your shirt ripped open? Did he cut you?"

"Maybe a little."

"Are you okay?"

"Of course not."

They bobbed and weaved. Mia hadn't looked up; navigating and evading had taken all of her attention. Right now, the big door track was ahead but not immediately so. Whoever had designed this storage area was a hoarder with a love for puzzles. It was kind of a mindfuck to just get through it. Or, perhaps more likely, it hadn't been designed at all. Someone had swapped for one thing he couldn't or didn't want to take home right away, and so someone had stuck it by the door. Then another and another and another, until it'd become this mess, waiting to bury the first person alive who bumped into it wrong. Then it would be like Jenga, only a lot more painful.

She whispered, "Maybe we should hide. Wait him out."

Hollis mumbled something. Mia didn't catch it, but the upshot seemed to be that Dr. Crazy wasn't one who could be waited out. This was the end of the last day in forever for Dr. Crazy, she imagined. He'd find Hollis before he went to sleep, or freak himself right the fuck out, to death, in trying.

"Ha!" came a shout. Not a normal-person shout, either. In Mia's experience, normal people didn't say "ha" much. It just wasn't a thing.

She looked back, through one of those flimsy garage storage units you could buy at Home Depot. It was full of miscellany, all tagged for pickup. The logistics of managing the Exchange struck her then, and for the moment organizing it all felt more daunting than a surgeon holding a murder knife.

The man tried to come through, now even more bloody thanks to the new wound. Two things bled like mad, and they were broken noses and scalps. Dr. Crazy had sustained both, plus maybe a concussion. He sure did look crazier than he had when he'd hopped atop Hollis, and he'd looked plenty crazy then.

He reached from his aisle to theirs, almost knocking the entire unit over. It would have gone, too, if the bottom hadn't been loaded with iron machine parts. The foundation was too strong; his insubstantial mass couldn't budge it.

So, trying not to lock eyes with him, Mia slinked back

against the aisle's opposite wall (a stack of abstract paintings, of all things) and pushed Hollis along.

"Where exactly are we going?" Hollis asked, already sounding tired again — not in terms of sleep, but in terms of no longer wanting to do ... well ... *anything* that wasn't surrendering to what might inevitably come.

"Out," Mia told him.

"That's what I used to say to my mom, when I wanted to hang with my friends."

He slumped. Fell to his knees. Anticipating total forfeit, Mia kicked him early, snagging the hand that'd gotten away from her, tugging him reluctantly to his feet.

"Not so rough!"

"That's what she said," Mia told him. Not because it was funny, but because it was the kind of thing he'd say.

It worked. Thinking her playful, he made that dumb grin that happened only in one corner of his mouth. Then he looked ready to flirt back, and that meant it was time to ignore him again, to go quiet, to pull anew. There'd be time for his crap later ... or, preferably, no time for it at all.

Although ...

She looked at him as they left the doctor behind and one aisle over, and saw something unnerving.

Eyes that were half-lidded, dilated like someone on good drugs. He was swaying on his feet, having trouble following her face even when talking right to her.

This wasn't good. She'd thought he seemed drunk right from Go, but now that the same effect was magnifying, she saw it for a species of delirium. Hollis had crossed from amusing-drunk to we-should-call-a-doctor drunk. Only, not drunk. Messed up somehow, though she wasn't sure how. Had he lost too much blood? Or was it simpler: Had he simply had *too much?*

The only thing still unaffected was his sarcasm. Oh, for joy.

Maybe he is dying.

The thought gave her a chill. She didn't like thinking about it, so she refused to.

He staggered. Tripped over his own feet. Then fell, knocking over an entire set of shelves that hadn't been anchored with heavy machine parts.

"Take me home," he said.

"Get up." She tugged, but nothing doing.

"I want to see Marcy."

"Who's Marcy?"

"You know. From *Peanuts*? She called Peppermint Patty 'sir.'"

"You're delusional."

"No, *you're* delusional!"

He got to his feet, then fell again into a pile of blankets on the aisle's other side. And, worse: People were coming. She could hear chatter not far away. She could hear a scramble, the pounding of feet. And maybe, on one level, that was fine. Who would bother them now? Even Brendan, if he was still alive, should be running the other direction. The mandate was to get away from the Exchange, and damn the merchandise. Damn the petty grievances, too. Brendan owed both of them a punch in the face or two, but that debt had settled before the aliens had arrived.

She heard sounds from outside the shell of the arena that she couldn't quite understand. Had the ships crossed the fence? Had more aliens disembarked from them — more of the insectile things apparently called "reptars," plus a few of the big alabaster ones. What had that blogger called *them*, again?

Pay attention, Mia.

Her mind was wandering. That happened. In the presence of an untenable situation, she tended to try and deflect. But what good would that do her now? She had a mad doctor behind them, and the remains of the Exchange's patrons streaming for the back door. Because, she saw now, that was definitely happening. The reptar must finally have moved away from it, perhaps making a circuit of the larger building, playing a deadly game of Hide n' Seek.

That, right there, made her wonder at its intentions. Hadn't it wanted freedom? She had, in her sideways, no-language sort of way, asked the thing for help. But it'd helped with its distraction, then devolved to hunting out those who weren't fast enough to make it through the doors. So: *Had* she really made the bargain she'd thought she was making? She was no longer sure. *Helping her* wouldn't have involved buckling the track on the front doors, leaving the arena with just one exit which (let's face it) just turned the whole *who-will-escape* thing into a twisted game. *Helping her* wouldn't have required the systematic extermination of every human it could find. And, adding to the puzzle, what about its goals? She'd sensed it wanting to leave, and the ships outside as wanting to seek it out. Neither goal was served by what it was doing now, seemingly far back over their shoulders.

It should have run. It should, by all rights, have made for the border.

Unless, Mia thought, it had taken its capture personally.

It was an ugly thought. One without a chance for recompense. She'd learned, in a college psychology course, about the difference between negative reinforcement and punishment.

Negative reinforcement was like a shock, applied until the subject's behavior changed.

Punishment, on the other hand, happened even if the subject started doing whatever the experimenter wanted.

You could stop negative reinforcement by being good, but punishment was unstoppable.

Like revenge.

She could hear the doctor, now behind them instead of aisles over. He'd found a cross-aisle, simple if you took the time to search ... or if the people you were chasing stopped because one of them could no longer walk.

Down on the floor, with a vaguely pleasant expression on his face, Hollis's eyes closed.

"Hollis," she said, slapping him.

Nothing. Just that dumb half-smile.

"HOLLIS!"

This time, she slapped him much harder.

"What the hell?" he said.

"You know what I hate about you?" she asked, letting go and stepping back, feeling a strange new hunch. "How desirable you think you are."

Mumbling, but with spirit: "Fuck you."

"But you're *not* desirable," she went on, still retreating. "You're not half as cute as you think you are. You're *boring*, Hollis. You're predictable, obnoxious, and ordinary."

His eyes opened more, as if waking up.

"Is that why you fucked me in your marriage bed?"

"I fucked you because I was using you."

"Bullshit. You loved it."

"I *tolerated* it," she spat.

The doctor behind Hollis. Coming fast by the sound of things, no longer making any effort at quiet.

"You're so full of it," he said, getting to his feet.

"I don't know why I came back for you. To *save* you."

"I came to save *you*," he said.

She manufactured a sneer, goading him, trying to work fast. It wasn't easy. She was used to having time to manipulate people, and the rush wasn't doing her any good.

"Save me," she mimicked, then rolled her eyes. "I was better off without you."

Now he was up. Face to face, inches away. He sure didn't seem injured now, with his dander up.

Careful, now ... he's still delirious, she reminded herself. The worst thing she could do, to break this spell, would be to try and return him to reality.

He was just staring her down, in some curious middle-ground between fury and lust that only a guy like Hollis could manage.

So she shoved him.

"Be a man," she said.

So he came at her, crossing the last few inches. He grabbed her upper arms and, being the most inappropriate at the most inappropriate time just like she'd figured, mashed his lips into hers.

She fell into it. Counting. Watching.

1 ... 2 ... 3.

Then, flipping the tables, she grabbed him and flung him around in what he probably took as a come-hither, throw-down-on-the-bed sort of move, and shoved him hard toward the open mouth of the aisle, where it spilled out into the apron of light that marked the back door.

"Wait," he said, looking around, some new species of mixed-reality awareness finally arising. "What's ... ?"

"Keep moving," she said, "and if you can manage to get your sorry ass out of here, I'll let you see my boobs."

For a half-dead guy, that somehow managed to light him up. The rascal's smile was back, tugging his lips up to show his teeth. Because — foggy or not, in imminent danger or not, slashed in a dozen places and losing blood or not — the basest things were still his trigger, if simply getting the machinery moving was the problem. And the truth was, he *hadn't* seen them. They'd kept everything on, that single time.

"Now that's my kind of ..." the revitalized Hollis started to say.

But in that moment, two things happened.

First, Dr. Crazy grabbed Mia from behind, putting his little scalpel to her throat. She could feel its stainless steel kiss against her windpipe, daring her to breathe too deeply.

And second, behind Hollis, the urgent crowd began to scatter.

To thrash, and turn to human mulch.

Because the reptar had returned, blind but not blind, coming to stillness directly behind Hollis's back.

37

MIA SQUIRMED. The scalpel bit her flesh. She felt a small drop, like a tear, begin to make its way down to the pit where her collarbones met. Her mind imagined what it might be like, if he cut her right where he'd laid the blade. She pictured her larynx, split like a seedpod. Would it look like a walnut inside? Her stomach churned, and it took effort to remind herself: *Focus.* As odd as it seemed, a knife to the throat wasn't the biggest threat here.

"Hollis." She swallowed, again feeling the knife's edge. "Don't move."

"Oh yeah? Show me your tits!"

A wave of sudden dispair hit her, disarming in its strength. She realized, helplessly, that she hadn't truly roused (and kissed) the real Hollis. The man before her was a doppelgänger that shared the same body, the same brain, the same time and place. But he wasn't in his right mind. He'd run out of gas, exhausted after being kept awake and beaten for days. The trick she'd pulled, in goading him to move, was one step up from reanimating a corpse. He was out of his head, operating as pure ID: Hollis Classic, as it were, replaying from instinctual memory.

His logical mind wasn't here. He didn't understand. He didn't see. It was like he was ambulatory drunk — a bottle of vodka in, his words and motives and world comprehensible only to others as inebriated as he was, or perhaps not at all.

The reptar, no more than ten feet behind him, was scenting the air. Or doing its own version of the same: psychic scenting, perhaps, as it searched the air for hopes and loves and fears.

Hollis, as he was, didn't understand. Not really. He could turn around and see it, and once he did, he might know what it was. But he wouldn't listen to her now. Couldn't.

She watched him sway on his feet, again like a drunk. Half smiling. Not knowing how close he was to death, and beyond her ability to talk to him, to reason.

She wanted to tell him: *Be calm.*

She wanted to say: *Let your mind go quiet.*

But he'd just stand there, ogling her chest, wanting to pick up the charade she'd already let drop.

To the man behind her, she said, "Let us go. Please."

In her ear, far too close: "I've got debts to pay."

"You don't owe Brendan anything."

"Debts," he said, "to you."

For whatever Hollis had done in the office before spilling to the Exchange floor. For the extra kick Hollis had delivered, the wrongs he'd bestowed. And for all that Mia had done to break them up — most particularly the fire extinguisher to the head. That was the debt, now, that the man behind her sought to bestow.

"The alien ..." she began.

"... will kill him first."

She watched Hollis, knowing it was true. The reptar,

using whatever sense it used in the absence of sight, had crept closer. How hadn't Hollis heard it? How hadn't he *felt* it?

"*You guys,*" Hollis said. "You crack me up."

Falling to his knees. Holding onto a shelf, keeping him from dropping further.

"Hollis," she said. "Be very quiet."

Hollis's grin, with no plan to be quiet at all. If anything, he was ready to be obnoxious. To be, in short, himself.

"What's wrong with him?" the doctor asked.

"Nothing."

"He's out of his mind."

"Nothing's wrong with him at all."

Mia slammed back with her elbow, but the doctor had seen it coming. His scrawny arm, with the blade as incentive, was plenty to hold her fast. He didn't need a body behind her, so he hadn't placed one. He was off to the side, her freest arm too far away to harm him.

He tightened up. Increased pressure on her throat. Another bead fell, then spilled.

The doctor's voice, now very close, quiet, and warm in breath, whispered in her ear.

"Watch," he said. "Watch what it does to him."

She thrashed again. Tried to raise a heel, to kick him in the groin. But he'd seen it all coming, was prepared for everything she had to throw.

The reptar was right above Hollis now, moving its helmeted head side to side.

It must hear him.

It must know he was there.

It raised an insectile arm. Probed. Found Hollis's shoulder.

"What's it doing?" the doctor finally asked.

"I don't know."

"Why hasn't it killed him?"

"I don't know," Mia told him.

"Why is it—?"

"I DON'T KNOW! I DON'T FUCKING KNOW, OKAY?"

Aware that, dammit, she was crying. In frustration, in anticipation of loss. There was nothing she could do. She'd failed, people were dying, and it was all her fault.

All your fault, her mind repeated.

The reptar, hearing her outburst, had raised its helmeted head. Curious. Deadly, yet striking no one. Behind it, through a narrow gap, the bravest of refugees sneaked through the door into the open air.

All your fault.

The darkness. The feeling of connection, of a deal made with death. Had she really believed she understood it? Had she really believed, in any way, that she wouldn't end up fooled?

Her mind went back there. Away from Hollis and his imminent death that, now, she could do nothing to stop. Away from the assailant behind her who held her just right, immune to just about anything she might to to try and break free. The assailant, she knew, who had nothing to lose — just like Hollis, who'd so recently given up, before her manipulative resurrection, also with nothing left to lose.

There was nothing to do.

No way out.

Nowhere to go.

Behind her was death. Before her was death. In between was Hollis's death, and Mia powerless to even make him aware.

Except that he *was* aware, wasn't he?

Seeing it now, horrified but in a childlike way, he stared

up at the thing above him, wanting to believe the helmet would make a difference — that if he stayed very still, it might not know he was there.

Another tear.

Her mind went back. Away. Away from it all.

Help me and do not harm me, she'd thought to it, *and I will free you.*

And yet the carnage.

Yet the revenge.

Was there method in its madness?

Its limb touched Hollis, curious. Curious in Mia's presence, perhaps *because* of Mia's presence. She could feel it now: that black cloud at her mind's edges, invisible to direct inspection, impossible to miss from the corner of her internal eye.

Trust, she thought.

She blinked, confused. Why had she thought that? Or ... really ... had *she* been the one to think it?

Of course. I'm the one who thinks my own thoughts.

But then she heard it again — still distant, still foreign, but different this time: *Believe.*

Words, inside her. From somewhere else.

Understand.

Which, she thought, felt like a question. Not saying that something *was* understood, but instead *desired* understanding. She felt curiosity. Wonder, even. And none of it her own.

It's coming from the reptar.

And as she realized, another one-word bolus entered her mind:

More!

Demanding, that last one. Immature petulance, like a child king, weak on the throne yet strong in will. It was the strangest sensation. She understood what was coming to her, but it wasn't truly language. It was more emotional — more instinctual — than that. She wasn't really hearing words. It came to her across many modalities. She didn't just think its thoughts. She also *smelled* them. *Tasted* them. Felt them on her skin, the way a snake senses sound.

More, the thought repeated. Mia's mind repeated. The reptar's will, inside her yet everywhere at once, repeated.

But more *what*?

She watched it move above Hollis. Saw it lean close, its exhale close enough to stir his hair.

A vision entered her mind. Its arrival was intrusive — thrust there, like a violation. In the vision, she saw the reptar, maskless now, open its mouth with its many rows of bright white teeth. Saw the blue spark inside the thing churn, reflected in Hollis's spellbound eyes. Then it snapped like a Venus Fly Trap, his head gone, a bloody stump remaining, blood spilling over the lip of torn flesh like—

The vison stopped, sudden like a scratching record. She'd closed her eyes against it, tucking chin low in defense, so as not to see. But of course it hadn't happened, not for real. As she opened her eyes, she saw that Hollis and the beast were just as she'd left them.

Hollis, frozen.

It, above him, helmet still in place, paused for some unknown judgment.

The doctor, behind her, had almost gone slack. She could probably get away from him now, if she wanted. He didn't understand what was happening, but it still must have left an aftertaste. The way a person feels when they enter a situation that isn't quite right — where something unseen is amiss? That, she knew, was how the doctor must feel now.

"Let me go," she said.

"I want you to watch him—"

But Mia cut him off. More forcibly, she said, *"Let me go."*

And that voice inside her said, *More.*

Hands sagged. Mia stepped away from the man behind her, his scalpel forgotten, his body frozen.

Standing solo now, she blinked. In the split-second her eyes were closed, she flashed back to the vision of horror that she knew the reptar had given her. In the moment, she hadn't understood. Now, she was beginning to. As she felt her fear and worry and sorrow leave her — drifting off, as it sucked away — she understood.

It wasn't just Hollis who was spellbound. The reptar was, too.

Watching her.

Sampling her thoughts, her emotions.

It provoked, then observed the reaction. Like a scientist.

Give me more.

Felt. Experienced. Not heard — not in words — but unmistakable just the same.

She looked at the alien. Felt its hunger. Then she let herself look at Hollis. Let herself feel.

There were new hands inside her mind. A new presence. She felt the new emotion leave her, traveling across some unknowable void.

And then it seemed to say, *And MORE.*

She stepped forward. Toward Hollis. Then past Hollis, toward the monster.

Hollis, finally understanding, turned. Returning, at least a little, to his true self. And now, between Hollis and the thing, she found herself in a curious cross-draft. She felt from the reptar, which was now feeling from Hollis. She saw

Hollis's mind inside her own, filtered through the alien's calculating intelligence.

"Hollis," she said. "Give me your knife."

"What?"

"Your knife."

How had she known he carried a knife. She had no idea.

She held out her hand, eyes now on the reptar. It was enormous. Hideous. It was larger than an automobile, broad like a spider but with a body that was less like abdomen and thorax and, up close, really more like a human torso — but dark ochre, covered in hard shell, and shining as deeply matte black as scuffed, long-owned dress shoes. Obvious impressions aside, Mia realized she'd never seen something so alien. It was nothing like her, not even a little. And yet she could feel it. Taste its sensations, recycled from her own, Hollis's own.

Something cool settled into her palm. She took it. Unfolded the primary blade.

Beneath her was Hollis, unmoving.

Behind them both was the doctor, stiff as wax.

"Mia ..." Hollis said.

And she replied, *"Shh."*

Her hand, touching the scales as she'd done before.

The knife, sliding along its neck, toward where the doctor, on her, hand held his own knife.

The doctor mumbled, beyond words. She wouldn't glance back, but now she could feel *him* through the reptar, too.

Terrified.

Desperate.

Curious.

But above all, fascinated.

"Don't," he finally managed to say.

Meaning: *Don't kill it. I want to know it. I want to see it do its horrors.*

But what a joke that was.

The knife blade slid through the helmet's leather strap like butter.

And then, over mutters of protest, she used both hands to lift the helmet from its head.

Its eyes were deep yellow. Merciless. Hideous. Lit from within, like phantom lanterns.

In the dark of her mind, she felt something new. Not a message; messages here didn't exist. But an impression. Watching its eyes, she cobbled something whole, from all directions at once, that she interpreted as:

I am not yours.

Which Mia knew. They did not know loyalty. They did not know morality, or fairness, or right. They did not have a sense of individuality, necessary for all those notions, even when they were as cut off as this one was. Even now — even separated from the others — there came from it a sense of abiding whole.

Of *course* it wasn't hers.

But it wanted to steal more emotion from her, and Mia knew how to give it.

"Take him," she whispered to the thing, "and see what vengeance feels like."

It doesn't understand taking, she thought. *It doesn't understand vengeance.*

Slowly, its horrible mouth opened.

But it wants *to understand those things.*

And when it leapt past them to separate the doctor from his head ... then, from Mia, at least, it understood both.

38

OUT THE DOOR.

Into the woods, toward the low hill behind which she'd left Carol and Theo — friends that now, she seemed to remember only from a very long time ago.

Hollis, apparently roused by trauma, began to stir as she pulled him along.

"How did we ... ? How did you ... ?"

"I don't know." And it was true. Feeling the beast was like holding onto a dream. Most of what she'd so recently been sure of was already gone, like cotton candy melting on the tongue.

"I feel drunk."

"You are."

"It's like someone stuck a hand mixer inside my head."

Mia could relate. This much she could, at least, still retain: Thoughts were like oil and water. You could scramble them, and in the scrambling feel loss. But there was a natural equilibrium there, and once the agitation stopped, the layered order would always return. She'd taken more than Hollis had — more by a mile. And though her brain had already forgotten most of what she'd known so clearly minutes ago, one thing remained: the sense of a hand inside her like a home invader, indefensible, leaving only when and if it chose to go.

"Are you ... Are you *crying?*" Hollis asked.

No answer. None to give. None, frankly, that she *wanted* to give. This, now, felt like the morning-after walk of shame. In the moment, things had felt normal and right. Now, they felt dirty. Embarrassing. The things she'd said, the things she'd thought, the things she'd felt? They'd had a time, and now that time was gone.

She wiped her face, fists raking cheeks like a grudge. She blinked, and that helped a little. She breathed deeply, and that helped a little, too. She looked away from Hollis. Toward the hill. Toward the goal, at the end of this terrible quest. And that, it turned out, helped most of all.

Carol and Theo were right where she'd left them. They looked like stuffed dummies of themselves, gawking like fools when they came over the rise.

"Holy shit," Theo said. "Holy shit; we assumed you were dead."

"We're not," Mia said.

"What the hell happened in there?" Then he saw Hollis. "Where was he?"

"Later."

"What did they do with you, Hollis?" Carol asked, coming forward, motherly, to inspect him with curious hands. Wherever she touched, he flinched. She didn't stop; she just moved more slowly. Raising the severed flaps of his cut-open turtleneck, which Mia had never gotten an answer to, about which she very much no longer cared. His wounds bled. She knew, from half-carrying him, that he had a fever — perhaps a deadly one. Any number of acute wounds hadn't yet been tended, and in the meantime he'd been dragged from place to place, kept sleepless, tortured psychologically as well as physically.

Some of this, she new from what she'd seen and things he'd said. Some, she just knew for no reason at all.

Grim, drained, and with no patience for emotion or circumstance, Mia sat on a stump. She wished she smoked. She wanted to travel back in time to pick up the habit, just so she could light a butt right now.

"Mia ... your feet."

Mia looked. Yes. Disgusting. There would be no fetish here, for the dying pervert.

"It's fine."

"You're really not going to tell us what happened?" Carol asked.

"A reptar got loose. *The* reptar, Carol."

Carol's hand went to her mouth. Her head swiveled, looking for escape. All she saw, so far as Mia could tell, were the last few running humans. They ran for the fences. The ships beyond them, curiously, were gone. Like the story she might eventually tell Theo and Carol about their adventures in the building, the means, way, and timing of the other aliens' departure — and, if known, the reason they'd come or gone — was a story for another day.

"We have to go," Theo said.

"You're wrong," Mia said, moving from the stump to the ground, to where Hollis half-sat, half-slumped. He was already flagging. People seldom got a second wind, but Hollis's week of Hell had forced him to dig deep and find ten or twelve. "We have to stay."

"We can't stay!"

"Then go."

She slumped, too, more tired than she'd realized. Her

head found Hollis's shoulder, but when he whimpered in pain, she sat up straight and instead leaned his head against her.

But then his eyes opened. With effort, he sat up and reached into his pocket. He came out with something that broke her heart: the locket Brendan had taken from her to leave as a taunt, now emptied of its spy device.

Hollis raised it before her eyes, one end of the chain in both hands. Then he leaned forward and reached around her neck, his body close, and fastened the clasp. She could tell, from his face, that even his fingers hurt, that the simple task took effort. But he did it, and she let him do it, and when he was done, he smiled.

"Bitch," he said.

"Asshole," she told him.

Carol and Theo, frantic above them, saw none of the subtle moment's beauty.

"Mia!" Carol said.

And Mia, settling back down now, said, "Let me rest. Let *us* rest."

The feeling wasn't totally gone. Inside, she'd felt emotions like a roaring river, all floodgates open. Now, two hundred feet away, she could still feel a trickle. She thought at Hollis. He, falling deep now, thought dreams at her. She felt at him. And he felt at her.

Mia closed her eyes.

"Do you hear me, Mia?"

Carol. Just a ghost now, lost in the darkness beyond the safety she knew — for now at least — was unbreakable and whole. *Here. There.* No matter where they were, this moment was protected.

"We won't leave you behind!" Theo said.

Another voice in the darkness, barely relevant.

"Then stay."

"We can't stay! There's—!"

"Then go."

Even with her eyes closed, she knew Carol was looking at Theo and Theo was looking at Carol. Caught between a rock and a hard place with some unknown and irrelevant future hanging in the balance, their companions — and, as things went, the only ones in their foursome with enough of the story to make a difference unwilling to budge.

Stay, go, she thought. *But either way, let us sleep.*

She didn't hear more words. She didn't feel more urgency.

There was just the release of darkness, and the secret whisper of shared dreams.

39

HOLLIS WOKE WITH A HEADACHE, not sure where he was in the way things are when you open your eyes in a strange place. Ordinarily, he'd be immune. Hollis, more than most people, had opened his eyes in many strange places — once a tent in a state he'd never before visited with a naked woman slapping him (no shit) with a large fish, once beneath a high-suspension pickup truck with its motor running. But this took the cake. This awakening didn't just have strange sights and sounds, though it had that in spades. Nope, it also had sensation. And bumps.

"Yo," he said.

Carol, ahead of him and pulling whatever he seemed to be laying upon, stopped and looked back. He'd had to crane his neck backward to see her. Before, he'd only seen the very strange rest of the scene.

"Hey," she said to the others, to Mia and Theo, "it lives."

Carol stopped. Hollis's conveyance stopped. Hollis found himself looking at an unmoving sky between the branches of tall trees — a sky that someone had thrown a bag's worth of tennis balls up into, only they'd been spray-painted silver, and they'd never come down.

All four of them looked down. He didn't say more, but his eyes were open, trying to wake from his quiet sleep and coming along only slowly. He had no idea how long he'd been out, but the light was different than he last remembered — and, really, of those last waking minutes he remembered very little. It could have been days. He hadn't slept so much as fallen unconscious. He hadn't truly slumbered; it was more like he'd died, then forgotten and woken back up.

"Is he okay?" Theo asked. "Hollis, are you okay?"

They knelt around him. He realized he was lying down, on an improvised platform that'd been being dragged. Everything hurt. Everything.

Given the situation, the first thing he could think of to say was to Mia.

"Take off your shirt."

"Excuse me?"

"You promised."

Mia, who seemed to think he was kidding, looked at Theo and said, "He's fine."

Carol knelt closest of all, fussing over him like a mother. She had a red box in her hand. She opened it, revealing an overstuffed First Aid kit. If Hollis had to guess, they'd scavenged the kit from somewhere, then found various medical miscellany to accessorize it the way a kid accessorizes a Barbie. Turning his head slightly, he saw that this particular kit had a full tube of Neosporin, a peach-colored roll of self-adhering Ace bandage, surgical scissors, and two bottles of what Hollis assumed were ill-gotten pain pills. There was also freeze-off wart remover. Because why not?

"You went shopping," Hollis said. "I wanted to go shopping."

"Try to lay still."

"You're not a doctor."

"Actually," Carol said, "I am. I have a doctorate in computer science."

"Me too," said Theo. He jumped in too eagerly, as if worried Carol would get all the nerd credit.

"Not the same."

"Don't knock it," Carol told him, checking other bandages he only now realized she'd wrapped around his various parts. "Mia told us how well your last doctor worked out."

Hollis looked again at the kit. Though it was extremely unlikely, he found himself hoping that some of Dr. Greensward's bag of horrors had helped build their little red kit. The good stuff, not the surplus props from the set of *Se7en*. It'd be nice, if that piece of shit's life ended up leading to some good — even if was only an antibiotic ointment here, a pair of tweezers there.

Hollis watched Mia make her rounds of his many injuries. When she sat back, trying to look more sure of things than she clearly was, Hollis asked, "Will I live?"

"I think so. I've decided that you're not bleeding internally."

"How?"

"By the fact that you're not dead."

"I don't think that's how it works."

"You're also still sexually harassing people."

"Also not how it works."

Carol sighed, sat back, and looked up at the others. They must have had this discussion before, because something unspoken passed between them. Hollis decided not to ask.

If he asked, she'd either tell him bad news (which he didn't want to hear) or ordinary news (which he was already bored of). He knew that his thoughts, for the first time in a long time, were completely clear. That was enough.

Oh, and the pain. When his thoughts had been fatigued and scattered, it'd been hard to focus on the pain. Now, it was easy. And that was pretty awesome.

"Am I still pretty?" he asked.

Mia said, "No."

Carol patted his shoulder. The sense of where he was and what was happening was in-focus now, and Hollis realized they'd been dragging him on travois. He also realized that, despite this charming conversation, his body hadn't told him to get up — or even sit up. That wasn't great; it probably meant he was more hurt than he wanted to admit. If there were still non-homicidal doctors, he'd need one. The rest, in all likelihood, wold just come down to time.

His attention moved from the heads above him to the treetops, then to the sky full of silver alien ships. They should have scared him, but they did anything but.

There were dozens.

Theo saw his gaze, then tipped his head high. They really must have been walking for a long time. It was like Theo had forgotten they were there.

"They're following us," Theo said.

Mia and Carol must have already known this, because the ball lobbed to Hollis, if anyone, for a response.

"Why?"

"No idea."

He seemed to remember Mia doing something with the aliens. The encounter with the big black bug was right there in the front of his mind, but it had the foggy feel of a nightmare. He didn't remember the details — only that Mia had gone close, had touched the thing, had seemed, in some weird way, copacetic with it. Had that been real? He recalled the alien biting the doctor's head off after Mia had removed its helmet, but leaving their own heads alone. Sort of like how, in other times and places, they'd seen these silver spheres lay waste to hundreds of humans at once — yet now, they didn't feel threatening at all.

"They were all around Brendan's property," Mia said. "They left before you and I came back out. These might be the same ones, or might not. They just ... showed up. A few ships at a time."

Hollis shifted his attention again and started to count. There weren't just dozens. That's how many were front and center, visible through the branches most directly overhead. But the whole sky above them was full, hovering through every break in the trees and surely past branches currently obscuring his vision. There were maybe forty of them. Fifty. A hundred. Or more.

"Where are we going?" Hollis asked. He also wanted to ask where they were, where they'd already gone, and perhaps what day it was, but decided it didn't matter. It wasn't more than a day because he still hurt too bad for it to have been less, but it was more than an hour because they'd clearly restocked. This wasn't Brendan's property; Mia was wearing shoes; even Brendan's shredded black turtleneck had been replaced. You've gotta be pretty out-of-it for someone to change your shirt without you noticing. And yeah, he had been. It'd been like someone had hit him with a sledgehammer, then blown pixie dust in his face to make him sleep. Only it'd been low-quality pixie dust, like tainted meth, made by pixies with tattoos and tract marks.

"Away," Mia told him.

"But where?"

"For now, just 'away.' In a few days, that should change."

"Why?"

"Because now you're awake."

"And the party can begin," Hollis supposed.

"Because," Theo said, "now you can tell us where your car is."

"My car?"

"With your phone in it."

"My phone?"

"Are you just repeating the last words I say?" Theo asked.

"I think it's actually Ricky's phone," Carol said. "You remember Ricky's phone, left in the car you stole from your friend Sonny?"

Ah. Yes. Now he did. And he remembered why they were interested in it, though Hollis's own interest in the same subject had substantially flagged of late.

"Why a few days?"

"Because you have to be ambulatory, if we're going after it."

"I'm fine."

He wasn't. And was fooling nobody.

"Theo told us you took pictures of everything in that old case of ours," Mia said. "You didn't tell him where those pictures were, though — on the phone inside the car. Luckily, you talk in your sleep."

"I do?"

"Yeah. And while we're out, do you want us to swing by your house? Grab your old teddy bear, Ralphie?"

Dammit.

"Where's the car, Hollis?"

"Off 360. In a subdivision."

"Can you be more specific?"

"Maybe we just let it go." Because Hollis, both conscious and unconscious, had been giving that old issue some thought. Based on what Carol and Theo had said when they'd accessed the Astral app's datacenter, the aliens had been playing with that same data. They were using it, somehow, to plunge deep into understanding human behavior. But they were also doing some yet-unknown mindfuckery with it — not just understanding what was there, but cobbling all that data into something new. Tying that knowledge into what he'd seen Mia do with the reptar, Hollis wasn't so sure he was interested in learning more. They'd been through enough. Let someone else deal with it.

"Hollis," Theo said. "If the aliens are really using that AI to build a neural analogue — if they're really training some sort of next-level AI with it ..."

"Meh."

"I want to see what they're doing, too, Hollis," said Carol.

"I repeat: *Meh.*"

"The more I think about it, the more I don't like it," Carol went on. "The working theory is that the aliens are connected to one another through a shared consciousness. We've seen how that prejudice — their preference for collective mentality, and maybe even their inability to imagine that any species could possibly think any other way — causes problems. They almost destroyed Austin when McCafferty and Garrett's armies were at each other's throats ... *because* they were at each other's throats. They're not just analyzing us; they seem to be *policing* us. And Mia ... well ..."

She looked at Mia, caught a look, and dropped it. That, Hollis remembered, too. Whatever Mia had done with that alien bug, she didn't want to talk about it.

"But other than that," Carol said. "What have the ships been doing?"

"Abducting folks," Hollis said.

"Sending ground troops," Mia said.

"Sending them why?"

Mia shrugged. Apparently Carol was leading this discussion, and the rest of them were just peanut gallery.

"As reconnaissance," she said, answering her own question. "Unless a fight breaks out and they engage, they mostly just roll through cities and observe. If we're right about the ones separated from the collective, that seems to happen so they can hide better behind enemy lines — assuming we're the enemy. The ships — both big and small — just hover unless they're provoked. It's been over a week, guys. Why aren't they ... well ... *doing whatever they came here to do?*"

"Maybe we just haven't caught them in the act," Hollis said.

"Or maybe they're already doing it," Carol said. "What about those lines of rocks they keep making, and the way they seem to awaken psychic ability?" She pointed up, at the ships. "Or what about these guys? I don't know about you, but those ships up there don't even scare me anymore. It's not that the aliens aren't a danger, but this crew above us isn't going to attack us. These fellas are ... well ... just curious."

Hollis peeked at Mia, remembering the way she'd acted in front of the reptar. He hadn't understood it all, but a few foreign thoughts had definitely come into his head watching it. At the time, he'd been half crazy, spiraling into delirium. He'd thought what he'd felt had been part of that, but now he wondered. Maybe they'd been real, instead. And maybe, if so, Carol was more right than she realized.

The reptar, curious more than deadly. The reptar's thoughts, inside his own head: *Give me more.*

Meaning more human thoughts. More emotion. More reactions, to things both good and bad, for it to feed on.

"So?" Hollis said.

"If they came to take anything from us, it begins here." Carol put one finger to her temple, indicating her mind. "They need to understand us. They want to see how we think, and they're not shy about how they go about it. Guys ... I remember what I thought, at the time, about the footprints in that databank. Now I wish I could go back and look again, with more context."

"Are you thinking of the throughput?" Theo asked.

"I'm thinking of a channel that seemed to be being built, to *process* throughput."

"What are you two yammering about?" Hollis asked. He'd managed to sit up, but didn't plan to go farther. But the rest had gone from kneeling to sitting, so it was okay. Equal footing, at least.

"The problem, as I see it," Carol said, "isn't whatever the aliens might be doing right now. It's what I think, based on my understanding of our technology and how a fresh perspective might interpret our technology, that they might be planning to do next."

"Which is what?" Mia asked.

"I don't know. And that's exactly why we have to find out."

"Let someone else find out," Hollis said.

They all looked at him.

"We've done enough," Hollis said. "We saved the damn city."

"And now we're going to do this," Carol insisted.

"Not if you can't get back into that database thingy. Not if I don't tell you where the car with the phone in it is."

Silently, Mia put her hand on his. Even that hurt, but

only a little. He tried not to look at her, but did so anyway. That little gold locket was hanging on her neck, a few strands of dark brown hair tracing its chain. Had he given it back to her, or had they found it in his pocket? He honestly didn't remember. It'd been a long few weeks, full of way more bullshit than usual.

Hadn't they all earned retirement? The world was about to go to shit, and they should find a bunker. Find new careers, perhaps as road warriors and scavengers.

Mia squeezed his hand, just a little.

"Ouch," he said.

"Does that hurt?"

"Yeah."

"Fucking baby."

She squeezed harder. They looked into each other's eyes, quiet between them.

"Fine," he finally said with a heavy sigh. "If you're going to be dickheads about it, I guess we can try and save the world."

THE STORY CONTINUES...

Save The World is the thrilling conclusion to the Save The Humans series —with more action, more secrets, and more twists than ever.

GET SAVE THE WORLD NOW!

A QUICK FAVOR

If you enjoyed this book would you please consider writing a review of it on your favorite bookselling site so other readers can enjoy it too? Just a couple of sentences would be fantastic.

Thanks!

Johnny B. Truant

ABOUT THE AUTHORS

Avery Blake doesn't want you to know where she lives, or what she does. She travels the world, moving from place to place quickly to ensure she can't be tracked. It's safer that way.

When she's not looking over her shoulder, you can find her in the corner of a cafe, facing the exit, typing as fast as she can.

Johnny B. Truant is co-owner of the Sterling & Stone Story Studio, an IP powerhouse focusing on books and adaptations for film and television. It's the best job in the world, and he spends his days creating cool stuff with partners Sean Platt and David W. Wright, as well as more than 20 gifted storytellers.

Johnny is the bestselling author of over 100 books under various pen names, including the Fat Vampire and Invasion series. On the nonfiction side, he's also co-author of the indie publishing mainstay Write. Publish. Repeat. and co-host of the weekly Story Studio Podcast.

Originally from Ohio, Johnny and his family now live in Austin, Texas, where he's finally surrounded by creative types as weird as he is.

ALSO BY SEAN PLATT

The Dead World Series

Dead Zero

Dead City

Dead Nation

Dead Planet

Empty Nest

The Beam Series

The Beam Season One

The Beam Season Two

The Beam Season Three

Robot Proletariat Series

En3my

Robot Proletariat

The Infinite Loop

The Hard Reset

Cascade Failure

Reboot

The Tomorrow Gene Series

Null Identity

The Tomorrow Gene

The Tomorrow Clone

The Eden Experiment

Karma Police Series

Jumper

Karma Police

The Collectors

Deviant

The Fall

Homecoming

Yesterday's Gone

October's Gone

Yesterday's Gone Season One

Yesterday's Gone Season Two

Yesterday's Gone Season Three

Yesterday's Gone Season Four

Yesterday's Gone Season Five

Yesterday's Gone Season Six

Tomorrow's Gone

Tomorrow's Gone Season One

Tomorrow's Gone Season Two

Tomorrow's Gone Season Three

Available Darkness

Darkness Itself

Available Darkness Book One

Available Darkness Book Two

Available Darkness Book Three

ALSO BY JOHNNY B. TRUANT

Robot Proletariat Series

En3my

Robot Proletariat

The Infinite Loop

The Hard Reset

Cascade Failure

Reboot

The Invasion Series

Longshot

Invasion

Contact

Colonization

Annihilation

Judgment

Extinction

Resurrection

The Tomorrow Gene Series

Null Identity

The Tomorrow Gene

The Tomorrow Clone

The Eden Experiment

Stand Alone Novels

Pretty Killer

Pattern Black

Burnout

The Target

The Island

Devil May Care

www.ingramcontent.com/pod-product-compliance
Lightning Source LLC
Chambersburg PA
CBHW010538100726
47903CB00011B/3047